X

1-15-96

DOCTORS
and LAWYERS
and *Such*

Other Milt Kovak mysteries

Dead Moon on the Rise
Chasing Away the Devil
Other People's Houses
Houston in the Rearview Mirror
The Man in the Green Chevy

About Kimmey Kruse

Funny as a Dead Relative
Funny as a Dead Comic

About E. J. Pugh

One, Two, What Did Daddy Do?

A MILT KOVAK MYSTERY

DOCTORS
and LAWYERS
and Such

Susan Rogers Cooper

St. Martin's Press ❧ New York

Library of Congress Cataloging-in-Publication Data

Cooper, Susan Rogers.
    Doctors and lawyers and such / Susan Rogers Cooper.
        p.   cm.
    "A Thomas Dunne book."
    ISBN 0-312-13468-1
    1. Kovak, Milton (Fictitious character)—Fiction.   2. Sheriffs—
—Oklahoma—Fiction.   I. Title.
    PS3553.06235D63   1995
    813'.54—dc20   95-32886
                                                        CIP

First edition: October 1995

10 9 8 7 6 5 4 3 2 1

I have a lot of people to thank for helping me with this book. I hope I put all their wonderful information down correctly—if not, please blame the recipient, not the giver.

For their technical advice, I would like to thank Jack Chandler, M.D., family practitioner, and his assistants, Sharon Stripling and Angel Powell; Terence C. Todd, Ph.D., Kinesiology and Health at the University of Texas; Juan Arojas of the Texas Department of Public Safety; Officer Wadley of the Tulsa, Oklahoma, Police Department; William G. Reid, assistant district attorney, Travis County, Texas; Manuel Mancias and Paul Knight, detectives, Travis County Sheriff's Office; and Judith Miller, M.S.W., C.S.W.

I would also like to thank Don and Evin Cooper for their unwavering support and willingness to put off supper until the chapter is finished. As always, my sincerest appreciation to the "black shoes"—Jeff Abbott, Jan Grape, and Barbara Burnett Smith.

Also, I would like to thank my editor, Ruth Cavin, for her constant support in this, our ninth book together, and my agent, Vicky Bijur, for her good ear and better advice.

DOCTORS
and LAWYERS
and Such

1

It was the eve of election day when the phone rang. Well, actually, no, it wasn't. It was really the morning of election day itself, but personally, I consider any hour before my alarm's set to go off to be the night before. I'm funny that way.

It was 2:00 A.M. when the phone rang. Now, when you're a peace officer, acting sherriff–variety, you come to expect this sort of thing. And when the only real-life psychiatrist in town, head of a six-bed unit at the local hospital, sleeps next to you, it's not all that unusual for the phone to ring in the middle of the night. But still and all, it ain't pleasant. This one most surely wasn't.

"Sheriff Kovak," I said into the phone. Which still remained to be seen. The electorate would go out that day, from 7:00 A.M. until 7:00 P.M., and decide my fate. I was running unopposed, sure, but you never can tell with voters. I mean, we had almost two full terms of Nixon, right?

"Milt?" the voice on the other end said.

I'm not real good with voices, especially when they wake me up. I'd a been okay if it had been A. B. Tate or Jasmine Bodine, my night deputies, but this wasn't either of them.

"Yeah," I said. "That's me. Who's this?"

"Lloyd Macon," he said. Lloyd Macon, in case you don't

1

know, is the mayor of Longbranch, Oklahoma, the county seat of the county for which I'm the acting sheriff. Me and Lloyd go way back, to the high school football team. Of course, I was a player and he was only the water boy, but I try not to hold that against him. Specially since he's been mayor now for close to twenty years.

"What's going on, Lloyd?" I asked, sitting up in bed and keeping my voice down so as not to wake up my wife. She was four months pregnant, sick most of the time her eyes were open, and mean when she wasn't sick. But that's life with a pregnant woman, they tell me.

Now for the life of me, I couldn't figure out why Lloyd Macon'd be calling me in the middle of the night. I answer to the county commissioners, not the mayor of Longbranch. He had authority over my best bud, Emmett Hopkins, chief of police of Longbranch. He was the one old Lloyd shoulda been waking up in the middle of the night, not me.

"Sorry to wake you up, Milt," Lloyd said, "but we got us a problem and I need your help."

"Well, sure, Lloyd, glad to oblige. What's going on?" I wiped sleep from my eyes and reached for a cigarette, then remembered I'd given 'em up (again) a month ago.

"Shirley Beth Hopkins just kilt herself," Lloyd said. No warning, no smoothing his way into it. Just up and said it like it wasn't gonna break my heart.

"Jesus H. Christ on a bicycle," I said, sitting up all the way in bed and dropping my feet to the floor. Shirley Beth was Emmett's wife—a sweet, quiet lady who'd been drinking herself to death since their boy J.R. died of leukemia something like ten years or so ago. "How in the hell did it happen?" I asked, hoping there was a way this was gonna be an accident. Anyway not to make it a suicide. How was Emmett gonna handle that?

"She used Emmett's sidearm—blew her brains out," Lloyd said. He sighed. "Milt, I can't have Emmett investigating his own wife's suicide—'sides, his gun was involved. And I can't

2

have none of the boys working under him look into this. Won't look right. That's why I called you."

"Well, hell, Lloyd, Emmett Hopkins's my best friend. . . ."

"I know that. But it would be less suspicious if you did the investigating rather than the city police. He don't have the power over you he'd have over his own men, know what I mean?"

"Where's Emmett now?" I asked.

"Here—at his house. That's where I'm calling you from. Emmett called me first thing after the paramedics. Not that they done much good. Poor old Shirley Beth's scattered all over the damned kitchen."

I grimaced at his words, hoping Emmett was far enough away not to hear. And nowhere near his own kitchen.

"Let me get my pants on, Lloyd. Be there in less than half an hour."

"What is it?" Jean asked from her side of the bed.

I stood up and pulled on my pants, which were lying on the chest at the foot of the bed. "Shirley Beth Hopkins killed herself," I told my wife.

Jean sat up. "Oh, baby, I'm so sorry," she said. Jean never had met Shirley Beth, since Shirley Beth didn't go out much (with her problems and all) and never made it to our wedding. Me and Emmett been talking about getting together as couples, sacrificing some chickens to the barbecue—but that never happened. Knew it never would. We just always talked like there was nothing wrong with Shirley Beth. Because that's what you did.

"Don't know when I'll be back. Maybe go straight on to work," I told Jean.

"Sure. No problem. Are we still going together to cast our votes?" she asked.

We'd planned on making a big production of it, just in case any of the local media—the *Longbranch Gazette* or the *Shoppe & Save*—wanted to capture the moment for posterity. Now the

3

whole idea just seemed kinda silly. Now that Shirley Beth Hopkins's brains were scattered all over the blue willow wallpaper of her spanking-clean kitchen.

"I'll call ya," I said, strapping my shoulder holster in place and covering it all with a light jacket. It was April. But still cold at night.

I went out and got in my new Jeep and drove the eighteen miles to Emmett's house.

Emmett Hopkins's house was a pristine little three-bedroom in an area of homes that looked a lot alike. The yard was real pretty, though, now that there were no bikes and toys to mess it up. The time Emmett would have spent with his son and a healthy wife, he now spent working in the yard, making something pretty in an otherwise-not-so-pretty life.

There was a city squad car and Lloyd Macon's '59 Cadillac (his baby) sitting in front of Emmett's house. The ambulance was gone, but neighbors still stood on the sidewalks and in their own yards, most decked out in nightclothes, some covered with regular coats, some with housecoats, all buzzing away trying to figure out what all the commotion was at the police chief's house.

Madelie Blakely, two doors down from Emmett's house, came tiptoeing through the dew-wet grass toward me. She was a big woman, well over six feet and weighing in, I'd bet, at close to three hundred, but with one of those pretty faces that always seems to make people say, "She'd be really pretty if she lost the weight." Which ain't necessarily true. Madelie was the solo soprano at my church and we spoke every now and then. But we didn't have the kind of relationship she was fixing to presume upon.

"What's going on, Milt?" she asked, all breathless and big-eyed.

"Police business, Madelie," I said.

"I saw the ambulance people coming out with somebody on

4

a stretcher, all covered up. Is Shirley Beth okay?"

"I'm not really sure myself what's going on, Madelie. Why don't you go on home? It's late." I touched her lightly on the shoulder. "You're gonna catch a chill out here. Hurt that pretty voice."

She looked longingly at the door to Emmett's house. "Well, if there's anything I can do . . ."

"I'll let you know if there is," I said, turning my back on her and walking up the path to Emmett's front door.

I knocked and opened the door, walking into the living room, which was right off the entrance. Emmett sat on the blue couch in the living room, bent over, his head in his hands. He'd pulled some work pants on over his shorts, but he was still in his sleeveless T-shirt. Funny the way the mind works. My first thought was that after all the years of knowing Emmett Hopkins, I'd never known he wore those old-fashioned, ribbed, sleeveless white T-shirts. My daddy wore sleeveless T-shirts like that. I guess I didn't even know they still made 'em.

My second thought wasn't quite as frivolous; I could still smell the cordite from the gun blast. And there was the underlying smell you get at a lot of violent death scenes—the sweet smell of blood.

Lloyd Macon was standing by the hall that lead to the kitchen. "Lloyd," I said, nodding, then walked over to Emmett. I sat down next to him and put my arm around his shoulder. "Hey, Emmett. It's me, Milt."

He leaned his body into me and I put both my arms around him and he cried like a baby. And I just sat there and held on to him. I've never been real good at that sort of thing, but it seemed sorta natural with Emmett. He needed some comfort and he sure as hell wasn't getting it from his boss, Lloyd Macon. I knew there was no family to call. Shirley Beth had been an orphan, raised by an aging aunt in Ardmore who died before she and Emmett met. Emmett was from Missouri and both his parents had died before J. R. had. He had a brother someplace up north, but they never talked and weren't close. So I was family, the only family he had.

Lloyd Macon cleared his throat. "Milt," he said softly, "thanks for coming. I appreciate you investigating this for us."

Emmett leaned away from me, wiping his dripping face with the bottom of that sleeveless T-shirt. "Milt," he said, his voice deep, sounding like he had a cold. "Thanks for looking into this for us. Under the circumstances . . ."

I patted him awkwardly on the shoulder. "You go in the bedroom and pack yourself some stuff. I'll take you on back to my place—"

Emmett shook his head. "No. Thanks, but no." He stood up and went to the window, staring out at the still-dark sky.

I got up and went over to Lloyd Macon. "He can't stay here," I said softly.

Lloyd shook his head. "I know. I'm gonna take him by the Longbranch Inn when we get through here. He shouldn't be spending the night here."

Lloyd turned and I followed him into the kitchen. It wasn't so bad really, except for that one wall—and the smell. She'd been sitting in a chair at the table in the breakfast room, her back against the wall that separated the kitchen area from the bedroom area. The blood spatter was contained, just a spot a couple of feet in diameter, smeared on the wallpaper and one of the decorator plates lined up on the wall—the Scarlet O'Hara plate. The John Wayne plate and the Elvis plate were untouched.

She musta had her head pretty close to the wall. The spatter was only a couple of feet wide, a few feet long as it had dripped. There was a little mucuslike tissue on the back of the chair and on the wall. The gun, Emmett's Colt .45 service revolver, lay on the floor by the chair, the barrel covered with blood and mucus.

Somebody had died in that kitchen, that I could tell you.

6

How it had happened, why it had happened—those things would have to come out later. I'd have to interview Emmett, much as I hated to. The how would come from Dr. Jim at the morgue.

Larry Joe January came out of the bedroom area. He was Emmett's right-hand man. I never liked Larry Joe much. He was a kiss-ass type who'd been after Emmett's job since the day he signed on with the department.

"Sheriff," Larry Joe said, extending his hand for me to shake, which I did.

"Larry Joe," I said. "How come y'all moved the body 'fore I had a chance to look things over?"

Larry Joe looked from me to Lloyd, then at the floor. Lloyd cleared his throat again. "That was my idea, Milt. I didn't think it was right to leave her here with Emmett just . . ." His voice trailed off. "Sides, Dr. Jim was here. He pronounced her dead. Had the ambulance people take her over to the morgue."

Larry Joe said, "I took plenty of pictures, though, Sheriff. Did everythin' by the book."

Which I didn't doubt for a minute. Larry Joe needed "the book" to figure out whether or not to hold his pecker when he peed.

"Get 'em developed," I said, leaving the death scene and heading back to the living room, "and get 'em over to my office, and," I added, giving him the same look I'd give to one of my own deputies, "bag that gun 'fore somebody touches it."

"Yes, sir," I heard behind me, almost feeling his fat lips on my shiny red ass.

Emmett was still standing by the window, staring off into space. I went up behind him and laid a hand on his shoulder. "How you doing?" I asked, knowing when I asked it what a stupid question it was.

Still staring out the window, Emmett said, "Now what, Milt? Now what do I do? They're both gone. My whole life. Both gone."

7

I squeezed his shoulder, patted him again, and left by the front door, getting back in my Jeep and heading to the hospital annex, where the morgue was stashed.

Longbranch is a different place in the wee hours of the morning. In the daytime, there's all the hustle and bustle you'd expect of a medium-sized town—farmers in town, shopping; businessmen picking their teeth outside Bernie's Chat & Chew while they try to sell each other just one more widget; young mothers pushing strollers from Tadum's Hardware, next door to the Allright Drugs; teenagers going too fast down the street in daddy's car, blasting country music loud as can be on the car radio; blue-collar workers hanging out in front of my brother-in-law's auto-parts store, telling lies about horsepower and gas mileage. But in the wee hours of the morning, the town is a different place.

When I first joined on with the sherriff's department, I had the graveyard shift. After about a month, I found I looked forward to it. Looked forward to the quiet, the unrealness of my town in the wee hours. Even the Sidewinder, on the outskirts of town, our only honky-tonk, closed its doors at 2:00 A.M., and that was only on Friday and Saturday nights. Weeknights, it closed up at midnight, and even then there were only a few diehards that stayed out that late.

Back in those days, those early days at the sheriff's department, I'd sometimes see ol' Alistair Peabody walking the streets, mumbling to himself. They say he'd been gassed during the war to end all wars—that was the first World War—and hadn't been exactly right in the head since then. I'd pick him up when I saw him and take him back to the County Home for the Aged, where he stayed. But ol' Mr. Peabody had died sometime in the mid-sixties, and as I drove from Emmett's house to the hospital, I didn't see a soul. The shops and businesses were closed up tight, with little night-lights burning. I passed one city cruiser as it went from street to alley, checking out the back doors of the businesses. I waved, but whoever was driving didn't wave back.

When I got to the morgue, I found Shirley Beth Hopkins lying on a gurney in the middle of the room, the only dead body in Prophesy County at the moment.

"Milt," Dr. Jim said as I came into the room. He didn't look up or move his hands from where they were working.

"Whatja got, Dr. Jim?" I asked.

"Fifty-five-year-old white female, dead," Dr. Jim said. He's never been known for his *good* sense of humor.

"Any reason not to think it's a suicide?" I asked.

Finally, he looked up at me. "Am I finished yet?" he asked. "Or are my hands still full of this poor lady's innards?"

"Well, you gotta have some preliminary feelings about this here, Dr. Jim."

"My *preliminary* feelings is that she's dead, Sheriff. My *preliminary* feelings is maybe the bullet in her brain's what done it. My *preliminary* feelings is that you best get the hell out of here and let me do my job."

I left the hospital and went on back to Mountain Falls Road, which is where I live, and fixed me and Jean some breakfast— which she threw up—got dressed in my uniform, which was fitting a lot snugger than it used to, and got back to work about 7:30, being the first one in and, therefore, able to make the coffee my ownself.

Gladys, our clerk, got there around eight o'clock. I was still standing by the coffeepot, so she didn't have far to go to get her juicy update.

"Is it true?" she asked breathily. "Is Shirley Beth Hopkins really dead?"

I nodded my head.

"And Emmett killed her?" Gladys asked, her eyes wide.

I swung around on this little lady who never knew how to

9

smile or laugh or say much of anything nice about anybody. "Who told you that?" I demanded.

Gladys backed up a step or two. "Why, that's what I heard at the station when I gassed up this morning."

"As far as anybody can tell at this moment, Shirley Beth Hopkins—"

"Is it true Emmett kilt his wife?" Dalton Pettigrew said, barging up to Gladys and me.

"No—" I started, but Mike Neils, our other day deputy, took that moment to pop in the front door.

"Hey, y'all hear about Emmett Hopkins killing his old lady?"

I stuck my fingers in my mouth and blew a loud whistle, holding up my hand like a traffic cop for silence. They all commenced to quieting down.

"Now listen up here," I said in my best acting-sheriff–soon-to-be-elected–voice. "Although this case is still being investigated, by this office, I might add, it stands right now that Shirley Beth Hopkins committed suicide. Unfortunately, she did it with Emmett's piece. Now you hear anybody say otherwise, you set 'em straight."

"Then how come Lloyd Macon took away Emmett's badge?" Mike asked.

I whirled around. "Do what?" I asked.

Mike took a step backward. "I was just talking to Troy on the city force and he told me Larry Joe told him Lloyd took Emmett's badge."

I slammed down my coffee cup and headed out the door. I had some city political ass to chew.

A few months back, my lady friend, Glenda Sue Robinson, was murdered. I knew, to a lesser degree, what Emmett was gonna be going through in the next few weeks. Yeah, I took a few days off, but by the third day, I was itching to get back to work—to do something, to stop the constant thinking, If only . . . 'Cause that's what you do when somebody you love dies a violent death. And I knew that's what Emmett was gonna be doing. My former boss, Sheriff Elberry Blankenship, took my shield and gun away from me then, too—but not until I'd stuck my piece halfway through his gut and threatened to give him a belly button–ectomy. But then, bosses tend to get a little testy when their subordinates threaten them with bodily injury.

There wasn't any reason like that for Lloyd Macon to be taking away Emmett's badge. No reason in hell for that.

I burst into city hall in a huff and marched up the stairs to the mayor's office. Margery Tompkins sat at the desk in front of the mayor's private office door like she had been doing through Lloyd's reign and those of two mayors before him. If age discrimination hadn't been against the law, Margery would have been forced to retire ten years ago. Although she was well into her seventies now, she could type rings around the younger women at city hall, took shorthand faster than most people can talk, and no one had ever been known to get around her to the mayor's door unless there was a damned good reason.

"Miss Margery," I said, doffing an imaginery hat.

She smiled sweetly. "Sheriff." Her smile faded and she said, "I was so sorry to hear about Shirley Beth."

"Yes, ma'am, that's why I'm here to see the mayor. I need to talk to him about the investigation."

"One moment, Sheriff." She turned a switch on the intercom thing on her desk, telling Lloyd I was outside. I heard his tinny voice coming through, saying to send me on in. I smiled and passed her desk, going into the inner sanctum of the highest office of Longbranch, Oklahoma.

Not that it looked like all that much. It was maybe one and a half times larger than the other offices in the city hall building, but it had the same high ceilings with the fancy molding; the desk was big as a normal desk, and the visitor's chairs were strictly city-issue. Nothing fancy. The walls, however, were adorned with pictures of the Longbranch Cougars football team and looked to include about every year since me and Lloyd shared a bench.

11

He stood up behind his desk and held out his hand. "Milt, glad you came by—"

I didn't take his hand. Instead, I leaned forward on his desk, my hands resting not too far from the double-frame picture of his wife and two daughters.

"What's this crap I hear about you taking Emmett's badge, Lloyd?"

He sat back down in his chair. "Now where'd you hear that, Milt? That's strictly confidential stuff."

I grinned to myself. At least, I thought, if nothing else, I can get Larry Joe January in serious trouble. "Larry Joe's been spouting off. One of my deputies gave me the news. No telling who else knows."

Lloyd rocked back in his swivel chair. "Well, shit-fire," he said. "And goddam."

"Why'd you do it, Lloyd?"

"Under the circumstances—"

"Under the circumstances, my ass. You got no call to be taking Emmett's badge. Just doing it makes him look guilty of something, and he ain't guilty of nothing, and you know it. His wife committed suicide—"

"With his gun—"

"So what? They lived in the same damned house! She knew where he kept his piece when he wasn't wearing it! Same as my wife! Same as the wives and husbands of every peace officer in this country, you asshole!"

Lloyd stood up. "Don't you be talking to me that way, Milton Kovak!" he said, his face going a funny shade of puce. I figured I'd just lost a vote, unless maybe he got to the polls real early.

"I can talk at you any way I want to, Lloyd Macon," I said. "You don't have any power over me. I work for the county commissioners, least you forgot. And another thing—"

Well, I didn't get the other thing out. Lloyd picked up the phone and dialed three numbers, standing there staring daggers

12

at me. After half a second, he said, "Larry Joe? This is the mayor." He waited for a minute, listening, no doubt, to Larry Joe blowing kisses over the phone wire, then he said, "You're the acting police chief. And you are now in charge of the investigation into the death of Shirley Beth Hopkins. The sheriff's department is no longer involved; it's all yours."

He hung up the phone and looked at me. "Was there something else, Sheriff?"

"Yeah, Lloyd, I was thinking I'd like me a glass a water. Surely you remember how to do that? You were so good at it in high school."

With that, I turned and walked out of the office.

2

There are 5,412 people in Prophesy County, according to the last census; 3,320 of them are registered voters. On that Tuesday in April, of that 3,320 registered voters, 1,003 showed up to cast a ballot on the county election. Three incumbent commissioners kept their jobs, two had retired, and two new people were voted in to take their places, and one commissioner got plumb voted out and replaced by a woman. Believe it or not. And I got 982 votes to become the elected sheriff of Prophesy County—which means twenty-one people voted against me, and I was running unopposed. Now ain't that a kick in the butt? Ten of those twenty-one votes were write-ins for ole Elberry Blankenship, the former sheriff, which pleased him a might. The other eleven voted for Wade Moon, the man who'd been running against me a month before but who was now of the deceased persuasion.

Jean and I celebrated my victory with Ovaltine and a good night's sleep. My first official act as sheriff was to write a letter to the mayor of Longbranch, officially telling him I thought what he done to Emmett was a crock.

Emmett spent only one night at the Longbranch Inn. After the ladies from the church had come by to clean up the mess in the kitchen, Emmett moved back in. I don't know if I coulda done that. But people handle grief in different ways.

I went by Emmett's every evening after work, but he was always just sitting in the living room in a sleeveless T-shirt, staring at the TV and drinking coffee. We never talked much, just sat there and watched *Jeopardy* together, not even bothering to yell out the questions, even the easy ones.

Thirteen days after that 2:00 A.M. phone call, Shirley Beth Hopkins's death was officially declared a suicide. Two days after that, Emmett was called into Lloyd Macon's office and received an official—in his file—reprimand for "allowing" his wife to use his city-issue service weapon to blow her brains out.

Which pissed Emmett off so bad that when Lloyd Macon handed him back his badge, Emmett just threw it in his face, said, "I quit," and walked out the door.

I found him an hour later at the Sidewinder Lounge on Highway 5 outside of Longbranch. To say Emmett Hopkins was three sheets to the wind was like saying the Pope's a Catholic—kind of an understatement.

That's when he told me what Lloyd had said and what he, Emmett, had done about it.

"Well," I said, patting him on the back, "there's only so much a body can take."

"Shit I reckon," Emmett said, tossing back another shooter.

"Let me drive you on home now, Emmett," I said.

He looked at me. His eyes were bloodshot; his shoulders stooped. He looked ten years older than me, and I looked damned old. In reality, Emmett was almost a year my junior.

"I ain't got no home to go to," Emmett said, staring at the wall of bottles behind the bar of the Sidewinder.

"Then come on home with me. Jean and me'll fix up that room upstairs. You can stay there a few days, till you figure out what you want to do—"

"Get the hell outta my face, Milt. You're like an old woman."

The words woulda stung, except I knew he was drunk. It was the booze talking, not my friend.

15

"Then go back to your house. Crawl under the covers and vegetate for a couple years. I don't really give a damn what you do, Emmett, but you ain't driving away from this place drunk as you are, and that's a promise."

He put his hand on my shoulder and pushed, but there wasn't much heat behind it. I barely lost my balance on my stool. "Don't go pushing at me, Emmett."

He pushed again. This time, I had to put a leg out to stay on the stool. "Emmett, I don't wanna have to arrest your ass."

That's when he socked me in the jaw. And that's when I took my best friend to the jailhouse. Ain't life just a pile of dog dookie?

The next morning, bright and early, I took a nice hot cup of coffee back to the cells and commenced to rattling and banging around till ole Emmett opened up those bloodshot eyes. He stared around him, figured out where he was, then looked up at me.

"I done stepped in it this time, huh, Milt?" he said, grinning sheepishlike at me.

I opened the cell door (we hadn't bothered to lock it) and handed him the coffee, taking a seat next to him on the bare mattress of the county-issue cot. "Up to your kneecaps, buddy," I said.

He looked at the bruised spot on the side of my chin. "I do that to you?" he asked.

"None other," I said.

He took a sip of coffee and stared at the floor. "Sorry 'bout that," he said.

I shrugged. "Happens with drunks," I said.

He shook his head. "Never did with Shirley Beth," he said quietly. First time he'd ever implied Shirley Beth was a drunk.

I didn't know what to say, so I didn't say anything. Just kept the old Milt trap shut—which is harder than you might imagine.

16

"She'd been trying to give it up, you know?" Emmett said. "She'd have days there toward the end when I'd come home and there'd be supper on the table and she'd smile at me all shylike." He sighed. "Reminded me of when I first met her. The way she smiled." He took another sip of coffee. He still faced the floor, not looking at me. I looked at the floor, too. It seemed the proper thing to do.

"There was almost a week without a drink. Longest time ever. Since before J.R. died. Since after they diagnosed him with leukemia. Then she'd slip up and I'd see the bottles in the trash and hear her crying in the spare bedroom." He finally looked at me. "We almost made love one of them times when she was sober. She—" He looked at the floor. "She touched me. Ya know?"

I nodded my head, but I wasn't sure he could see. "And I kissed her. And she kissed me back. But then the phone rang." A sob racked his body. "I thought she was getting better. After all those years, I thought she was getting better."

I left him sitting there in the cell and went upstairs to use the phone, calling my wife and asking her if she made house calls— in this case, jail calls. She agreed and showed up less than twenty minutes later, making her way down the stairs with the aid of her crutches. Jean had polio when she was a kid—left her with partially paralyzed legs in braces and the need to get around on a set of crutches. But she does get around, let me tell you. Jean went down to the holding cell and stayed there for over an hour. When she came up, pulling herself and her swelling belly up the stairs, Emmett was behind her.

"Okay if Emmett leaves now?" Jean asked me.

I nodded. I'd never officially booked him, so there was no need to officially sign him out. The two left the office together and got into Jean's car. And I breathed a sigh of relief. She'd take care of it. Help him cope. That's what she did. And she was good at it.

Later that night at dinner, I asked, "How's Emmett?"

17

She looked up at me, those hazel eyes dancing in the kitchen light. "It will take time," she said.

"He tell you about Shirley Beth trying to stop drinking?"

She took a bite of the chicken on her plate and said, "Um-hum." She swallowed. "That happens a lot with alcoholics. They know they have to quit—something's telling them it's time—but quitting alcohol is very hard. Very hard. If an alcoholic attempts suicide, it's usually when they're trying to quit, or when they finally realize they can't."

I sighed. "Ya know, I've known Emmett a hell of a long time, but I only met Shirley Beth a few times before J.R. got diagnosed. Before she started going downhill. Seemed like a real sweet, quiet lady." I thought for a minute. "Just like after. Just like when she was drinking. Real sweet, real quiet."

Jean nodded her head.

"When you think Emmett'll be ready to go back to work?" I asked.

Jean looked up from her plate. "I thought he quit his job?"

I nodded. "Yeah. But I still got that slot for chief deputy open at the sheriff's department. Can't think of a better man to fill it than him."

Jean smiled. "Interesting," she said. "What about Mike Neils?"

I looked down at my plate. "What about Mike?" I asked, knowing full well what about Mike. He'd been salivating over that job since I'd vacated it to become acting sheriff. But it had been vacant for five months without me putting Mike in there. That shoulda told him something.

"He's really expecting that job, Milt," Jean said.

I looked at my bride of two months. "Now how would you know that?"

"Melissa told me."

Melissa. I shoulda known. Melissa was Glenda Sue Robinson's daughter, who'd come back to Prophesy County for her mother's funeral and stayed on because of me. Or that's what I'd thought. I'd thought we had a nice family thing going—me being the adopted grandfather of her daughter, Rebecca, and her working for Jean, who was now my wife. She lived right down the road from us, in the old Munsky farmhouse. But then there was Mike.

I can't really say what it is about Mike Neils that chaps my butt, but whatever it is, it chaps it real bad. He's like a hyperactive puppy with a weak bladder. Cute only goes so far. His endless chatter and pushy personality have been a boil on my butt since he signed on with the department five years ago.

I knew Mike and Melissa'd been sniffing around each for a while now. Knew that probably those nights we baby-sat for Rebecca, Melissa was out gallivanting around with Mike Neils. But I didn't want to talk about it—or think about it.

"What'd Melissa say?" I finally asked.

"She said Mike was wondering when you were going to give him the job 'officially.' He thinks he's been doing the work; now he just wants the title."

I barked out a laugh. "He thinks he's been doing the work? Hell, that boy couldn't investigate a dog turd."

"Before you offer the job to Emmett, I think you'd better talk to Mike."

"Why?"

Jean sighed. That exasperated look on her face she gets after talking to me for more than ten minutes at a stretch. "Because it's the polite thing to do. You need to let him know you're looking elsewhere to fill that position."

"Well, hell, I don't know why he thinks I'd give that job to him. Come to think of it, Dalton's got more seniority than Mike!"

Jean barked her own laugh. "Dalton Pettigrew as chief deputy?"

"I never said that! I just said that if I were Mike, I'd assume I might go on seniority."

"Mike's not stupid enough to think you'd give that job to Dalton."

"Well, he's stupid enough to think I'd give it to him."

Jean got up from the table, balancing herself on one crutch while she took her plate to the sink.

"Just talk to Mike first, Milt. It's more businesslike. Classier."

Okay. I figured I could try the classy route once in a while. Couldn't hurt. After all, I married Jean—the classiest thing I'd ever done.

The next morning, I called Mike into my office and asked him to shut the door.

"Mike," I said, clearing my throat and trying to remember exactly how I'd rehearsed my little speech to myself the night before, "I think we got some air clearing to do."

"Sure, Milt, no problem. Whatever you say. Clear air's a real good idea. I think it would be just great if we cleared—"

"Shut up, Mike."

"Sure, Milt. Whatever you say—"

"Mike, about the chief deputy job—"

"Milt, I swear you won't regret it! I swear. I'll be the best damned chief deputy ever—'cept for you, of course—I mean, well—"

"Mike, just shut your mouth, okay? Don't say another word. I got something to say and I gotta just say it." I took a deep breath and looked into those cow-patty brown eyes. "Mike, the thing is, I'm thinking of offering that chief deputy position to Emmett Hopkins."

You ever seen a balloon deflate when somebody sticks a pin in it? Well, that's exactly what seemed to be happening to Mike Neils. His chest sorta caved in, his shoulders went down two inches, and his neck got long and loose. It was a pitiful sight, and I wasn't real proud of myself for causing it.

"You're a real good deputy, Mike, you know that—"

" 'Scuse me, Sheriff," Mike said, then stood up and walked out the door. I stood and followed him. He walked down the long hall to the bull-pen area, where he and Dalton had desks and where Gladys manned the counter. He went through the opening in the counter, out into the lobby, and through the front door. And kept on walking.

Course, it was about then I thought about how much of an idiot I was gonna look like if Emmett Hopkins declined the job.

Which is exactly what he did later that evening. I stopped by his house, like I'd been doing every night for over two weeks. He was sitting there watching the TV, just like always. I asked real politelike, "Okay if we turn off *Jeopardy* for a little while? Something I gotta talk to you about."

He didn't even look at me. "This guy here, the one from Missouri, he might make five-time champion today. Don't wanna miss that."

I walked to the TV and punched in the off button. "We won't miss much," I said, taking a seat next to Emmett on the couch. "Something I need to talk to you about."

He wouldn't look at me. Just stared at the TV. "Said I was sorry about punching you. Need me to say it again?"

I shook my head. "No, that's not it. You know that job of chief deputy at the sheriff's department's been vacant now since I become acting sheriff. I figure now that I been elected, it's time to fill it."

There was no sound from the other end of the couch.

"I'm offering you the job, Emmett. You're the best man for it."

Still he didn't look at me. "Mike Neils's in line for that job," he said.

"Not rightly, no. Senioritywise, it'd belong to Dalton, but no one in their right mind would wanna see Dalton in that job. And just between you and me, Mike's just too young and inexperienced to handle the responsibility. Besides, he irritates me, and I don't think the sheriff should find his right-hand man irritating, do you?"

Emmett let out a small laugh. "No. Irritating right-hand men tend to take over your job. Like old Larry Joe January took over mine."

"Emmett, it was your decision. You gotta remember that. I know they treated you like dog shit, but they were gonna give you your job back. You're the one threw it back in their faces."

He finally looked at me. Okay, glared at me. "Easy for you to say. Nobody ever done nothing like that to you."

"I'm not saying you didn't do the right thing, Emmett," I said. "I'm just saying the right thing or the wrong thing, it was your decision."

He made a *humpth* sound and turned back to the blackened TV screen. "I'm doing okay, Milt. Don't need a job or nothing right now. I got my retirement pay—they give it to me in a lump sum when I quit. I can live off that for a while, specially when I sell the house."

"You selling the house?" I asked. First I'd heard of that.

"Yeah, talked to Marcia Knight over at Knight-Bridger Realty today. They gonna have somebody come appraise this sucker, then put it on the market."

I sighed. "Emmett, you've lived in this house for—"

"For fifteen years. My boy died in this house and my wife died in this house. See any damned reason why I should keep this pile a shit?"

"You're right. A new start. Get yourself one of them condos they're building over in Bishop—"

"Thought maybe I'd buy me an RV. Take off for a little while," he said.

I stood up and walked to the TV. Before I turned *Jeopardy* back on, I said, "Well, Emmett, the job's yours if you want it. At least for the next six months. I ain't giving it to Mike no matter what you say. And I won't advertise it for six months."

He nodded his head. "Turn *Jeopardy* back on, wouldja?"

I turned the TV on and left the house.

* * *

22

That weekend, Melissa had to go down to Dallas to visit a sick friend, and me and Jean kept Rebecca. Good practice for the upcoming baby, and besides, Rebecca's the sweetest little thing you ever did see. Never did get on much with kids—till I met Rebecca.

That Sunday evening, Melissa pulled her little red Miata into our long driveway and we went out to greet her—me, Jean, and Rebecca. Unfortunately, she wasn't alone. Mike Neils was sitting beside her. I hadn't seen Mike since he'd walked out of my office on Friday morning. The day's schedule had to be rearranged to make up for his absence. Though under the circumstances, I hadn't wanted to gig him for it. Now, seeing him sitting in the car with Melissa, after what was obviously an illicit weekend in "Big D," I wasn't so sure.

Melissa ran and picked up Rebecca in her arms, swinging her around. Then Rebecca held out her arms to Mike, who took her and hugged her hard. Which didn't just piss me off. I was thinking maybe of making Mike Neils the permanent jailer. A rotation job everybody hated. It was boring and nasty and seemed to be just perfect for the likes of Mike Neils.

"Can we come in and wind down a minute?" Melissa asked, addressing Jean, knowing better, under the circumstances, than to address me.

Jean smiled real big. "Come on! How about some coffee? I was just about to fix some fancy decaffeinated."

Everybody agreed that sounded great. But I took over for Jean. I didn't feel like being in the same room with those two any more than I could help it.

After I brought in coffee and fixings and sat down, Rebecca on my lap, Melissa said, "Well, Mike and I have some news."

I noticed Mike sitting there on the side of the couch he shared with Jean, squirming fit to beat the band. Then it hit me—they'd run off and got married.

"Y'all run off and got married, didn't you?" I said.

First Melissa's eyes got wide, then she burst out laughing. "Good God! Why would you think that? No!"

"I wish," Mike muttered.

Melissa sobered and looked first at Jean and then at me. "I sorta lied—about the sick friend in Dallas."

"No kidding," I said, eyeing Mike.

"I went to Dallas for a job interview. It's as head social worker for a large psychiatric clinic, and the pay is outrageous. Of course, so is housing in Dallas. So I guess that works out. Anyway, they offered me the job."

I looked at Jean and Jean looked at me. Neither of us said anything.

"Look, I know this comes as a shock to both of you. Jean, I'll be able to give you a full two-week notice. But this is such a great opportunity for Rebecca and me. . . ."

Jean leaned forward to where Melissa was perched on the hassock in front of my chair and put her arms around the girl, hugging her tight. "Don't worry about that. I'll find someone to take your job. I'll never find someone to replace you—but I'll find someone for the job."

Four-year-old Rebecca was asleep in my arms. I looked at that beautiful little face, the coffee-colored skin, the slight thickness to the lips and spread of nose that bespoke her father's ancestry, then looked at Melissa. "You're taking Rebecca away from me?" I asked. I felt tears stinging the back of my eyes and handed the sleeping child to her mother and walked into the kitchen.

I leaned against the sink and gulped in air. I'd only had Rebecca in my life for five or six months, but it had seemed like forever. Like she'd been my own flesh-and-blood granddaughter for all of her four years. Ain't it funny how you can get attached to kids? Ain't it really just goddamn funny?

I washed my face at the kitchen sink and went back into the living room. Mike stood when I walked in. "I'm going with Melissa to Dallas, Milt. I done turned in my applications at the county and the city down there. See what happens. May have to go back to the Academy, seeing as how that's Texas and all—"

"You getting married?" I asked.

"Well, now, Milt, I asked, believe me, I asked. . . ."

"Milt," Melissa said, laying the baby down on the couch next to Jean and coming up and putting her arms around me. "You know I don't do things the simple way. Marriage is an institution—I've never felt the need to be institutionalized."

"So you two are just gonna go live in sin in Dallas with my grandbaby?"

Melissa grinned up at me. "Sure as hell looks that way," she said.

3

Two weeks later, we had a going-away party for Melissa and Rebecca. Unfortunately, we had to include Mike.

It was early May and nature was doing her thing. The road I live on, Mountain Falls Road, winds straight uphill from the highway and circles up the mountain, then down again, hitting the highway about half a mile from the other entrance. Jennifer Creek, which runs behind Melissa's house—across the road from me—originates from an underground spring at the crest of the little mountain, runs half a mile, then drops straight down into what used to be a dammed-up pool at the bottom when my old friend Haywood Hunter had a camp and RV park there. A tornado a while back busted the dam and Haywood got paid a pretty penny to move, which he did. During the summer months Jennifer Creek is just a little trickle and the water at the end of the falls stays pretty much put in the pool. Come spring, though, when we get the rains, the north end of the road is underwater and there's only the one entrance to my place.

It had been raining off and on since mid-April, so that whole north end was a gushing river. The county—in the guise of me—had put up roadblocks to convince anybody stupid enough to come that way that maybe they best rethink their options.

The night of the party, the rains slacked off and we had real pretty weather, although we told everybody to come in the south end of the road.

Things had been buzzing around the sheriff's department since Mike's resignation had been announced. I planned on moving Jasmine Bodine from nights to days and had hired a new man for the night shift. Hank Dobbins was twenty-three, newly out of the Academy, and a lifelong resident of Longbranch. His parents were the first blacks to own their own business in Longbranch and not get run out of town on a rail for being so uppity. They owned Dobbins' Dry Cleaning over on State Street, which is just off the central business district of downtown Longbranch. Hank'd be riding with Jasmine for a couple of weeks to get the hang of everything, then Jasmine would move to days, replacing Mike.

Two days before the party, my sister Jewel had called, asking if she could bring some extra company to the party.

"Hell, you and your brood alone'll take up the whole downstairs," I said, jokinglike.

"Well, a party's no fun unless you have to fight your way to the punch bowl, right?" she said. "And you tell Jean I'm bringing some of those fancy appetizers she likes so much. And anything else she wants me to bring."

I refrained from asking out loud what cooking of my sister's Jean could possibly have liked. I figured Jean'd just been being polite—saying something nice about some concoction of my sister's before spitting it out into the nearest receptacle.

"You finally dealing with this Melissa-Mike thing?" my sister asked.

"I'm fine," I said abruptly.

She giggled. "Oh, you sound just swell."

"You said you were going to bring company to the party?" I said, by way of changing the subject.

"Oh! Yes! Remember me mentioning Libby Fortuna?"

Did I remember my sister mentioning Libby Fortuna? Only

about a hundred million times. Libby Fortuna had been Honey Lancaster's roommate at LSU. Honey Lancaster was my sister's next-door neighbor and best friend when she'd lived in Houston. And I'd heard the story a million and eleven times. Jewel'd always brag about "knowing" Libby Fortuna—which I figured meant she'd been introduced to her once. But according to Jewel, the three of them had been big buddies when Libby had been working for a local station in Houston. About ten years ago, she'd gone to one of the big networks. I suppose you've heard it often enough: "This is Libby Fortuna, reporting from the White House." When Jewel lived with me, there was only one network news show we watched and that was the one with Libby Fortuna. And every time we watched it, Jewel would say, "Did I tell you I knew her in Houston?"

Which I don't know was all that much to brag about. Libby Fortuna had one of those obnoxious, grating voices with an attitude, like so many of her ilk.

"So what about Libby Fortuna?" I asked my sister, hoping I could get off the phone sometime in the next century.

"She's here in Longbranch!"

Well, now, did Longbranch finally make the national news? Maybe it was that exciting sheriff's race a while back. "What's she doing here?" I asked.

"You will not believe this."

"Try me."

"Remember the Gallagher twins?"

"The Gallagher twins?"

"Phillip and Daniel—"

"Oh!" I said, light dawning. "Old lady Gallagher's change-of-life babies. Yeah, what about 'em?"

"Well—" my sister said, always one to drag out the juicy stuff—"you remember that Daniel went to law school and was in Washington for several years, working as an aide to Congressman Spohn?"

"Well, no, not as you'd notice. Don't keep up like I used to," I said, all sarcasticlike. Went right over her head.

"He and Libby got married!"

"Huh," I said.

"And . . . they've moved back to Longbranch. Libby's working on a book about her days at the White House during the Reagan years—she calls it an exposé—and Daniel's opened his own law practice. Anyway, Honey went to the wedding, and when she found out where Libby and Daniel were moving to, she almost died! Can you imagine?"

"Uh-huh," I said, reading a handout from the State Highway Patrol on DUI arrests in the state for the month of February.

"So, anyway, is it okay if I bring Libby and Daniel? And, of course, his mother. She seems to go everywhere with them."

"Old lady Gallagher? She still alive?"

"Seems to be," my sister said, getting a little sarcastic her ownself.

"Sure, no problem," I said. "The more the merrier."

Which is exactly what we got come Saturday night—more, and more, and more. We musta had close to a hundred people in my little house on Mountain Falls Road. A. B. Tate would be manning the dispatch for half the night; then Dalton would go replace him so A.B. could come to the party, too. Everybody else from the sheriff's department was there—Gladys and Jasmine and Hank Dobbins and, of course, Mike. Former sheriff Elberry Blankenship and his wife, Nadine, came, of course, for Mike and for Melissa, who they'd grown fond of, too, in the short time she'd been in our midst. Lots of people from my church showed up and lots of people from Jean's church, 'cause Mike was a Catholic, too. Half the hospital personnel were there. (Even some of the inmates of the locked psychiatric ward were there, I think. Or maybe just some people who should have been).

Emmett Hopkins was conspicuous in his absence—but maybe just to me.

It was pretty early, around seven-thirty or eight, I guess,

29

when Hank Dobbins and Rebecca discovered each other. There aren't a whole lot of black people in Prophesy County, and Rebecca's always been the only black child in her day care. The major minority in Prophesy County has always been Native American, so Rebecca hadn't seen that many black people. Hank and I were standing next to the food table (my favorite place at any gathering) when he spotted Rebecca.

"Who does she belong to?" he asked.

"She's my granddaughter," I said.

Hank looked at me with surprise, then looked at Rebecca. "No kidding?"

"Of the adopted variety," I said. "Her mama's not really my kin, but she was almost my stepdaughter once."

"Oh." He walked up to Rebecca and squatted down. Rebecca looked at him shyly at first, but before I knew it, they were sitting on the couch together eating chips and dips and talking up a storm. Maybe, I thought, moving to the big city will be good for her. Maybe she won't feel like such an outsider—one of the few of her race in a town that had treated her badly once upon a time. And maybe I could learn to live with Melissa's decision. Maybe I could—if it would be good for Rebecca.

Around nine o'clock, Jewel Anne showed up with her famous friend and all hell broke loose. Libby Fortuna wasn't much to brag about on TV—just one of them hair-spray journalists with a toothpaste-ad smile. Close-up and personal, she was a knockout: velvety smooth olive complexion, dark, dark brown hair, and blue eyes that could bowl you over. She was wearing what my mama called in her later years a pants suit, but Libby's looked to be made out of silk, a deep red that made her own coloring stand out all the more. I got good TV reception, but my TV never recepted the true colors of Libby Fortuna.

Daniel Gallagher stood next to her like he had the prize jewel in his possession. I vaguely remembered the twins. They were a few years older than Jewel and several years younger than me, but Mrs. Gallagher had been a great friend of Mama's, so I'd seen the little boys often enough over at our house. Grown up, Daniel Gallagher was a handsome man: blond hair, blue eyes, tall and thin—the kinda guy women like to see in a pair of tight blue jeans, which just happened to be what he was wearing, along with a camel-colored suede jacket and a white button-down shirt. I studied him for a minute, thinking that except for the tight jeans, I could pull off something like that. Jean had been after me to dump my seersucker suits for something sexier.

Looking at the two of them, Libby and Daniel, I figured they were gonna make some beautiful babies together—but then, I been thinking about making babies a lot lately.

Mrs. Gallagher stood on the other side of her son, beaming with pride at both of 'em. She was a little dumpling lady—short and plump, with gray hair pulled back in a messy bun that always seemed to be springing a leak. She came up to me and hugged me to her soft bosom.

"Oh, Milt, as I live and breathe! I haven't seen you in so long!" She pushed me away from her and her face slid into a sad frown. "I was so sorry about your mama—and so awfully sorry I couldn't make it to the funeral."

"We got your flowers, Miz Gallagher, and we surely appreciated 'em," I said.

"Seems hard to believe Margurite's been gone almost ten years," Mrs. Gallagher said.

"Have you met my beautiful, famous daughter-in-law?" She pulled Libby gently toward her. "Libby, honey, this is Milt. His mama was my best friend in the whole world. Forever and ever. And he's Jewel's brother!"

"Hi, Milt," she said, grinning and sticking out her hand.

Figured there was something wrong with the sound on my TV, too. Her voice wasn't at all like what I heard coming to me live from the White House.

31

"I'm a big fan of yours," I heard myself saying.

Another hand found its way into mine. "Remember me?" Daniel said.

"Well, now, I either remember you or I remember your brother—who ever knew?"

Daniel laughed politely.

And then I lost sight of 'em as the partygoers realized there was a celebrity in their midst and engulfed Libby Fortuna and her family in a sea of people.

Around about midnight, the table was getting bare. Jean and Jewel were in the kitchen trying to find something extra in the cupboards to feed the tons of people who didn't seem to be leaving anytime soon. I made the mistake of going in.

"Y'all need some help?"

Jewel snorted and Jean gave me the ole rolly-eye bit.

"I'm just asking!" I said.

"You still have that stash of beer and potato chips upstairs?" my sister inquired.

The answer, of course, was no. While Jewel and her kids were living in my house, I'd been relegated to an upstairs room—and not allowed to drink beer in front of her children. After a couple of weeks, I'd bought myself a small refrigerator and a TV for my upstairs room and spent a lot of time, according to Jewel Anne, "swilling beer and farting in front of a ball game." After she moved out, I moved my beer and other goodies into the refrigerator in the kitchen. It was, after all, my frigging house!

"No," I said. "I don't. Don't have any pretzels stashed under the mattress, either."

Jewel said something to Jean and they both giggled. I know when I'm out of the loop. I'm no fool.

"Popcorn!" Jean yelled, heading for the pantry.

You know how you're supposed to learn from your mistakes? Well, I'd always wondered about that. How can somebody learn from a mistake when each mistake is brand-new? Not like you're gonna make the same mistake again. You keep making new ones. Like the one I made right after me and Jean got married. She and Jewel got extremely pissed at each other and I set about making things right between them. How was I supposed to know that having them two be friends was gonna make my life a living hell? Their idea of womanly bonding is to gang up on me.

The next day, I helped Mike Neils pack the last of Melissa's and Rebecca's stuff into the U-Haul.

"What are you gonna do about the house?" I asked Melissa.

"Billy Moulini offered to buy it back," she said, naming the man she'd originally bought the old Munsky farmhouse from and who now owned all of the mountain—except my house and land.

"Oh, goody," I said, "now he gets to play feudal lord again."

"When was the last time Billy was even on the mountain, Milt?" Melissa asked.

"That's not the point—" I started, but she'd grabbed me in a bear hug, and I thought now was no time to get petty.

She pushed me away and looked up into my face. "You've been better to me than I deserve, Milt Kovak."

"Oh, now—"

"You have. You're the daddy I never had."

"Well—"

"I love you," she said, and hugged me tight. All I could do was hug her back.

I smothered Rebecca with about a million kisses and made her promise to write as soon as she learned how, then shook hands with Mike.

"Take care of my girls," I told him, my voice husky. "You don't, I'll come gunning for you."

His face was sober as he said, "I don't take care of 'em, you can just shoot me like a dog."

Jean kissed everybody, and Mike got behind the wheel of

the truck and Melissa and Rebecca got in the Miata and they caravaned out of the driveway and down Mountain Falls Road, little Rebecca waving at me as long as she could before her mama drove her out of sight. I took that opportunity to show my wife I wasn't too damned macho to cry.

The next week was thankfully a busy one and I didn't have much time to miss Melissa and Rebecca. Jean had hired someone to take Melissa's job, a girl—excuse me, woman—named Nancy Anderson, who was about twelve and fresh out of the OU MSW program. Okay, so she was twenty-four. She *looked* twelve. She was one of those freckle-faced redheads that don't look their age until they reach a hundred or so. I had lunch on Tuesday with her and Jean, and let me tell you, she didn't act much older than twelve, either. She was a giggly mouth-breather and I had to wonder why in the hell Jean chose her. But it wasn't my place to ask, so I didn't.

We were shorthanded on day shift, with just me and Dalton, so I made a deal with Elberry to come in two days a week to help with the paperwork. The county commissioners okayed this, and I figured it would work out okay until Elberry started telling me what to do and how to do it. Which happened, of course, twenty-seven minutes after he showed up the first day.

Jasmine reported to me, in her usual sad, Eeyore voice, that Hank Dobbins was doing real well.

On Monday of the second week without Mike, Jewel Anne came by my office, bringing Libby Fortuna with her. Libby looked like she just stepped out of an L. L. Bean catalog, all decked out for country living.

"Libby and I thought we'd stop by and say hi. We're on our way to Tejas County to that new antique shop they've got over there."

"Well, I hear the prices are sky-high, but I wish you luck," I said. "I'm sure you two'd have a good time at a dump."

Both women giggled. "That's true," Libby said. "But"—and here she beamed at my sister—"we came by to tell you that you and I have something in common."

I looked quizzical, as I knew I was supposed to. "Oh? What's that?"

"I'm pregnant!" Libby said, almost shouting.

I laughed, got up from the chair, and went around the desk, hugging the new mother-to-be.

"Congratulations!" I said, trying not to think how nice she felt to be hugging. I'm not one of those men who hug women willy-nilly. Standing back and giving her stomach a look, I said, "How far along? And are y'all gonna have to have the amnio?"

Libby nodded. "Already had it done, and I'm four and a half months. I didn't want to tell anybody until we were sure everything was okay. He's fine!"

"A boy?" That deserved another hug. I'll admit I was getting to like it. "Well, hell, our kids'll be about the same age—in the same Little League, Cub Scouts—"

"Jean and I can be den mothers and room mothers."

We prattled on for a while, Jewel Anne beaming down like a proud aunt.

That afternoon, when I made my run by Emmett's house, which I'd pared down to about once or twice a week, there was a SOLD sticker on the FOR SALE sign in front of his house, and a huge Winnebago sitting in the driveway.

I got out and knocked on the front door, hearing Emmett yell, "Come in!" from deep inside the house.

I walked in and found him with his head in the cabinet under the kitchen sink. He looked up when he heard my footsteps.

"You and Jean use a half-empty can a Comet and a used Brillo pad?" he asked.

I shrugged. "Why not?"

He pulled himself to a standing position, using the rim of the sink, and put the Comet and box of Brillo pads into a cardboard box. "Got some frozen stuff and refrigerator stuff in here won't fit in the RV. And some dishes ain't worth storing or taking. You want 'em?"

I shrugged again. Knowing Jean, she'd just throw it all out, but I figured it would give Emmett a feeling of accomplishment.

"See your house got sold," I said.

"Yeah, young couple from Tejas County. He just got a job working at the refinery up the Tulsa Highway—figured this'd be a closer commute than Taylor. Got me a good price for it, too."

"Well, that's great. Nice-looking RV out there."

Emmett glanced out the kitchen window at the Winnebago in the driveway. "Yeah. Got it used. People had it 'fore me got it all fitted out. Sold me ever thing—including plates and cups and stuff. Real good deal."

I nodded my head. "Well," I said. "When you thinking about taking off?"

Emmett looked around the kitchen. "Movers are coming tomorrow to take my stuff to storage. I got ole Miz Renfroe coming in after that to clean up the place. Paying her fifty bucks." He finally looked at me. "I'm leaving right after the movers," he said.

"Well, maybe I'll come by—"

He shook his head. "Naw. That's okay." He held out his hand. "Milt, I couldn'ta got through this without you."

I shook his hand. "Well, yeah, you coulda, but—"

"No. I couldn't have. Thanks."

"Emmett—"

He picked up the box of junk he was giving me and put his free arm around my shoulder and headed me toward the front door. "You take good care of Jean and that baby, Milt, hear?"

He shook my hand again, handed me the box, and shut the door in my face. I could take a hint. I left.

* * *

About a month later, me and Jean had Jewel and Harmon and Libby and Daniel over for dinner on a Saturday night. Daniel was a nice guy, I decided, after the ladies took their leave after dinner, going into the new nursery to show off. Jean and Jewel wanted to show Libby the cradle Jewel had given Jean—the one my daddy and I had made when my mamma was pregnant with Jewel. Long, long time ago.

Us three he-men sat in the living room discussing politics and football, just like men are supposed to do. Daniel, having lived in Washington and having worked for Prophesy County's own congressman, had a lot to say on the subject of politics, and most of it was so downright god-awful, you just had to laugh. My tax dollars at work, my ass. When the women came back in, Libby joined in the discussion, talking about her days at the White House, through Reagan and Bush. The lady was downright funny, and I think my wife figured out halfway through the evening that I was getting myself a nice, innocent little crush on the pretty lady from Washington.

At least that's what I figured when later that night in bed she said, "Well, you certainly made a fool of yourself."

"What?" I demanded, sitting up in bed. "What'd I do?"

I could see the hormones flashing in her eyes and knew I was in for it. She turned over, giving me her back. A trick she learned from my cat, Evinrude. "You know," she said, her voice muffled by her pillow.

"Now, Jean, listen here, I don't know what you're talking about. What'd I do?"

She whirled around in the bed, glaring at me. " 'Oh, Libby, you're just so funny,' " she said, I guess trying to imitate me. Did a piss-poor job of it, I might add.

"Well, she was telling some funny stories—"

"I never knew you were so politically insightful, Milton," she said. Just like my mama—if Jean used Milton instead of Milt, I knew I was in deep dog doo.

I wonder sometimes how people ever have more than one child. This hormone business had me by the nuts. "Honey," I said, all soothinglike, "I was just being polite to our company. Jean, you're letting those hormones get you again—"

I, of course, am not allowed to talk about her hormones. I am not allowed to say anything about hormones.

She glared at me, laid back down, her back to me, and was asleep in about a minute and a half, while I stayed up most of the night trying to think of ways to save my marriage.

Which I needn't have done. Next morning, Jean was bright-eyed and bushy-tailed, and horny as the devil.

Women, go figure.

The following Monday afternoon, I was driving over to the high school for my end-of-school "Drugs—Just Say No" speech when I got the call from Gladys about a suspicious car parked behind the Stop N Shop off Broadway. It was getting on to three o'clock in the afternoon when I pulled in behind the silver Lincoln Town Car. The call from Gladys had said it had been sitting there most of the morning and most of the afternoon and it was causing problems with delivery trucks getting into the dock area of the Stop N Shop.

The sun was beating down hotter than a two-dollar pistol, but the Lincoln Town Car was buttoned up tight. I peered into the front seat, not seeing anything, and was just about to go back to my car to call a wrecker to come tow the thing off when a peek of color—red—caught my attention in the backseat. The windows of the Town Car were tinted, but when I stuck my face right up to it and shielded my eyes with my hands, I could see in. On the floor of the backseat was a heap of clothes, red-and-blue-striped. Unfortunately, that heap had a human arm sticking out.

4

I got the slim jim out of the trunk of my squad car and popped the lock on the front door of the Town Car and unlocked the back door. There are those that say I got the stomach of a flat-iron skillet—constitutionwise not shapewise—but the smell coming out of that locked-up and overheated backseat was bad enough to knock a buzzard off a manure wagon. I got the hand-kerchief out of my back pocket—where my daddy had encour-aged me to keep one since I was old enough to wear long pants—and reached for the body on the floor. Because that's what it was. Even without Dr. Jim to declare it dead, there wasn't any way that thing on the floor could be living. It took me a full minute of bending over the body before I realized I was looking at what used to be Libby Fortuna.

Part of me was in shock—that part of me that has a wife and a baby on the way and a sister and friends and believes in God and motherhood and apple pie. The other part of me—the cop part—took over, because it had to. Maybe it was Libby Fortuna on the floor of that car, somebody I knew, but chances were pretty heavy in such a small county that whoever had been on that floor, I woulda known them.

I quickly backed away and went to the squad car, calling Gladys and telling her to send Dalton and Dr. Jim over right away. I stayed by the squad car, not wanting to go back near the Lincoln, not wanting to see what was left of that formerly lively, lovely lady. When I thought about that baby that had been brewing away in her body, I almost cried. But I steadied myself and waited for the real work to begin.

Dalton and Dr. Jim got there about the same time. Dalton stood with me while Dr. Jim crawled into the backseat of the Lincoln and looked at the body.

Crawling back out again, he came up to me and said, "Throat's been cut. Lots of lacerations on other parts of the body, but I'd say the throat's what did her in. And, just preliminary speculation, but looks like the other lacerations might have been done after she was already dead."

I nodded my head and went back to the Lincoln. Over my shoulder, I said to Dalton, "Call Floyd and have him come over here to take the body to the morgue."

Floyd Ackerman was the local funeral director. His hearse doubled as an ambulance and was used by the county. Dalton nodded and got on the radio while I looked around in the front seat. Hell, I didn't even know if this was her car. There was no key in the ignition, no purse on the front seat. I tried to open the glove compartment to see if there was any ID in there— proof of insurance, car registration—but the glove compartment was locked. I'd have to wait until the ambulance got there to move the body, to see if maybe her purse was under her, the car keys lying on the floor of the backseat.

I told Dalton to seal the car as soon as the ambulance attendants had the body out—you have to spell everything out for Dalton—and then have the car taken to the parking lot of the sheriff's department so we could go over it. Meanwhile, I had the worst part of my job to do: notifying next of kin.

I knew Daniel's new law office was in an old building within walking distance of the Longbranch Inn. I'd met him there at lunch once or twice. I drove over there and got out of the squad car, going into the building and walking up the flight of stairs

40

to Daniel's office. The building was an old one, built in the 1920s, with lots of high ceilings and marble floors and with the smell of rot and mildew a lot of old buildings get kept down to a minimum.

The door to Daniel's office had a pane of frosted glass, just like in an old movie, and the name DANIEL GALLAGHER, ATTORNEY AT LAW was stenciled on the glass. I opened it and walked in. Mrs. Gallagher, Daniel's mother, was sitting behind a desk, typing away on a word processor. She looked up when I opened the door.

Her face broke into a huge grin. "Well, Milton! How are you?"

I worked hard to smile back. "Miz Gallagher," I said. "Daniel in?"

She stood up. "He sure is! Let me just tell him you're here!"

She turned and walked to a door a little ways from her desk, knocked quickly, and opened it. "You got a visitor!" she said in a singsong voice.

I followed her lead and walked to the door of Daniel's office and looked in. He was sitting behind a large desk, papers and law books spread out before him. He grinned when he saw me. "Well, if it's not the long arm of the law! Hey, come on in!"

I thought for a moment Mrs. Gallagher was going to follow me, but she didn't. She shut the door and went back to her desk. I stood in front of Daniel's desk, and if I'd had a hat, it woulda been in my hand.

I guess Daniel could tell something was wrong by my face. He sat up straighter and his face got serious. "Have a seat, Milt," he said.

I declined. "Daniel, I got some real bad news."

Daniel stood up slowly. "Libby . . ."

I walked around the desk and put my hand gently on his shoulder, encouraging him to sit down at his desk. "Daniel, Libby's dead."

His face turned ashen and his whole body began to shake.

"Oh my God, oh my God, oh my God—how? What happened?"

"Just a minute, Daniel," I said. I went out to the front room for Mrs. Gallagher. Briefly, I told her what I'd told Daniel. She rushed into her son's office and held on to him as he began to weep. "What happened?" Mrs. Gallagher said, looking at me over her son's head, where she clutched it to her breast.

I sighed. Things were bad enough. But I had to tell them. "She was murdered," I said.

Daniel pulled away from his mother and stood up. "What?"

He came at me. Mrs. Gallagher grabbed his arm, but still he came. I put both hands out in front of me, encouraging him to back off. "Daniel, I'm sorry. I'm real sorry. We don't have any leads right now—"

"What'd they do to her?"

"Daniel, no," Mrs. Gallagher said, her voice shaking, tears streaming down her face.

"Your mama's right, Daniel. Not right now—"

"What the hell did they do to her?" he screamed.

So I told him. Briefly. No punches pulled. Just the facts, ma'am. The brutal, horrible, ugly facts.

The fire went out of him. He fell back against his desk. His mother went to him, holding him in her arms as he wept, the horrible sound of a man not used to crying filled the room. I left.

The town didn't take the news of Libby Fortuna's death well. She was the first national celebrity ever to live in Prophesy County, and no one liked the idea that her residency had been cut so short—or why. The national news, especially her own network, began showing up later that same day.

And wouldn't you know it, the one newshound I actually knew, and one of my least-favorite people in the world, showed up at the office just hours after the news of Libby's death had been released. I was in the bull pen, trying to coordinate the investigation. Dalton was outside in the hot sun, trying to keep the journalists at bay. But Dalton being Dalton, and remembering this particular fella fairly well, he let him in when the guy just barely hinted at me expecting him.

The door opened, the voices from the rabble outside rose in protest, and I turned around. Marv Bernblatt. And the only thing changed about him was there was a little more gray in his mostly fuzzy black hair. Tall, thin to the point of skinny, his hair still too long, his Hush Puppies still worn down on the sides, his jeans still bell-bottomed, and he was wearing the same faded red T-shirt with the legend "Eschew Obfuscation" in dirty white he'd had on the last time I'd seen him. I figured if he was still wearing the same clothes, it was doubtful his personality had changed all that much.

Couple of years back, a lady who worked as a teller in the bank in town had died of carbon monoxide poisoning—and the rest of her family had died along with her. Marv Bernblatt had come to town, claiming to be with the *Washington Post*, and gave me some information that helped, in a very slight way, with my investigation. And the whole time he wasn't trying to interfere with my investigation or just bug me for the pure-dee joy of it, he was trying to bed my sister, Jewell.

Seeing him walk in the door did not make my day. Turning to Hank Dobbins, I said, "Get that slime outta here!"

Marv sidestepped Hank and made his way over to me. "Now, hold on, Milt." He held out his hand. For me to shake, I suppose. I didn't take him up on it. He scratched his dirty hair instead. "Now, Milt. Don't be that way. You know you wouldn't have cracked that Lois Bell case without me."

"Shee-it," I said, turning my back on him. Something else that chaps my ass about the boy—I get real redneck the minute I see him, start doing a sorta imitation of Rod Steiger in *In the Heat of the Night*. He just don't exactly bring out the best in me.

He handed me a card. "I'm really representing the *Post* this time," he said. "I called them up a couple of hours ago, told them about my relationship with you, and they couldn't wait to send me down here."

"Go away, Bernblatt," I said, bending over a desk where a map of the county was laid out.

"Come on, man! We got history! Just give me a little edge over what you tell the other guys, huh?"

Which got me up and out the front door for my brief but meaningful press conference. Damned if I would give Bernblatt something I wouldn't give Peter Jennings.

All I could tell 'em was all I knew—it had been Libby's car; her purse and keys were missing, as were her wristwatch and wedding and engagement rings. Mrs. Gallagher said Libby'd been wearing a pair of diamond stud earrings, a carat each, that were also missing. We swept the car for prints, but the only ones found were the ones that were supposed to be there— Libby's, Daniel's, and Mrs. Gallagher's. Dr. Jim's autopsy revealed what he'd suspected when he first saw the body—the slashed throat had happened first, the other lacerations had been done to the corpse, and her body had carried a twenty-two-week healthy male fetus. Healthy, that is, until his life-support system, his mama, had died.

When I finished, I told them all "no questions" and headed back inside the building, leaving Dalton to stand guard at the door and telling him in no uncertain terms that Bernblatt was not allowed back in.

I got Jasmine and Hank working days, Jasmine and Dalton working overtime, covering nights. Hank was too new for double shifts. We rousted people at the Sidewinder and the no-accounts who lived at the Holiday Hell in Bishop, the old, beat-up transient trailer court.

We managed to confiscate three handguns, arrested four people for possession of controlled substances, and found a young man who'd been on a wanted poster from Oklahoma Highway Patrol for over a year.

We also had two people call in to tell us they knew who'd done it: who'd killed Libby Fortuna. One was a call from a lady who just knew it was her ex-husband. Turned out, after a couple of phone calls and a lot of meaningless excitement, that the man, James Cleary, had been working in Texarkana the day in question but did owe his ex-wife a heap of back child support. The other caller turned in a guy whose dog had been using his flower beds as a shithouse and was getting damned tired of it. People never cease to amaze me with what they will do to their fellows.

But basically, we got no place and we got there in a big hurry. The first forty-eight hours in a murder investigation are the crucial time—at least that's what my law-enforcement journals tell me. But in that first forty-eight hours, all we found out was that Libby Fortuna had been killed by person or persons unknown.

I spent almost the whole of those first forty-eight hours at the office, trying to find out something. When I finally went home, tired, hungry, my back hurting, it was to find Marv Bernblatt sitting in my living room, having herb tea with my wife.

"What the hell are you doing here, boy?" I said, looking and feeling meaner than a junkyard dog.

Jean pulled herself up from the couch. "Milton!" she said. "We have company!"

"That ain't company," I said. "That's a pain in the ass."

"Milt, you old rascal," Bernblatt said, smiling and standing up to pat me on the back. "Married and with a bun in the oven! I'll be damned!"

"Get away from me, Bernblatt," I said, moving away from him.

Still smiling, he said, "I don't mean to keep you two from dinner, or whatever"—at this point he leered at my bride—"but if you'll just tell Jewell I'm here—"

This is where I started grinning. "She don't live here anymore," I said. "Actually, she moved out when she got married.

She and the kids have moved in with her new husband." I put a little emphasis on the words *married* and *husband*.

If it had been anybody else, I might have felt a little bad watching as his face fell, but remembering that his proposal to my sister had been that she come out to D.C. and move in with him, *without* benefit of marriage, and that if she thought they needed a bigger place, he'd be happy to move anywhere *she* could afford—well, remembering all that kept my pity in check.

"Oh. Well." He moved to the door. "It was really nice meeting you, Jean. But how a classy broad like you got herself mixed up with this redneck, I'll never know." And with that, he was out the door before I had a chance to kick his butt.

But, as they say, there's no rest for the weary, and Jean was fit to be tied about me behaving like an "illbred, uncouth slob" to our company.

"Honey, you don't know this guy," I said, sinking down into my easy chair.

"Neither do you, apparently. In the few minutes I spent with him, I found him to be an articulate, intelligent man with some delightful insights."

"Oh, really?" I said, wondering just what it was that slob of a guy had that made women like my sister and my wife take to him.

"Yes, really. And I found your behavior to be beyond rude, Milton. I found it reprehensible."

"Oh, really?" I said. No one could ever fault *me* for my witty reparte.

Jean got herself up on her crutches and shot her way into the bedroom, slamming the door behind her. I went to sleep in my chair.

Jewel Anne took Libby's death real hard. She spent a lot of time with Jean, the two of them going over it and over it and both pissed as hell at me for not figuring out in a hurry who'd done it.

46

Libby's funeral was a full-blown affair, with people showing up from all over the country and even a couple of foreigners besides. There was one guy from France who was with the government, and even a Russian from the embassy in Washington. Miss Libby did know a few people, and that's a fact.

The service was held at the Lutheran church in Bishop and was open to the public. The graveside service was private. Jewel and her family had been invited. Me and Jean hadn't. I understood that. It hurt, but I understood it. I was the bearer of bad tidings. And I was the incompetent fool who hadn't found out yet, and maybe never would, who had killed Libby Fortuna.

Jewel had invited us over to her house after the private graveside service, and we went. No one would be going to the home of the bereaved, as is usually the custom, because Mrs. Gallagher had specifically requested that no one come. She said, and probably rightly so, that Daniel couldn't handle that. So Jewel had opened her own home to the mourners from the cemetery. People brought the food there. Jewel would take it over to the Gallaghers' later.

The first person I saw at my sister's house was Marv Bernblatt. I couldn't believe it. I marched over to my sister. "What the hell's he doing here?" I asked.

My sister was all wide-eyed innocence. "Who?"

"You know who! That damned Yankee newshound!"

"Oh! Marv! I couldn't for the life of me think who you could be referring to—"

"Stow it, Jewel. Does Harmon know he's here?"

"Of course. Harmon's taking Marv out later to look at his motorcycle collection."

She smiled sweetly and I left her, trying to avoid contact with good old Marv Bernblatt.

I'd seen Honey and Chuck Lancaster at the church service, but not to speak to. They were up front with the family, while Jean and I had been relegated to the rear of the church. I knew she'd be at Jewel's; I knew she was staying there, she and

Chuck. When Jewel had had her trouble back in Houston, when her husband, Henry, had been murdered, Honey Lancaster and I had worked together trying to figure out what had happened. Just 'cause I'd kissed Honey once, I didn't think it would show.

As usual, I was wrong. She was standing by the fireplace in Jewel's large living room, a cup of coffee in one hand, talking to the minister. When he left, I took Jean over.

"Milt!" Honey cried, throwing her arms around me. Not good.

Honey's about five feet nothing and earned her name because of her color—hair, eyes, and skin, all the smooth silk of honey. And she's got this overbite. . . .

"Hey, Honey," I said, removing her arms from around my neck. "Want you to meet my wife, Jean McDonnell. Jean—"

"Hello," Jean said, not bothering to let go of a crutch and offer her hand.

Honey removed her arms and smiled at Jean. "Hi! I heard the old rascal got himself a woman, but I hardly believed it."

Jean's smile was tight. Like the noose around my neck was gonna be later that night.

"Real sorry about your loss, Honey," I said.

She sighed. "I just can't believe it. Libby was . . . Libby . . . oh, God," she said, and buried her face in my shirtfront.

"I'll just leave you two alone," Jean said, and marched off.

"Is she gone?" Honey whispered from the depth of my chest, wiping her tears on the new power tie Jean had just bought me.

"Yeah, she's gone and I'm in big trouble."

Honey grinned up at me. "Good. You should be. Getting married like that without even asking my permission."

"Well, now, I thought about calling, saying please, but then I just said, shoot, a man's gotta do what a man's gotta do."

Honey's face sobered. "What are you doing about this, Milt?"

"This? You mean Libby?"

48

"Yeah, what are you gonna do about it?"

I sighed. "I'm doing everything I can. I won't close this case."

She poked me in the stomach with a finger. "You bet your ass you won't! Daniel has to have some resolution. There has to be an end to this."

I nodded my head. "I'm trying, Honey."

She cocked an eye at me. "You want me to stay and we can play Nick and Nora again?"

I didn't get a chance to reply. A beefy hand with the grip of Arnold Schwarzenegger fell on my shoulder. "Well, sweet Lord Jesus divine, if it ain't ole Milt! Hey, man, how in God's glory are you?" Chuck Lancaster poked me in the stomach with a finger as large as a fifty-cent pickle.

I doubled over and he slapped me on the back. He wasn't trying to hurt me. With Chuck, a former Houston Oiler turned insurance salesman, this was called manly affection.

"Hey, Chuck," I said in a strangled voice while staring at the fibers of my sister's carpet. "How you doing?" I glanced at Honey with what was supposed to be a quizzical look— probably came off looking like I was constipated. Chuck Lancaster's language had left me baffled. When I'd known him before, he'd been a grand user of the *F* word, putting it in some of the strangest places and using it in front of everybody and their brother—or mother. I don't think I'd ever heard him utter a single sentence that wasn't heavily dusted with the expletive.

Honey mouthed, "He's found Jesus."

I wondered, but didn't ask, how Jesus felt about that.

"Man, ain't this disgusting?" Chuck said, referring, I assumed, to the demise of Libby Fortuna.

I straightened gingerly. "Yeah, it surely is," I said.

It was that night, after the funeral, that I woke up in the wee hours with a start. I don't know if I'd dreamed it or if I just woke up with this thought fully formed. The thought being: Jewel said Libby Fortuna had been writing a book. An exposé on

Washington. If so, how interested might someone there be in what she had to say? In other words, what had Libby Fortuna been about to tell the world that someone might murder to hush up?

I slept fitfully the rest of the night and was up and ready to go to work an hour before usual. Jean had had a bad night, too, getting up to go to the bathroom every hour on the hour—whenever Junior stuck a foot on her bladder. We ate breakfast in sleepy silence and were both out the door in a hurry.

I waited till around ten o'clock before calling Daniel Gallagher and asking him if I could come over. He was obliging. When Mrs. Gallagher had raised the boys in Longbranch, back when she and my mama had been so thick, they'd lived in a house not much different from ours—a small two-bedroom Depression-era bungalow. That's not where she lived now. When Libby and Daniel had moved back to town, they'd bought a large, sprawling ranch-style house on about fifty acres between Longbranch and Bishop. I drove up, spotting the white rail fence that surrounded the property right away. A white rail arch with a gate covered the driveway, but the gate was open, since they knew I was coming.

The house itself was dark-stained wood, a long and low one-story structure with a long porch running half the length of the front. I got out in front of the house, took the step up to the porch, and rang the doorbell. Mrs. Gallagher answered my ring.

"Milton," she said, stepping across the threshold and hugging me. "Thank you for coming by," she said.

"How's Daniel?" I asked. I'd had a hard time, the day before, even looking at him during the funeral—his grief had been so open and so obvious. Libby's family, her father and mother and two brothers, some aunts and uncles, had left directly after the funeral. They all seemed to be of the stiff-upper-lip variety, and Daniel's grief had seemed even more poignant by comparison. Little Mrs. G had held her son up through most of the service, her tear-streaked face and rumpled appearance only slightly less pitiful than that of her son.

Mrs. Gallagher shook her head in response to my question about Daniel. "It'll take time," she said. She sighed and walked into the house, with me following.

We were in a foyer of Mexican tile covered with Navajo throw rugs. On the right of the foyer was the living room, one step down from the foyer, with broad plank hardwood floors also covered in spots by colorful Navajo throw rugs. On the left, off the foyer, was the dining room. In the quick second I stood there, I got the impression of soft woods, muted colors, style and grace. I followed Mrs. Gallagher down a hall, passing a large family room dominated by a fireplace and wall-to-wall books, to a door of another room. She knocked briefly and opened it.

"Daniel, Milt's here." She turned, touched my arm briefly, and walked away.

The room was small and fitted out as an office. There was a desk with a computer, bookshelves, and a large overstuffed easy chair, which is where Daniel was. He started to stand, but I shooed him back down.

"Don't get up," I said. I went over and shook his hand, glancing at the walls as I did. This had obviously been Libby's room—her study. The walls were covered with pictures of her—with Ronald Reagan, with John Chancellor, with Lee Iaccoca, with Barbara Bush, and one of four women sitting at a table, obviously having a good time—Libby Fortuna, Connie Chung, and two other TV news types whose names I didn't know. There was also a picture of her from her Houston days, with Honey Lancaster and my sister, Jewel, displayed as prominently as the one with the President.

Daniel obviously noticed me studying the walls, because he said, "She was something, wasn't she?" The pain in his voice was a heartbreaking thing to hear.

"Daniel, I was wondering about that book Libby was writing. . . ."

He nodded his head. "Yeah. That's what you said on the phone." He pointed at the desk. "It's there—the hundred something pages she had of it, and all her notes. I've boxed up stuff for you, including some discs. I think they have notes on them, too."

"Thanks," I said. "I'll get them back to you."

He stood up and headed for the door. "Keep them as long as you need to. The book won't be finished now. Just . . . keep 'em." He walked out the door and I picked up the box off the desk and headed back the way I'd come. Mrs. Gallagher met me at the den.

"Could I get you something to drink, Milt?" she asked.

"No, ma'am, thanks, I best be on my way." With that, I took my leave, depositing the box in the locked space in the back of the Jeep where the spare tire and tools belonged. The spare tire was in a bracket on the back door of the Jeep, so there was ample space for Libby's box. I locked the compartment and took that key off my key chain and put it in my wallet. I got behind the wheel and drove on back to the sheriff's department.

It was later that night, after Jean had turned in, before I had a chance to get the box out of the Jeep and examine the contents. On top was a large loose-leaf binder, inside of which was the 185 pages of Libby Fortuna's manuscript. I opened it to the first page:

LIBBY FORTUNA AT THE WHITE HOUSE
OR
THREE THOUSAND, SIX HUNDRED AND FIFTY
DAYS IN HELL, BUT WHO'S COUNTING?

I was born Elizabeth Margaret Cutter Fortuna in New Orleans, Louisiana, the product of six generations of breeding that all led to one inevitable conclusion: that I would grow up to be, not a doctor or a lawyer, or even an Indian chief, but a lady. Instead, I became a journalist, thereby causing six generations of Cutters and Fortunas to turn over in their mausoleum vaults.

The last argument I gave my parents, the one that convinced them this was a workable solution to my life, was of historic note. Who in the family had not heard the fabulous tales of Great-Great-Grandmother Estella's four years as a Washington hostess, the four years she spent getting information that was passed on to her Confederate cohorts? What, I said to my parents, was reporting, if not spying? How could the family deny me a life they'd been so proud of for my foremother? We southerners are a proud people, proud of our heritage and our ancestry. Therefore, I had them by the proverbial balls.

I smiled to myself, seeing Libby write this. It was just the way she talked. I read all 185 pages and learned that she considered Ronald Reagan to be very charming, but her description of Nancy made Kitty Kelly's book look like a tribute. She was definitely nonpartisan in her funny, cutting insights—what she had to say about the Reagans and the Bushes differed little from what she had to say about the Clintons. But in all, there was nothing that could cause a scandal, no secrets, no Watergate or Iran-Contra ballyhoo uncovered. It was just one journalist's real opinions of the people who governed our country. And it was definitely a declaration that she never intended to go back to Washington as a reporter. Serious bridges were being burned with that book, but nothing that would cause anyone to kill her—at least not in the pages I read.

It was after two o'clock in the morning when I finished reading the manuscript. I put it back in the box and headed to bed.

The next day was one of the days Elberry was working, and

he took the opportunity to show me what I'd been doing wrong on the paperwork since he'd left. That opportunity took almost the entire day, as Elberry tended to start talking about his days as sheriff and how much better they'd been. I kept my mouth shut out of courtesy to my old friend and mentor, but damned if he didn't chap my ass just a little bit.

Elberry left a little bit before five and I dug the box out from under my desk, where I'd stashed it that morning. I figured if it wasn't safe in the sheriff's own private office, then it wasn't safe anywhere. Moving the manuscript aside, I started going through the steno pads, where Libby had kept notes. They were in a strange shorthand—abbreviated words rather than symbols—and I could make out some, if not all, of it. But still there was nothing there that would call for a CIA termination.

Everybody had left for the day and A.B. had shown up for night duty but was busy in the jail with our one inmate—a drunk who was getting a little noisy. Hank was out on patrol, so the bull pen was empty. I went out to the computer to see if the discs in Libby's box would work on our machine. I don't know much about the blamed things, but it didn't take long to figure out they were compatible. After several fits and starts, I had the first disc in and had pulled it up on a screen, only to find out I had the original copy of the manuscript. I hadn't been able to figure out what was on it by her labeling. That disc had been labeled LFN. Two more were labeled LFN-2 and LFN-3. I figured this was more of the manuscript. I was right. LFN-3 was some that hadn't been printed out. Again, it was good, funny, easy to read, but nothing worth killing over—and nowhere near ended. Even if Daniel had printed out this last disc, there'd be less than three hundred pages of text, and no ending. It could probably be finished by somebody but I didn't think Daniel wanted to consider that right now. Maybe in a few years, as a tribute to her memory, but not right now.

There were four discs labeled J, J-2, J-3, and J-4, and one labeled CRAP. I put CRAP in the computer, and that's exactly what I pulled up: household budgets; lists of vendors and repair people, some in Washington, some in Longbranch; expenditures on the new house; a list of Christmas presents from the year before—crap.

That left me with the J files. I stuck the first one in and hit paydirt—Libby Fortuna's personal journals.

5

J, and J-2 weren't much. Half of J was of her time in Houston, and she had some rather scathing things to say about the people she worked with at the station there, but their names were all just initials. I couldn't really tell who she was talking about. If any of the stuff had been important, I figured Jewel could straighten it out, but none of it was—important, I mean. The rest of J was about her move to Washington, and there was a lot of stuff about her insecurities:

10/1/84—How'd I get myself into this? I'm small-town. This is network. I can't do this. Who the hell do I think I am? R. was right when he said today that I'm entirely too stupid to be reporting from the White House. Okay, so he didn't exactly say stupid, but that's what he meant. Wouldn't it be best to just quit and go back to Houston before I get fired and thrown out of Washington in disgrace? I hate this apartment. It really sucks. I hate this town. Why did I decide being a little fish in a big pond was better than what I had? In Houston, people knew me—they wanted to see me; they liked me. Here, I'm just one of thousands. Every network, cable, and print media in the world has reporters here. And every damned one of them hates the new kids on the block. I've been warned about tricks the old-timers play on the new—but is being warned a trick in itself? It could be. I feel very alone.

It wasn't until J-3 that I got to the good stuff:

6/12/92—D. is seriously cute. But he's a congressional aide. I'm not about to compromise my journalistic integrity for a pair of cute buns. Besides, stupid, he hasn't even asked you out. But, my God, he's cute. Blond, blue-eyed. Wearing an Armani suit. Okay, so every other lawyer in this damned town wears an Armani suit. But none of them look as good in them as he does.

6/24/92—D. asked me out. It's just dinner. How compromised can I get with dinner—integritywise? He can compromise my womanhood all he wants. Yuk, yuk. Besides, his man is on a main committee. It wouldn't hurt to cultivate someone in his position. (Standing or lying down. Yuk, yuk.)

6/30/92—He's wonderful. Dinner was wonderful. The food was wonderful; the service was wonderful. He was wonderful. He's so honest. I had no idea a congressional aide could do that. But we never talked about his work or mine. He comes from this little town in Oklahoma—okay, enough said. Anyway, there's this café there called—I'm serious here—Bernie's Chat & Chew. I mean if nothing comes of this relationship (?), at least I'll have a funny story for Washington parties, right? Bernie's Chat & Chew!!!!!

The phone rang. I looked at my watch. Damn. It was after nine. A.B. was at the switchboard. I hadn't even noticed him come up from the jail.

"Milt? It's your wife?" A.B. said.

Gingerly, I picked up the phone. "Hey, babe," I said.

"Milt, are you all right?"

"Sorry, honey, I got to working on something, didn't notice the time—"

"Well, I certainly hope you're not expecting any dinner, because I ate it all."

"I'll grab something on the way home—"

"Go by that pizza place, okay? Mushrooms and anchovies. And black olives!"

I laughed. "Jeez, you sound like you're pregnant. Sure you don't want some ice cream on that?"

"Ben & Jerry's Cherry Garcia. The Stop N Shop carries it. But not on the pizza, Milt. I'm not that far gone yet."

I hung up and headed for my errands. Knowing my wife, she'd probably be asleep before I got home with the food. Which would be a shame. I hate mushrooms, anchovies, and black olives.

I thought on my way home about trying to talk the county commissioners into buying another computer to go in my office. For some reason, I didn't want to sit there in front of a full bull pen reading Libby's private journals. I felt enough like a voyeur as it was. Having witnesses would just make it worse. Or was it because I didn't want to share Libby with the rest of the staff? I pushed that thought out of my mind and drove home.

Jean was asleep, but the smell of the pizza brought her out of the bedroom. She was having more and more trouble getting around on her crutches the larger she got. The swell of belly in the front queered her equilibrium something awful. She was using a wheelchair at the hospital and we were thinking about getting one at home until the baby came. She managed to get to the table and I set out bowls and paper plates for the ice cream. Lately, Jean liked to take a bite of pizza, a bite of ice cream, a bite of pizza—but she wouldn't mix 'em, no, not her.

I told her about the manuscript and we discussed it and Libby and how my sister was taking all this and how Daniel was doing. I never mentioned the journals. I'm not sure why I didn't, but I didn't.

I got to work before six o'clock the next morning. A.B. left usually around one or two in the morning, switching the phones to whoever was on call—which was usually me. The place was empty at six in the morning. I went straight to the computer and punched up J-3.

7/4/92—The fireworks were wonderful—especially from the Capitol bldg. What a view! D.'s congressman's office looks out over the Mall, so we could see everything. And we had the whole office to ourselves. Fried chicken and Dom Perignon. What a combo. I wonder if the congressman will notice how his desk had been occupied the night before? Or does really great sex linger only for the participants? Yuk, yuk.

7/22/92—D.'s man's committee held a secret meeting today and I've been dying to ask D. what's going on. And I was worried about him compromising my journalistic integrity! What a crock! I can't ask. I just can't. Besides, if he told me, I'd probably think less of him, and if he didn't, I'd probably be pissed. So just don't ask. You have other sources. Use them. Leave D. alone. Got it? Got it.

7/26/92—He won't tell me anything about that secret meeting. I know it had to have something to do with Bosnia. That's really heating up over there and this committee oversees foreign investments, etc. I know something hot is brewing and D. won't tell me anything! What's the good of having a boyfriend who works for Congress if you can't get the skinny? This is crap! Besides, I just found out he lives with his mother! Okay, his mother lives with him, but is this the mature man I at first thought? I think not.

7/30/92—We broke up. Okay, I broke up with him. I have my pride. I have a job to do and he's hampering it. I probably would have found out what was going on way before Donaldson scooped me if I hadn't been dating D. I have my career to think about. He was good in bed. Period.

8/12/92—I can't stand it. I miss him so much. I miss the way he laughs, and his stories about his silly town in Oklahoma. So what if he lives with his mother? I mean, if his mother lives with him. It's really kind of sweet when you think about it. He's a bachelor—why shouldn't he take in his widowed mother? This way, he has a hostess. Oh, God. I'm so incredibly stupid. I love my job, in a strange kind of way, but you certainly can't curl up next to it late at night.

8/17/92—D. called. Oh, God, the sound of his voice. That quiet drawl. It reminds me of old Gary Cooper movies. He even looks like Gary Cooper. I think I'll rent *High Noon* tomorrow night. D. wanted to see me. I said no. Why did I do that? Why am I so stupid? And on top of everything else, I got "scolded" by J. today. What kind of job is this for a grown woman? Spying on the people in power, then tattling to the rest of the world. I'm losing my humanity. I'm losing my mind. Maybe he'll call back. Maybe I'll call him.

8/20/92—I got roses today. Twenty long-stemmed white roses. The card simply said, "I love you." What I want to do is borrow a mink coat, put it over my birthday suit, and show up at his front door. But I can't—his mother. I'm thirty-eight years old and I'm in love for the first time in my life and it scares me to death. That's what this has been about. I know that now. I've been a journalist for twenty years—when you consider college papers, etc. Is this what I want to do forever? Is this what I've always wanted to do? Wasn't there a time in my life, when I was ten or eleven, or sometime, when I thought about being a wife and mother? No, I don't think so. Is it so stupid to want that now? To change my mind? How much further am I going to go here? I'm thirty-eight. I doubt the network is going to give me my own prime-time mag. That suit will be sitting anchor for another thirty years. They allow men to grow old on the tube. It isn't even fun anymore. It isn't even exciting. I don't really care anymore. Or is this just rationalization? Oh, God, I wish I knew. Call him. Just call him.

8/21/92—Called D. last night. His mother answered. I acted like a socially retarded thirteen-year-old and hung up. But D. knew it was me. He called back immediately, but I let the machine pick it up. I could hear his voice. I could hear him saying, "Libby, are you there? Pick up, Libby, please." Please. He's always so polite. A gentleman. I had no idea there were any left in this world. I just want to see him. Look at his face. It's been so long since I've seen his face.

8/22/92—I went by the Capitol bldg. today. I knew D.'s man had a committee meeting today and that he'd

61

be there. He was in the hall outside the door of the committee room. He was talking with some woman. But I saw his face. And his body. He didn't see me. Why am I doing this? I want to see him—why don't I just do it? Call him or answer the phone when he calls! What is making me act like this? God, I can't stand it. If he calls right now, I'll answer the phone. Right now. Ring. Ring, phone, ring!

8/24/92—D. called tonight. I answered the phone. I'm so proud of myself! You idiot! He's coming over. I have to make this a short entry. I have to wash my hair and put on makeup and find the proper attire for my gentleman caller. My wonderful, beautiful gentleman caller.

9/17/92—D. wants me to meet his mother. Everything he's said about her sounds like she's a wonderful woman. How long has it been since I've met a "boy's" mother? A thousand years, at least!

9/22/92—She is wonderful! A sweet little pumpkin lady, as my daddy used to say. All dimples and doilies. Sweet, funny, and I think she liked me. I really think she liked me! Hot damn!

10/4/92—D. asked me to marry him. Boom. Just like that. "Libby, I want you to be my wife. I want to be with you forever." If he just hadn't said that "forever" part. I didn't say yes. However, I didn't say no. Do I want to marry D.? Yes. I do. Heave large sigh here. Okay, I'm calling him.

10/8/92—I agree with D. that there's absolutely no reason to stay in D.C. We both want children—and quickly. Do we want to raise children in D.C? Absolutely not. I mentioned New Orleans, but I wasn't really serious. Living in the same town with my mother? God forbid! But we'll be married in New Orleans. At least we're talking about that. He mentioned moving back to his home in Oklahoma. Why not? Fresh start. Sounds like a wonderful place to raise children. Lots and lots of children.

I heard the front door open and glanced up, to see Gladys moving toward the bull pen. I got out of the J-3 file and turned off the machine, taking Libby's discs with me back to my office.

There was nothing in any of the discs that shed any light on who had murdered Libby or why. I knew in my heart that it was one of those senseless, random things that happen sometimes. She was in the wrong place at the wrong time. But I would finish reading her journals. There was no question in my mind about that. She was talking to me, and I wanted to hear it. I wondered fleetingly if Daniel knew about the journals, if he'd read what she'd said about him. Somewhere deep in that nasty little part of me I like to keep hidden from the general public, I hoped he hadn't read them. I hoped I was the only person who ever had, who ever would.

I tried concentrating on forms and files and all the other crap that accumulates in an office like mine. I tried filling this one out and delegating that one, but all the time my hands would stray to those discs, like just holding them was something special. Around noon, I called my wife and asked her to lunch. Yeah, I was feeling guilty. No two ways about that.

When the day crew left at five o'clock and the night crew came on, Hank went off to start his rounds and I sent A.B. out on an errand, telling him I'd pick up the switchboard. I put the J-3 disc back in the computer:

10/10/92—We talked about our plans today with D.'s mother. She's all for moving back to Longbranch.

63

We'll all be going there in a week or two to look at houses. I'm giving my two-week notice tomorrow. They'd prefer longer. I could give a shit.

10/22/92—Longbranch is much, much nicer than I thought it was going to be. I'm not sure what my image of small-town Oklahoma was, but it wasn't this. It's a lovely town with huge trees and beautiful old homes. And we found a dream of a place —a ranch house on fifty acres! There's plenty of room and the former owners had an apartment fitted into one wing of the house for their married daughter—just perfect for Mrs. G.! She loved it. Now I have to start packing, and answer my mother's 1 million phone calls about the wedding. I told her just to handle it, but she wants me involved, for some reason. Maybe I'll have Mrs. G. call her back.

The rest of the entries were no longer diary, but more like a calendar—just dates and times of wedding appointments, then the move to Longbranch and appointments with plumbers and electricians, the cable company and the telephone company, and so on. I went through to the end, but there was nothing more. No reason, I guess, to talk to a journal now—she had Daniel.

I printed out all the entries on the J files and took them home with me—hidden under the front seat of my Jeep.

The weeks passed. Jean got bigger and bigger and we had to get a wheelchair for the house. Jewel and Harmon came over one weekend and Harmon and I built a ramp on the front steps and one from the kitchen into the master bedroom, which had two steps down. We made Jean try it out, see if she could get up and down the ramp by herself, and laughed like idiots when she had to back up to the far wall of the bedroom and take a running

64

start to get the chair up the ramp. She didn't find it nearly as amusing as the rest of us.

Sex was becoming a thing of the past. The doctor said we could do it if it was comfortable for Jean. Try as we might, we never could find a comfortable way of doing it.

One Saturday, me and Jean went to K Mart to buy me underwear. I'd never bought underwear in my life until my ex-wife, LaDonna, up and left me. My mama always bought my underwear; then, for my brief stint in the air force, Uncle Sam had issued me my drawers. After that, of course, I married LaDonna and she took over.

But number one on the list Jean handed me shortly before she agreed to marry me, a list entitled "Noncompromise Positions," was that she wouldn't buy my underwear. Number two was that she wouldn't do my laundry or put away my clothes. Number three was that she refused to put down toilet seats I left up. You get the drift? One of the drawbacks of marrying an independent woman. I, of course, did not come to that meeting with a list, but I've been drawing one up since the wedding night and pretty damn soon I'm gonna hand it to her, I can promise you that!

Anyway, we went to K Mart to buy me underwear and they had briefcases on sale. Since I was the newly elected sheriff of Prophesy County, I thought it behooved me to have one, so I bought it.

I got into a pattern of going to bed after Jean, sometimes an hour or more. I'd bring home my briefcase every night, and that briefcase had one item—Libby's printed-out journal entries. I'd sit up late at night reading and rereading those entries until I almost had them memorized.

It was a particularly hot, humid day, the third week of July, almost a month after Libby Fortuna's murder, when there came a knock at the door of my office. I was knee-deep in county, state, and federal paperwork, wishing to hell I'd run for dogcatcher instead of sheriff, so my response to the knock was a mite gruff.

I looked up when the door opened and saw Emmett Hopkins standing in my doorway. Emmett's usual pasty complexion was now a healthy tan and he had dropped at least thirty pounds, but not in a sickly way. He looked trim, muscular, and disgustingly healthy. And now he looked a good five years younger than me. His normally medium brown hair had been bleached by the sun to a light coppery color and the smile on his face was something to see.

"Well, I'll be goddamned," I said, standing and walking around my desk. We did the man hug and I encouraged him into a visitor's chair. "Well, damn if you don't look like a movie star," I said.

"Been down to the Florida Keys," Emmett said. "Real pretty, even if there is too much commercial crap and some real strange hairdos."

"So how long you back for?"

"Depends," Emmett said. "That chief deputy job still open?"

And that's all she wrote. All he ever needed to do was say yes.

A week later, in the middle of the night, I got a call from A. B. Tate on night dispatch.

"Milt, that ju?"

"Yeah, A.B., what's up?"

"We got a suicide?"

I sat up in bed. "Who?"

"Linda McKenna, over in Bishop?"

"Don't know her," I said, pulling on my pants.

"Hank's heading over there, but thought you might wanna know," A.B. said.

I got the address and headed over there my ownself. Hank was a little new to be handling a dead body on his lonesome. I thought I'd give him a little backup.

Linda McKenna had lived in a nice four-bedroom colonial in one of Bishop's more expensive subdivisions. It was all white brick, redwood, and glass, with a landscaped yard and tall oak trees. Hank was already in the house when I got there. A husband and two kids—one of each flavor—were sitting in the white-on-white living room, all huddled together. Hank directed me to the master bedroom, where Linda McKenna lay sprawled across the bathroom floor, a .22 pistol on the floor near her right hand. Blood dirtied the pristine white tile and clashed with the peach-and-cream wallpaper, towels, and so on. She was wearing a white cotton nightgown with little rosebuds printed on it. Funny how you notice the little things.

"You call Dr. Jim?" I asked Hank.

"Yes, sir," he said. "And the ambulance."

"Okay," I said. "Guess we need to go talk to the family."

Abel McKenna, the husband, was about thirty-five, tall, dark-haired, and handsome. He was an accountant, with his own business in Bishop, and looked, by the house anyway, to be doing okay financially. The kids, a thirteen-year-old girl named Marnie and an eleven-year-old boy named Jason, were handsome as their daddy, even tousled from sleep and wearing their nightclothes.

Except for the big black bruise on Jason's cheek and the scratches down his left arm, which could be seen from his short-sleeved Batman pajamas.

It took about ten minutes for me to separate the boy from his father. We went to the kitchen to see about getting drinks for everybody. Once there, I asked him, "How'd you get that shiner, Jason?"

He opened the refrigerator door and stuck his head in. "Had a fight at school," he said.

"Your arm, too?"

I saw the back of his head nod from the depths of the icebox. "Jason, what happened here tonight?"

He started to shrug his shoulders, but they just wouldn't

work for him. He began to sob and ended up sitting on the floor in front of the open refrigerator door. I knelt down beside him and moved him enough to shut the door. I stroked his silky head and said, "Bubba, I know you been through it tonight. I just need to know who done this to you."

His body shook, but he didn't respond.

"Did your daddy do this?"

Finally, the boy looked up, his eyes large. "No," he said. "Mama." And he began to cry again.

A voice from behind me said, "Leave him alone, Sheriff. Please." I stood up. Abel McKenna stood in the doorway of the shiny-clean kitchen. "Come with me," he said.

I motioned Hank into the kitchen to take care of the little boy, and Mr. McKenna and I stepped out the French doors of the living room and onto the deck that overlooked the back-yard. McKenna sank heavily onto a cushioned patio chair. I joined him on its twin. It was still hot out, and what breeze there was just blew the hot air around. I was sweating before I sat down. McKenna didn't seem to notice the heat, or much of anything else.

"Linda . . . Linda is . . . was . . . a clean nut . . ." he said, his voice slow and halting. "She loved to have the house clean as a whistle . . . everything in its place. . . . She just couldn't stand it . . . she just couldn't stand it if somebody messed up the house. . . . I mean, she'd just get . . . really . . . mad. . . ."

He stopped, took a gulp of air, and went on. "When Jason was little, she'd get so . . . mad . . . because Marnie had been such . . . such a quiet baby, so neat . . . but Jason . . . Jason was a little boy." He sighed and a sob caught him and shook his body. I waited. "He was messy. . . . He was active . . . like a little boy's supposed to be . . . but Linda . . . I'd come home and I'd bathe him . . . and I'd find . . . bruises . . . bruises on his little body . . . and she'd say . . . Linda would say that he fell . . . and I believed her. . . ." He began to sob in earnest. I awkwardly patted him on the shoulder.

"Mr. McKenna—" I started.

"Then when he was five, he broke his arm," McKenna said, sitting up straighter, his voice stronger. "She called me at the office and I rushed home and we took him to the hospital. She said he was playing in that tree," he said, pointing to a large oak with low branches in the backyard, lit by spotlights around the trunk of the tree, "and that he fell out of it." He laughed without much humor. "And I bought it." He looked at me. "Would you buy that? If your child was always bruised and then got his arm broken and your wife—who's alone with him all day—tells you he fell out of a tree, would you buy that?"

I didn't want to think about that. So I didn't. "Mr. McKenna, did you shoot your wife?"

McKenna stood up so abruptly, he knocked the lawn chair over. "What? God, no!" He sighed and straightened the chair, sitting back down. "Last year, she concussed him. Hit him so hard, he fell on the foyer floor—it's Mexican tile—and got a concussion. I guess Marnie'd had enough. She was there. Saw the whole thing and called me." He sighed. "I guess I knew, in my heart, I knew for a while that Jason wasn't that accident-prone. I knew. But when Marnie called me and told me what Linda had done, then I had to deal with it. Finally had to deal with it."

"What'd you do?"

"I confronted her. Told her to get some help. Told her that if she didn't, I'd divorce her and take the kids. She started seeing a psychologist in Longbranch—Dr. Marston," he said, mentioning the name of the woman my sister and I had gone to when we were having domestic problems—as in living in the same house together. "And she got better. Dr. Marston told her that when she got that feeling she should go in another room, get away from Jason, as far away as she could, until the feeling

69

passed. And that's what she did. Until tonight."

"What happened tonight?" I asked.

McKenna leaned forward, resting his elbows on his knees, and stared at the old oak tree with the low branches. "I was working late. Marnie had ballet class and Jason had Little League. Linda dropped Marnie off at class and picked Jason up from Little League. He . . . he got the car dirty. It rained yesterday; the field was still muddy. His cleats were caked with mud. She told him to take his cleats off before he got in the car, but he forgot. She saw all that mud on the floor of the car and went berserk. Backhanded him. When he tried to get out of the car—I'd told him if she started something when he was around other people to go to another adult for help—he was trying to get to his coach. That's when she grabbed his arm and raked it with her nails. It started bleeding, all over the seats—that just made her madder. Jason said she ran red lights and drove really crazy all the way home—drug him into the house by his hair—" McKenna started sobbing again. He stood up and wiped his face with his sleeve. "Jason told her to stop. He pulled away and said, 'Mama, stop or I'll tell Daddy.' He said that's when she ran into the bedroom and slammed the door. He called me and I came home as quick as I could. The bedroom door was locked. I could hear her talking to somebody—on the phone, I guess. Marnie got a ride home from ballet class, so I fixed the kids some dinner and sent them to bed. And I just sat in the living room, trying to figure out what the hell to do. I fell asleep at some point. The gunshot woke me up."

I stood up and patted his shoulder again. "I'm sorry, Mr. McKenna," I said. "Real sorry."

He nodded his head.

Just to be on the safe side, I had Hank use his AA kit for the nitrate test. Since Hank was new, I watched as he got out the Q-Tips and swabbed the hand area on Mr. McKenna and both kids, then made sure he sealed each swab in a different sterile tube and labeled and signed them. He'd send them off to the state lab, and it would probably be three or four months before we got the results.

But Dr. Jim's autopsy, two days later, concluded suicide. Two suicides and a murder in four months, in such a quiet little county.

6

10/3/91—Why do I always find photographers so
sexy? Maybe it's the way they dress. That casually af-
fected Indiana Jones look. But for some reason, when
they're photographers, it's forgivable. Maybe it's those
big zoom lenses. Yuk. Yuk. Anyway, I met another one
today. He's not like B. at all. Seems very levelheaded.
His name is Peter; he's a Brit (okay, so I'm hitting two
biggies here—a photographer and a Brit—sometimes I
just can't help myself). He's just back from Moscow
and is very interesting. He asked me to dinner tomorrow night and I accepted.

10/4/91—I'm home early and writing in this journal
because I had a splitting headache. Okay, so I lied. I've
been out with men before on first dates where they
talked about themselves a lot. Men do that on first
dates, and quite often it's just because they're nervous.
P. does it because it's the only thing he finds really fas-
cinating. We'd barely gotten into the entrée at dinner
when he said I would definitely enjoy having sex with
him later that evening. His hotel room was quite nice
and he'd laid in some supplies! Supplies????? This is a

man who could make a woman's biological clock stop ticking. I wouldn't have touched this guy with a ten-foot medical clearance. Okay, back to square one. Somewhere there's a man for me. I just know it.

I put the journal entries down and wished I had a cigarette. Evinrude, my orange tomcat, jumped in my lap and proceeded to knead my groin area until I picked him up by the scruff of the neck and deposited him on the living room rug, where he sat with his back to me. He's real sensitive, Evinrude. It was three o'clock in the morning. Jean was sound asleep and I wasn't. I wondered about her—Libby. I wondered if she was happy those last months with Daniel. I wondered what she'd been like as a little girl. And somewhere there was a Brit named Peter I'd like to sock in the jaw. Just for the hell of it.

I stretched in the chair, pushing my legs straight out in front of me and stretching my back. I should have been in bed. But I'd already tried that. Didn't work. I kept thinking about the conversation I'd had earlier that evening with Jean.

She'd come home upset because one of her patient's had committed suicide. When I tried to question her about it, she told me it wasn't my jurisdiction. The girl had lived in Long-branch and the police department was handling it.

"Larry Joe January couldn't handle his own pecker," I told her. "Babe, something's going on here. That's three suicides in four months right here in Prophesy County. Something's going on. Larry Joe won't pay any attention to it. And really, rightly so. Shirley Beth's suicide was four months ago. He won't connect 'em—"

"So you tell him about the woman in Bishop. Maybe he'll share his information," Jean said.

I snorted in an imitation of a laugh. "Yeah, right. Larry Joe's a real cooperating type." I gave her the old winsome smile—sometimes it works. "Why don't you just tell me what happened, okay?"

73

I doubt she woulda done it if it hadn't been bothering her, losing a patient and all. But I think she had about as much confidence in Larry Joe January as I did.

"Her name was Lori Nabors and she was fifteen. She's been suffering from anorexia for about two years. The school nurse discovered it when the girl passed out at school four months ago—"

"What do you mean discovered it?" I asked. "I thought anorexia just meant you didn't eat and you got skinny and you died."

"Succinctly put," my wife said in her most sarcastic manner. "Most anorexics know how to hide their problems by the clothes they wear. They choose layers or big baggy sweaters and sweatshirts. Lori had been doing that—the big clothes. When she passed out, the school nurse started to lift her head and discovered how light she was. When she got her in a closed room, she looked under the baggy shirt. At that time, Lori weighed eighty-five pounds. And she was five feet seven."

"How come her parents didn't notice this?" I demanded.

"You obviously have never lived with a teenaged girl, Milt," Jean answered.

I mentioned my sister's daughter, Marlene, who at fifteen had shared a bathroom with me for more than a year. I definitely knew more about teenaged girls than I ever wanted to.

"Even the seminormal ones require the privacy of a CIA agent," Jean said. "Most parents rarely see their teenaged daughters in any form of undress, and even if they do, it's for very short periods of time. Most parents wouldn't think to question why the bathroom door was locked or why their daughter dressed a certain way. Most parents think their teenagers dress like slobs, anyway. So what if she's always wearing sweatpants and baggy sweaters? She'll just say it's the style, and what parent would question that? Remember, most parents of teenagers today lived through the sixties. Who are they to question style in their teenagers?"

74

"So what was happening with Lori?"

Jean sighed. "I thought she was getting better. We'd had her in the locked ward for a month. She was putting on weight and the mortality watch had passed. She'd almost reached one hundred pounds. She was released from the locked ward two weeks ago to go home. But she was seeing me on an outpatient basis daily. And her mother was really good. She felt very guilty about what had happened to Lori—when she was a preteen, Lori had gotten chubby. Her mother had encouraged her to diet. Mrs. Nabors blamed herself for the whole thing. So, anyway, she was keeping an eye on Lori, monitoring her calorie intake. I think Lori was trying some bulimic techniques. She'd never done any B and P before—"

"B and P?" I asked.

"Binge and purge." Since I still looked blank, Jean sighed, like she would with a really slow first-year med student, and explained in words of one syllable or less: "Bulimics' standard eating disorder is to go through an almost-ritualistic eating binge—eating everything they can get their hands on—then they purge themselves: a finger down the throat to induce vomiting, usually, after a true ritualistic eating binge. But that's the high end of the bulimic spectrum. The most common form is the technique of eating whatever they want normally—not necessarily bingeing—then using diuretics, laxatives and even a vomit-inducer like Epicac to neutralize the effect of calorie intake.

"A really 'good' bulimic knows the whereabouts of every public bathroom that has some privacy in their town. Most people with eating disorders are very sneaky, very cunning.

"Anyway, I think Lori was using some of those techniques. Probably nothing more than her finger down her throat every time her mother made her eat a meal—which was three times a day. Mrs. Nabors would have been on the lookout for laxatives and diuretics. I know this because Lori'd been losing weight again. She and I talked about it yesterday—"

Jean stopped and looked down at her swelled belly. "I wish there'd been someone else I could have sent her to."

"Why, babe? You're the best—"

She looked up. "I'm big as a house. A girl like Lori sees me and thinks, Who is this woman to tell me I shouldn't diet? Do I want to end up looking like her?"

"You're pregnant!" I said. "And gorgeous."

Jean grinned. "Well, gorgeous, yes. And pregnant, yes. And Lori knew I was pregnant. But remember, this is a disease that manifests itself in some strange ways. Even though Lori knew that everyone around her would perceive her as too thin—which is why she covered herself with baggy clothes—when she looked in the mirror, she saw fat. Now if her mind could make those wild leaps of reason, why would the simple explanation that I'm pregnant remove the repugnance she must have felt every time she looked at me?"

"Baby, you're beautiful—"

Jean laughed. "Milt, I'm not feeling insecure about my appearance. I'm not fishing for compliments. I'm trying to explain a disease process. This is what Lori saw." Her face got a very sad look on it. "That's why I wish there'd been someone else to send her to. Maybe I should have insisted the family send her to Tulsa to one of the hospitals up there—"

"How did she do it?" I asked. "How did Lori kill herself?"

Jean sighed. "Her parents have a hundred and fifty acres that back up on the railroad. There's a train that comes by every morning around two A.M. Lori was standing on the tracks in her nightdress. The engineer saw her—hit his horn and his brakes. But you can't stop a train like you do a car."

"Ah, hell," I said.

Jean had gotten up then and excused herself to take a long bath and go to bed. I'd watched TV for a little while, finally ending up with Libby's journals in my hands. But even Libby's journals couldn't keep me from wondering what the hell was going on.

76

Now I had a new name to add to that of Shirley Beth Hopkins and Linda McKenna. Now I had Lori Nabors. Three women dead in four months. Four women if you count Libby. But there couldn't be any connection with the four deaths. Hell, it was hard to imagine a connection with the three suicides, much less connect Libby to them. I suppose if you're a real suspicious type, which I'm supposed to be—being sheriff and all—you could question the two suicides with handguns. We hadn't checked Emmett for powder residue after Shirley Beth's death, and we still didn't have the results on Abel McKenna and his children.

There are a lot of things I don't know in this world, but one thing I did know: Emmett didn't kill his wife. I knew that like I knew ice cream melts in the sun and brussels sprouts taste like crap. It was a given.

I decided it was time to go to bed, before I had conspiracy theories coming out my ears.

It was nine o'clock in the morning and I was feeling a little bleary-eyed from my late-night journal reading and soul-searching. When the phone on my desk rang, I forgot to identify myself and just said, "Hello," which just shows to go ya how tired I was.

"Milt?"

"Yeah?"

"It's Bill Williams," the voice on the other end of the line said. Bill Williams, chief deputy sheriff of Tejas County, one county over. We were ass-chewing buddies—which meant we could chew each others asses off about some infraction or other and still remain semifriendly.

"Hey, Bill," I said, yawning. "Sorry. Didn't get much sleep last night."

"What I tell you about living with a pregnant woman? Have you up to all hours finding her weird foods? Or was she just discussing at length your manly faults?"

"Naw, last night was my own damn fault. What can I do you for?"

"Well, you know that notice you sent me about the stuff was stole when that newswoman of yours got killed?"

I was all of a sudden wide awake. "Yeah?"

"Well, you know Berle Canton owns the Canton Jewelry & Hock over on Misty Road?"

"Not to say hey to," I said.

"Well, he just called me. Said some guy come in trying to sell him a one carat diamond stud earring. Gold setting. Got a little bitty *L* engraved on the back."

"The seller still there?"

"Yeah. Ole Berle's a member in good standing of the American Legion. Tied the guy up in the back room and called me. I'm on my way over there now."

"I'll meet you there," I said, standing and hanging up the phone.

It took about twenty minutes to get to Misty Road. Canton Jewelry & Hock was a Mestex steel building on the outskirts of Taylor, the county seat of Tejas County. It had two big plate-glass windows in the front, both covered almost completely with filigreed cast-iron bars. There were three cars in the parking lot—a Tejas County sheriff's car, a white-on-white Cadillac, and a beat-up '72 Ford LTD with missing tags and slick blackwall tires. It didn't take a rocket scientist to figure out which car belonged to who.

Bill Williams was standing in the main room of the store, leaning on a glass case of watches, talking to a tall, thin man behind the counter. Bill's always been a big, burly blond. Berle Canton looked like his negative. His thin, lean face was high-colored, like he was about to blow a stroke. His dark hair was slicked back with the greasy kid stuff. Although he was a tall, lean man, he had a protruding belly that stuck out a lot like Jean's, right in the front. He wore a fancy Sooner belt buckle, buckled beneath the protrusion.

"You got him?" I asked Bill.

"Milt Kovak, Berle Canton," Bill said, being unusually nice. Figured maybe Berle was holding some belonging of Bill's Bill might be worried about getting back.

"Hey, Mr. Canton," I said, shaking the hand of the man behind the counter.

He nodded. "Guy you looking for's in the back room," he said. He came out from behind the counter and took a large ring of keys off his belt, fingering them until he had the right one. He'd just stuck the key in the lock when we heard the engine start up outside. Bill and I whirled around. The LTD was moving at a fast clip out of the parking lot.

"Shit," Berle said.

Bill and I ran out of the store, hopping into our squad cars, and commenced to chasing the LTD. I gave Bill the lead. It was his county, his jurisdiction, *and* he knew the roads.

Well, there was good news and bad news. The bad news was the '72 LTD had a heap bigger engine than either of our county-issued cars and the seller was making good time and leaving us in a cloud of dust. The good news was he obviously wasn't local and didn't know the roads. And he was stupid. We lost him five minutes into the chase. We found him when he came tearing out of a dead-end side road and managed to pull the LTD right between me and Bill. Bill slammed on his brakes and did a side turn. I did the same. In his panic, the driver of the LTD, by the look on his face, musta accidentally hit the accelerator. My sheriff's car was sideways to the front of the LTD. The driver hit it T-bone, knocking me slanchwise and killing the LTD's engine, and any fire left in the bad boy.

He was banging his head on the steering wheel when Bill and I approached his car, guns drawn. I had a gash on my head that was bleeding like a stuck pig. I got my handkerchief out of my back pocket and sopped at the blood. My unit was a total. You could tell that just by looking. I radioed back to my county, asking for the wrecker to come and get the car.

Thirty minutes later, I was sitting across a table from the man who'd tried to sell Berle Canton a one carat diamond stud earring, gold setting, with an *L* engraved on the back. His name was Howard Cleveland. He was in his mid-thirties, had dirt-colored hair, the nose of a heavy drinker, and a pockmarked face. He was a slight man, about five feet five, weighing maybe 135 on a day he ate regular. He was dressed in worn khaki work clothes. A name had been sewn at one time on the breast, but it was missing. The khaki was a little darker where the name had once been. He was smoking a nonfilter Camel and staring at the Formica-covered tabletop like it had a list of his sins written on it that he was studying just in case he could find one that didn't fit.

"Howard," I said. He didn't look up. "Howard." I said it louder. He looked up that time. "Where'd you get that earring?"

Looking me straight in the face, he said, "I found it."

"Uh-huh," I said. "Where'd you find it?"

"Next to a Dumpster behind this store."

"What store, Howard?"

He shrugged.

"What store, Howard?"

"Hell, I don't know. A store."

"Here in Taylor?"

"Naw. Someplace else. I was hitching a ride from Oklahoma City. Got dumped in some little burg. I was scrounging the Dumpster for something to eat when I saw the ear bob. Just picked it up."

"So where'd you get the LTD?" Bill Williams asked.

"Huh?" Howard said.

"The LTD you were driving, Howard. Where did you get that if you hitched a ride from Oklahoma City?"

Howard began studying the tabletop again.

I tapped Bill on the arm. "Howard, we don't care nothing about the LTD. What we wanna know is where you got the ear bob. Now think. What town were you in when you found it?"

He shrugged, still looking at the tabletop. "I dunno. All these hick places look alike to me."

"What was the name of the store?"

The shrug was getting on my nerves. Howard was getting on my nerves.

"Howard, you gotta talk to me. If you don't, Bill here's gonna release you to my custody and I'm taking you back to Prophesy County, where we're gonna put you in lockup and charge you with murder."

That got Howard's attention. "Murder? Shit!" He stood up, looking around for an escape.

"Sit down, Howard," Bill said. "The door's locked. You ain't going anyplace. Except maybe over to Milt's county for charging."

"I didn't—I never—who? Hell, I didn't kill nobody! I found the ear bob! It was on the ground right by the Dumpster back of this store, man! I swear on the heads of my children! I never kilt nobody!"

"What store, Howard?" I asked.

"Ah . . ." His face scrunched up in an exaggeration of concentration. "It was like a little store. Not like one of them big chains, but not like a Seven-Eleven, either. I mean, hell, man, I was at the back of the store. I didn't even see no sign or nothing! I was just trying to get some grub out of the Dumpster. I didn't have nothing to eat all that day, man. I was hungry. Then I saw that ear bob just laying there—"

"Whatja do with the other one?" I asked.

"Huh?"

"Earrings come in twos," I said. "Two ears. Two earrings. What you do with the other one?"

"Man, I swear, there was only that one. Only one ear bob just laying there in the parking lot, right next to the Dumpster."

"When was this?" Bill asked.

"Ah, yesterday. Day before. I dunno."

Bill gave me a signal and we walked out of the room, leaving

Howard Cleveland to worry. Once out in the hall, Bill asked, "Your boys go over that area?"

"Yeah," I said. "They swept it. Coulda missed something as small as that ear bob, though, I guess." I shook my head. "Hard to believe it's been sitting there by that Dumpster all this time and nobody noticed it."

"Yeah, that's real hard to believe. But it's also kinda hard to believe that numb nuts in there woulda held on to it this long without selling it."

"Unless he's been selling all the other stuff."

"Why sell just one earring? No way you're gonna get as good a price for two earrings separately as you would for a pair. Right? What woman's gonna buy one earring?"

"Sell 'em for the diamonds, not the earring. Sell two one carat diamonds separately, make more money than if you try to sell the earrings as a set?"

Bill shrugged. "It's what, fifty miles, maybe a little more between that Stop N Shop and here? It's been how long? Six weeks? What's this creep been doing all that time? Where's he been selling the other stuff? Everybody in Prophesy County or Tejas County's seen the handout on the stolen items. Most people'd call in."

"Most," I said. "What are you saying here, Bill?"

Bill sighed. He looked at the floor, then looked up at me. "There's a real good chance this bozo's telling the truth, Milt. He found that ear bob at the Dumpster behind the Stop N Shop. Your boy's just didn't see it."

I sighed my own sigh. I halfway thought Bill was right, but I didn't wanna give up a suspect in any all-fired hurry. "I wanna hold this guy for a while. See how this thing plays out."

"Well, that LTD sure don't belong to him."

I nodded my head. "Okay. You keep him here on auto theft. We run wants and warrants through the state, may even have time to run him through national. See if this guy's got any violence in his past."

Bill shook my hand. "Sounds good to me."

"I'm gonna go on back. Scare the crap outta him with the murder charge. See what comes up."

"I'll keep you posted," Bill said, turning and walking back to the room where Howard Cleveland waited.

Jasmine Bodine came and picked me up in one of the squad cars and we drove back to Prophesy County. Emmett was sitting at his desk in my old office, his feet propped up on the top, a county report in his hands, pretending he was studying it. I motioned for him to join me in my office. That was my perk as sheriff.

When Emmett came, he said, "Whatja do to your head?" as he got himself arranged in my visitor's chair.

I told him what had transpired in Tejas County.

"Yeah, well, Bill's probably right," Emmett said. "That dog turd probably didn't do nothing other than find the earring and steal a car."

"Probably. But I'll wait 'til his rap sheet comes in before I make a judgment." I leaned back in my swivel chair and stared at the map of the county that covered one wall of my office. "Still and all, it would be nice to get that ear bob back to Daniel."

"Who?" Emmett asked.

"Daniel Gallagher. Libby Fortuna's husband."

Emmett's eyes narrowed. "I didn't know she was married to Daniel Gallagher," he said.

"Yeah. Guess you missed a lot of this 'cause you were out of town and all."

"Speaking of being out of town," Emmett said, "remember when you were down in Houston with Jewel and her troubles?"

I snorted. "Can't hardly forget that."

"Well," Emmett said, leaning back in the visitor's chair and taking the liberty of putting his feet up on my desk, "interesting thing happened in town then. Maybe you heard about it?"

"Well, I don't rightly know until you tell me what it is, now do I?" I said, wondering why he hadn't asked permission to put his feet on my desk. I'd a asked Elberry's permission. If I'd ever had the guts to even *want* to put my feet on Elberry's desk.

"We had a house bombing over on Mulberry Terrace."

"Yeah, now, I've seen that burned-out house. Didn't know it was a bombing, though."

"Well, at first we just thought it was a leaky gas line or something, but then Norris Babcock,'" he said, mentioning the name of the chief of the volunteer fire department, "said all them houses on Mulberry Terrace are all electric and he wanted to call in an arson specialist he knew in Tulsa to look the house over. Lo and behold, he found the charred makings of a bomb."

"Well, now, this is all real interesting, Emmett, but what's this got to do with the price of beans?" I asked. His feet were getting on my nerves.

"Only one fatality in that bombing, Milt. Well, now I guess the born-agains might say two. The lady was pregnant."

"And?"

"Her name was Cassie Gallagher. Phillip Gallagher's wife."

7

"I don't rightly remember all the details," Emmett said, "have to get the file from the city department for a lot of it. But I do remember a few things—like Phillip Gallagher was in St. Louis when it happened, at a medical convention."

"He's a doctor? What kind?" I asked.

Emmett squinted with remembering. "OB-GYN, I think. Anyway, I remember we checked him out seven ways from breakfast when we discovered the insurance."

"Insurance?"

Emmett laughed. "That perked you up some, huh? Yeah, insurance. Great, heaping gobs of insurance. Close to three-quarters of a million when all was said and done. And we did what you did for the Fortuna woman. We rousted every bad boy from here to hell and back. Nothing concrete to go on at all." Emmett sighed. "But I kept going back to Gallagher. I checked his alibi until I was blue in the face. It wasn't airtight by any means. He was in St. Louis, sure. But there's planes. There's rental cars, buses, trains. One doctor at the convention had dinner with him—finished, I don't know, about nine, something like that. Then Gallagher had a breakfast meeting at seven the next morning. That leaves ten hours unaccounted for. He coulda got back to Longbranch."

"So why didn't you charge him?" I asked.

"Never found anything that could put him in Longbranch. His name and description couldn't fit anything any flight attendant could remember for any flights from St. Louis to Tulsa or to Oklahoma City—or to Dallas, for that matter. Couldn't get him identified at any car-rental place. Never found no hard evidence—like a Visa slip saying he rented a car or bought a plane ticket. And far as anyone I interviewed, couldn't come up with a motive, either. Except that damned insurance. Everybody said Phillip and Cassie Gallagher were the 'perfect' couple. Both real excited about the baby coming.

"The twin, Daniel, had left for D.C. about a year before, but the mother was still living in town. She was no help. Got the drift that I was asking whether or not Phillip coulda done in his wife, I thought the old lady was gonna castrate me, she got so mad.

"But we never got a lead. Never got nothing. Cassie's parents gave us a real hard time, wanting to know what we were going to do about it. I said we were doing all we could. Finally, the case kinda petered out. Then, not quite a year after it happened, Phillip Gallagher up and moved out of town."

"Huh," I said.

"Huh's right," Emmett said. "You ever see that movie about them twin brother doctors, true story, about these two sickies that liked surgery a little too much?"

I grimaced. "That thing with that English dude? What's his name?"

"Yeah, that's the one."

"Never got through the credits. Nasty credits," I said. "You insinuating the Gallagher twins are a little strange?"

Emmett shrugged. "One of 'em's a doctor. Both their wives are murdered. What's the odds?"

I started doodling on my desk pad. "Call around," I said. "Find out what kinda insurance Daniel had on Libby."

"Yeah, I was thinking that."

"Also, call New York. One of them big publishing houses. I'd like to know what an almost-finished book by Libby Fortuna would be worth."

Emmett nodded. "Good thinking."

"I think I'll talk to Daniel Gallagher. Never did ask him what he was doing the day Libby died."

"Well, maybe you shoulda," Emmett said.

I glared at him.

"Then again," he said, grinning, "who'd a thunk?"

Libby Fortuna had been insured for $500,000, double indemnity in case of accident. Murder is considered an accident in the insurance biz. That meant a cool million bucks would go to Daniel Gallagher. If the case was ever closed. The insurance company had a policy of not paying up in a murder case until the police had declared the case closed, which I wasn't about to do.

The New York editor Emmett talked to said normally the book would go for mid-five figures. But in this case, with Libby's murder, with maybe somebody who knew her—one of her cohorts in D.C.—writing a tragic epilogue to the end of the book, he said we could be talking low to mid-six figures. And that was just up-front money.

"That's what they call the advance," Emmett said. "This guy says, though, that with good sales, the royalties could be hefty, and then there's the paperback deal, and the foreign-rights deal, and maybe even a movie. He says a book like that, in the end, could be worth a million or more."

"Shee-it," I said.

"And he said since the book isn't like a novel, where it needs a plot or whatever, that it could stand just the way it is. What'd you say, less than three hundred pages? Hell, with a good epilogue—"

"I get your drift."

Emmett grinned. "It was kinda cool."

87

"What was?"

"Talking to that New York editor."

I grinned back. "Feel like a real sophisticate, do you?"

"I could live with it—long as I don't have to drink bubble water," he said, grinning.

I leaned back in my swivel chair, losing my grin. "I hate to think I been wrong about Daniel Gallagher." What I really hated to think was that Libby had been so wrong about him. That Libby had waited all those years to find the right man, only to have him betray her in such a brutal and ultimate way.

"You talk to him yet?" Emmett asked.

I shook my head. "No. I was waiting for you to find out about the insurance."

"Want me to do it?"

I looked at my old friend. I smiled and shook my head. "Thanks for the offer. But I best just do it."

I got up and left the office. The July heat was of the suck-you-dry variety. Sidewalks shimmered like they were wet; tar bubbled in the streets. A fat dog was breathing hard, lying under a tree by the courthouse, and all the old men who usually sat on the bench in front had moved indoors for the season. The temperature was pushing a hundred, and if this kept up or got worse, which it surely could, we'd start having heat prob-lems—like finding out ole Aunt So-and-So hadn't been seen in a week, only to find out she'd died of heat prostration in her unair-conditioned house; or Minnie May had had about enough of Jay Bob as she could handle and took the butcher knife to him 'cause he hadn't got around to paying the electric bill; or the lovelies out at the Sidewinder who get meaner just 'cause it's hot; or the guy stuck on the side of Highway 5 with an overheated car who punches out the wrecker driver when he finally shows up fifteen minutes late. You know, heat problems.

I drove my Jeep over to Daniel's office and got out, leaving the windows down so the car would be somewhat bearable when I got back in. There was nobody much about to say hidy to—real heat can be like real cold—nobody much wants to get out in it.

Daniel had been back to work for a couple of weeks. Mrs. Gallagher was busy at the word processor when I walked in the office. She smiled shyly when she saw me. "Hi, Milt. How are you?"

I smiled back. "Just fine, Miz Gallagher. Daniel in?"

I tried not to think how much the scene reminded me of the day I'd told Daniel that Libby was dead.

"Sure. But I think he's on the phone. Let me just check."

She came back in a minute and said, "I thought he was. I was right. Why don't you just sit down here and wait for him? Would you like some coffee or a soda? We got diet or regular."

"Diet Coke if you got it," I said. I hated the stuff, but I was fighting a middle-aged spread that had been winning for a while now. Which reminded me that when I got through with Daniel, I needed to go by Dobbins' Dry Cleaning and see how they were coming with my uniform. For some reason, after my few years in civvies as head of the Homicide Unit, my uniform didn't fit like it oughta. Hank Dobbins's mama was gonna see what she could do about letting out a few seams.

Mrs. G. came back in a few minutes with a can and a glass of ice. I poured myself some Coke and sipped while I waited for Daniel to get off the phone.

It probably didn't take more than five minutes or so, but it gave me time to work out in my mind how I was going to approach him. When Mrs. Gallagher ushered me into Daniel's office, I was ready.

We shook hands, but there was none of the witty dialogue we'd shared in the past. I hadn't seen Daniel since the day I'd picked up Libby's journals from him, the day after her funeral. He'd lost weight and there was gray in his blond hair. The white shirt hung on him and his tie was loose. The bags under his eyes were prominent and he had a sickly pallor about his skin that made me want to walk out the door and not question him like I was about to do.

I settled down in the visitor's chair across from his desk and said, "Daniel, I know this is gonna be like an invasion of privacy, but I gotta ask."

"No, you don't. That was my insurance agent on the phone. I know you've been checking up on Libby's insurance."

"It's something we gotta do, Daniel."

He nodded his head, his right hand playing aimlessly with a sleek gold letter opener. "I'm surprised you didn't suspect me before this, Milt. Usually the spouse is the first suspect."

"Well, I'm glad you're gonna cooperate, Daniel. How come so much insurance? Half a mil seems steep."

Daniel smiled. "Not in D.C. The salary Libby was making there justified the policy. It was the one the network took out on her. She had it transferred to a private policy when she quit. She made me the beneficiary when we got married. Just like I made her the beneficiary on mine. My policy is face value one million even. Double indemnity."

The insurance seemed plausible. But I'd check it out. Have Emmett call the network and then call the insurance agent back to see if Daniel's was as large as he said. It probably was. He wasn't stupid. He knew I'd check.

"I also need to ask you about your movements on the day Libby was killed," I said.

Daniel dropped the letter opener and leaned back in his chair. "Wish you'd asked me earlier, Milt. It's been so long and so much has happened, I don't really remember." He leaned over and pushed a button on the intercom on his desk. "Mama," he said into it, "would you bring me my book for last month, please?"

Mrs. Gallagher brought in the appointment book for June, raised an eyebrow at Daniel, then, getting no response, quietly left the office.

Daniel thumbed through to Monday, the twentieth of June, then cleared his throat. He didn't speak for a moment, just stared at the page. Finally, he said, "I was taking a deposition in Tulsa in the morning. Left the house around seven and got back to the office a little before noon. I'd called Mama before I left Tulsa and she had lunch ready for me when I got here, so I just sat at my desk and ate and went over some papers. What time was Libby killed? Was that ever determined?"

I cleared my own throat. His voice was real even, but his skin had gotten even paler as he'd talked. "Dr. Jim reckons between nine in the morning and one in the afternoon," I said. "Something about stomach contents."

Daniel looked toward the window, where heavy curtains had been pulled back, exposing the bright, hot day. "I guess my only alibi is my mother—from eleven-thirty until nearly one o'clock. I had a client drop in." He glanced at the book again. "It's not down here, but I billed for the time. It should be on Mama's computer."

"If you could get me a printout of that," I said.

"Sure. Would you like a copy of my calendar?"

"That would work," I said. I had a hard time looking at him. Did he look so bad just because of normal grief? The normal grief of a man who'd lost the love of his life? Or did he look like this because he finally realized the money hadn't been worth it? Was guilt making Daniel Gallagher look like a ghost of himself?

I cleared my throat again and steeled myself to look in his face. If he had killed her, if he had murdered Libby, then he'd pay. I'd make him pay. But there were other questions that needed to be asked. "Daniel, tell me about your brother."

"Phillip?"

I nodded my head.

"What about him?"

"I understand he lost a young wife, too."

He looked away from me, back to the window and then to

91

the appointment book still open on his desktop. Finally, he said, "Yes, that's true. Quite a coincidence, isn't it?"

"I was thinking that," I said quietly.

"Cassie was killed when a bomb went off in their home. The police never determined who set the bomb or why. But Phillip had his suspicions, and so do I."

"What suspicions?"

His fingers picked at the gold letter opener. "Phil worked three days a month at a women's clinic in Tulsa. He performed abortions. He'd been getting a lot of hate mail and some death threats. He told the police that, but they didn't pay any attention to it." He looked at me. "That guy in Florida may not have been the first murder by these zealots. I think, and Phil's always thought, that Cassie and her baby were the first." He laughed without humor. "Isn't it ironic? Here they are trying to stop abortions by killing the doctor—and they commit their own abortion. And in the last trimester yet."

"Did Phillip have any names of people he thought might have been responsible?" I asked.

Daniel shrugged. "I don't really remember. I wasn't even in town then. I came back when it happened. Sat with him for days." He stopped. "Which is more than he's done for me."

"Where is Phillip now?"

"Los Angeles. He moved there about a year after Cassie's death."

"You hear from him?"

He shrugged. "Not much."

It was six o'clock that evening and Emmett and I were sitting in my office, each with a cold beer. I wasn't on call. I'd called Jean to tell her I was running late, but she was still at the office, too. Her secretary said she had a patient who was acting out. It could be a while for her, as well.

"Yeah, I remember something about that," Emmett said.

"Gallagher was real hot about the right-to-lifers. Had these letters he kept sticking under my nose."

"You have the letters? Keep 'em in your file?"

Emmett squinted. "Well, now, I think maybe I did make copies of some of 'em."

"So what you think our chances are of getting that file from Larry Joe January?"

Emmett laughed. "What's the chances of you winning Miss Longbranch?"

"Well," I said, pushing myself up from my chair, "all's we can do is ask. Then again, maybe you can hold him while I rifle the filing cabinets."

Emmett got up, too, and headed for the door. "Can I pummel him while I'm holding him?"

"Sure," I said, opening the back door and heading for my Jeep.

"Great," Emmett said, "I never have pummeled anybody. Might be fun."

I think Emmett was a might disappointed that he didn't have to pummel Larry Joe. Though for a minute there, I woulda held him and given Emmett instructions on just what to do.

We caught Larry Joe coming out of the courthouse door on his way for his evening repast at the Longbranch Inn. It was nearing seven o'clock and, although the sun was still pretty much up, the day had begun to cool down enough that you didn't have to stand in the shade.

"Hey, Larry Joe," I called, jogging slightly to catch up with him. "Got a minute?"

Larry Joe looked from me to Emmett and smirked. "Well, a little bitty one," he said. "I'm on my way to some dinner."

"Won't keep you but a second," I said, smiling my sincere smile. "We might have a connection between Libby Fortuna's murder—"

"Who?" he asked, sucking on a toothpick and looking longingly at the Longbranch Inn a couple of blocks down.

"That TV news lady—"

"Oh, yeah. Connection?"

"Between her death and a death happened here in town few years back. Cassie Gallagher?"

Larry Joe shrugged. "Don't rightly recall—"

"The bomb, you dumb shit," Emmett said.

I got between the two. "Now, Emmett," I said, real sweetlike, "no name-calling. Larry Joe's being real cooperative here."

"I don't have to cooperate with you at all, Milt," he said. "And I sure as hell don't have to deal with that"—he pointed at Emmett—"at all. Now you get him outta my face, maybe we'll talk."

"I ain't in your face now, numb nuts, but I will be in a New York minute!" Emmett said, reaching around me to get at Larry Joe.

"Emmett!" I shouted. Emmett backed down. "You go on now and wait in my car." He didn't move. "Go on, Emmett. Now."

Larry Joe smirked. "That's right, Emmett. You do what your boss tells you to do."

Emmett turned quickly and headed back to the Jeep, but not before I saw the fire burning in his face. I turned to Larry Joe. "You ever talk to him like that again, January, they're gonna be scraping bits of you outta my teeth."

He got all huffy. "You ain't got no call to talk to me like that—"

"You used to be a toad, Larry Joe. Now you're just a toad with a little bit of clout. Now I'm through being nice. We can do this the easy way—you just give me a copy of that file—or we can do this the hard way. Like I go to Judge Lorimer, who so kindly married my wife and me, by the way, and I tell him what an asshole you're being—standing in the way of justice and all—and see if I don't get me them files quick as lightning. Of course, doing that's gonna just outright tell the judge and anybody else watching what a slimy little toad you are."

He turned and walked back into the courthouse. Fifteen minutes later, I came out carrying a copy of the file.

I got into the Jeep, not looking at Emmett. He wasn't looking at me, either. I knew he was pissed because I'd embarrassed him. But he'd pushed me to it. Given time, he'd realize that.

"Wanna go by the Longbranch Inn for some dinner while we look this over?"

"Naw. How about Bernie's?" Emmett offered. Which made me remember that the Longbranch was where Larry Joe had been headed. Emmett was right: We didn't want to go there.

I started the Jeep's engine and headed to Bernie's Chat & Chew. It's a little hole-in-the-wall with cracked linoleum floors and Formica and chrome tables and a long bar with bar stools covered with genuine Naugahyde and masking tape. But the food was good, if you liked grease, and hot. We both ordered hamburger platters and iced teas and opened the file on the bombing and murder of Cassie Gallagher and her unborn child.

The gist of it was about what Emmett had recited earlier. The bomb had gone off at about 11:00 A.M. on the morning of February 14—Valentine's Day—1989. Cassie's body was found in the kitchen, where the device had obviously been set. That's where most of the damage had been done. But if she'd been in the bedroom, she'd probably still be dead. The bomb had been strong enough to knock out the neighbor's windows, according to the first officer's report. There wouldn't have been time for her to get out. The explosion had been so bad that the Gallagher's dog, in the backyard, had also been killed.

Phillip Gallagher had been reached at his hotel in St. Louis at about three that afternoon. He'd managed to get back to Longbranch early the next morning. Mrs. Gallagher, the twins' mother, had been notified, as had Cassie's parents. The initial investigation mentioned the possibility of a ruptured gas line.

The follow-up investigation mentioned the fact that Mulberry Street had all-electric service and that an arson investigator from Tulsa, Ronald Dewey, had been contacted to come check out the scene. Dewey's report was also in the file. There was a lot of jargon and technical stuff, but the conclusions at the end of the report were in layman's terms: "It is my opinion, based on my investigation, that an incendiary device, most probably composed of dynamite, was the basic causative factor in the demolition of the house at 1842 Mulberry Street in the city of Longbranch, Oklahoma, and most probably the causative factor in the death of the one occupant of said house."

Dr. Jim's autopsy report was also in the file. I won't go into detail on that. It was gruesome and something I wished I'd never read.

Also in the file were copies of five letters, all addressed to Phillip Gallagher, some at the clinic in Tulsa, some at his office in Longbranch, and two to his home address. The first letter, dated in August of the year preceding the bombing said, "You are a killer of babys. You should die. Sincerely, Madelyn R. Carey." The second, coming sometime in October of that year, said, "And the Lord Jesus said, 'Blessed are the children.' You are doing the Devil's work and you will burn in hell." That one was unsigned. The third was dated in November. It read, "Cease and desist. You must seek forgiveness for your sins. Take reason and sanity and good Christian ethics as your watchword and stop the abominations. What you are doing is Wrong!!!!! You are killing living souls. Repent and be forgiven." This, too, was unsigned.

The fourth one, dated in January, less than a month before the bombing, said, "I've tried to reason with you. I've tried to set you on the path to forgiveness and righteousness. You have ignored my warnings. You will not do so again." Unsigned. The last one, dated one week after the fourth and in very similar handwriting, said, "We are soldiers in the army of the Lord. The Lord forgives those who must act in His name. We are the one's who will be forgiven. You will burn in hell." The last two were sent to the Gallagher home.

I tossed the letters at Emmett. "You ignored this?" I said,

pointing specifically at the last two letters.

"Ah, hell, Milt, these crackpots just like to blow off steam."

"Yeah? What about that crackpot in Florida who blew off a little more than steam? Like that doctor's head?"

Emmett looked at the letter. "Yeah, well, that hadn't happened yet when this went down. It just never seemed, I don't know, relevant, I guess."

"You know any right-to-lifers here in Longbranch?" I asked.

"Yeah, your own church is involved in a group. Your church, Jean's church, and that fundamentalist bunch out on Highway Five. It's called an interdenominational group. They're vocal but not violent."

"Only takes one person with a screw loose to do something like this."

"Well, okay, fine. Some screwball born-again blew up Phillip Gallagher's house and his wife and baby because he did abortions in Tulsa. Fine. What in the hell has any of this got to do with Libby Fortuna?" Emmett said.

"Hell if I know," I said, "but we're fixing to find out." I finished my hamburger.

8

I was lying on the bed, my head resting lightly on Jean's stomach, listening to Junior do his thing, when he kicked me in the ear. Jean and I both busted out laughing. It was a real charge, feeling that little fella kicking around in her belly. She thought so, too, when he wasn't waking her up from a deep sleep with his aerobics. Lately, I'd caught her rolling her wheelchair around and around the living room, trying to sooth Junior back to sleep.

Jean stroked what was left of my hair. "I've signed us up for Lamaze," she said.

I lifted my head from her belly and looked at her. "Us?" I said.

She nodded her head. "Yes, dear, us. You have to go."

"Why?"

I hadn't totally decided yet whether or not I wanted to be in the delivery room. I'd asked Bill Williams if he'd ever been in the delivery room for any of his kids.

"The last one, little Bubba," he said.

"And?"

Bill just shook his head. "Wouldn't take a million dollars for the experience," he said. "But I wouldn't do it again for a million, either."

That didn't help my decision-making abilities a bit. I knew Jean wanted me to be there. And part of me wanted to be there, too. After all, I'd been there for the fun stuff—the conceiving—it just stood to reason I should be there for the not-so-fun stuff. But, even though I'd seen more than my share of grief and carnage in my career as a peace officer, I wasn't sure I could stomach watching my lady go through the hell of childbirth.

"You have to go," Jean said, "because I want you to go. I'm pregnant and hormonal and you don't want to upset me. So you'll go."

I leaned back on my side of the bed. "Honey, I still haven't made up my mind about being in the delivery room."

She laughed—one of those laughs that are meant to signify humor. "It must be nice to have a decision to make, Milt," she said. "You see, I don't have the choice. I have to be there. But I'm glad you feel this is a decision for you. I'm happy for you that you feel a decision is what you have here, rather than a given."

I sighed. "What time's the Lamaze class?" I asked.

Monday morning I had to go by Bishop on my way to work—out of my way to work, if the truth be known—to take my sister, Jewel, some papers to sign. We were selling the burial plots Mama and Daddy had bought us when we were little, when they bought theirs, because there wasn't enough room for Jewel and Harmon and me and Jean, not to mention the kids. Besides, having a burial plot from the time you're a kid puts a real burden on a body. It's like you're expected to die. Not a nice thing to think about, but then, Mama and Daddy weren't doing anything more than providing—which is what parents back then thought was the be-all and end-all of parenting.

I pulled through the open gate that began the property on which Jewel and Harmon's little twenty-two room love nest resided.

Harmon and Jewel had fallen in love when Jewel was a teenager and Harmon was a no-good dropout, one of many sons of a no-account pig farmer in the north end of the county. Harmon didn't look so good to Daddy, who had his sights set a bit higher for his baby girl. So he'd had me, a new deputy sheriff, scare off the boy. Which I did. Harmon ran off and joined the service and Jewel grieved something terrible, then went off to OU and got knocked up by Henry Hotchkiss.

Sixteen years, a move to Houston, and a mortgage later, Jewel found herself a widow, with three kids on her hands and no skills to speak of. Of course, she really didn't need any skills, 'cause Henry, an accountant, had provided well for his family. She moved back to Prophesy County and took up residence in my house.

Now, while Jewel was having babies and moving to Houston, Harmon Monk had come back to town, taken over his dead daddy's pig farm, and turned it into an auto graveyard and used-part shop. By the time Jewel came home to Prophesy County, Harmon owned a dozen or more used and new parts shops all over our end of Oklahoma and drove a brand-new Cadillac. It took him about a week to dispose of his wife—a prissy thing from Oklahoma City who always thought living in Bishop was too beneath her for words—and move her back home to her daddy and come courting my sister. They were married a month before me and Jean.

Now, I been in Jewel's house in Houston, where she and Henry and their three kids had lived for several years. It was a nice upper-middle-class tract home on about a pint of land—which is just about all they give you to go with a house in Houston. Chez Monk was not exactly the same thing. It was kinda like Tara—in *Gone With the Wind*—except bigger. Great big white house with columns holding up the front and a big double door and circular drive with roads leading off to the stables to the left and the barns to the right. The grounds boasted all sorts of blazing flowers in colors nature never originally intended, surrounding little boy statues pissing into fish ponds.

It's what passes for elegance in Prophesy County.

I pulled my Jeep around the circle, past the pissing statue, to the front doors, got out, and rang the doorbell. Deep inside, I could hear the chimes making music—"Lara's Theme" from *Dr. Zhivago*. It took a minute for Miz Bertha to answer the door. Miz Bertha's Harmon and Jewel's housekeeper. She's three hundred pounds of trouble on feet that shouldn't be able to hold up an anorexic—tiny feet, tiny hands. Miz Bertha had been Harmon's housekeeper from his first marriage, and she was so relieved to get rid of the first Mistress Monk that she's actually nice to my sister.

"Sheriff," she said, blocking the door—and it's a real big door.

"Hey, Miz Bertha. My sister in?"

"Is she expecting you?"

"Yes, ma'am, she surely is." I wiggled the papers in my hands as mute explanation of my visit, then felt resentful. I mean, this was my sister! I could damn well visit anytime I wanted. If it was okay with Miz Bertha.

"She didn't mention it to me," Miz Bertha said, still blocking the door.

"Well, then, why don't you ask her if it's okay to let me in?" I suggested.

"Bertha, it's okay," Jewel said from behind the larger woman. I could see her head bobbing up and down like she was jumping up to get a look at me. "Let him in."

Miz Bertha moved away with a shrug, like she was saying it wasn't her fault if Jewel would just let any ol' riffraff in.

Jewel's house is in a constant state of redecorating. The former Mrs. Monk was into the formal look—lots of French provincial phonies, with a few real antiques thrown in. Jewel was into whatever the former Mrs. Monk wasn't. Everytime I'd been over there, one room or another had been under reconstruction. Today, it was the foyer. There was a man on his hands and knees, using a tool to loosen up the black-and-white marble tiles that had been laid for the previous lady of the house. The walls were already stripped of their former silk brocade wall lining and I could see wallpaper swatches and heavy oak paneling leaning up against the walls.

"Wainscoting," Jewel said with a flourish of her arm, taking in the large foyer. She went over to the wallpaper swatches and held up two. "The bottom half in oak, then topped with one of these. Which?" One was tiny rosebuds in a buttery yellow with a pale blue stripe on a cream background. The other was tiny rosebuds in a pale blue with a buttery yellow stripe on a cream background. God, the decisions!

"Well," I said, smiling, "I think either one would look real nice."

Jewel tossed the swatches against the wall. "Oh, thanks. You're just heaps of help. Come on."

She led me into the living room, or the parlor, or whatever you call one of many such rooms in a house this size. This was the one in front, or the main one. Jewel had already redone this room—the first one she'd done. When I first saw the house, right after she and Harmon started seeing each other, the room had been very formal, with Louis the whatever chairs, heavy velvet drapes, and antique silk brocade couches, the floor covered with huge Oriental rugs. Now the parquet wood floor was mostly visible, except for a few spots covered by light-colored throw rugs. My sister swears the room is "Country French." Looks kinda Early American to me. But it's a comfortable room.

We sat down and I showed her where she needed to sign the papers.

"You want some coffee or something?" she asked.

"Yeah, fine. If Miz Bertha made it instead of you."

"I'm taking cooking classes," she said.

"Harmon's a smart man."

"I'm going to have you and Jean over the minute I get my certificate. I'm planning on beef-tongue soup, an endive salad—"

"Um, um, cow mouth and weeds. Just what I want after a long day of work—"

"Bertha!" she called. "Fix my brother some of the bad coffee, okay?"

Once Miz Bertha had grudgingly brought us the coffee and fixings, along with some not-so-bad-looking pastries, I settled back. "I know this is gonna seem kinda weird, maybe 'cause you think you already told me, and maybe you did, but you know I never listen to you—"

"I'm sorry, were you speaking?" she said.

"—but I'd like you to tell me about Libby. About how you met her, what you know about her prior to her Washington time—"

Jewel stopped the joking around. She set her cup down. "Why?"

I shrugged. "I'm not sure why. It just seems to me the more I know about her, maybe the easier it'll be to find out what happened."

Jewel sighed. "I don't see how what she did over ten years ago in Houston would have any relevance to this, Milton."

"It probably won't. Humor me?"

Jewel lifted her coffee cup and leaned back on her couch. "What exactly do you want to know?"

"Everything. Anything."

The French doors were opened to the side patio. The temperature hadn't started to rise yet, even on this first day of August, so the still-cool morning weather wafted our way, along with the sweet sounds of a songbird. I could hear the far-off whinny of one of the horses in the stable and the distant voices of two of Harmon's hired hands. All the sounds faded as Jewel began to talk. I was back in Libby land, a place I seemed to be going to a little too often.

"Well, I'm not sure where to begin. I guess at the beginning. Henry got this huge promotion and raise. We'd had this little two-bedroom in the Heights and it was getting crowded. I was about eight months pregnant with Carl when we found the house off Fondren. It was about two years old and in wonderful condition. The day we moved in was the day I met Honey for the first time. I'll never forget it. I hear this voice—'Yoo-hoo'—and I look up from the back of the truck, where I'm busy handing Henry the stuff I can still pick up, and there's this little doll of a woman with a basket of blueberry muffins in one hand and a Thermos of coffee in the other.

"Well, I'm so pregnant, I can't help much with the unloading, and Leonard and Marlene weren't old enough to be much help to Henry, so here comes Chuck. 'Hey, you need some effing help?' " Jewel laughed. "I thought Henry was going to have a heart attack when he saw Chuck. But somehow, they took right to each other. Mutt and Jeff in more ways than one. Anyway, Honey decides to take over the kids and the three of them go in the backyard, which was a muddy mess. It had rained the day before and Honey spent hours out there with the kids making mud pies. We had to hose all three of them off after that." Jewel sighed and poured herself another cup of coffee. "I really miss Honey sometimes. She's something else."

"Yeah," I said, having to agree. "She surely is."

"We became friends so fast, it would make your head spin. It was like I'd known her all my life. And when Carl came, you would have thought she'd given birth to him. She spent all her time over at our house those first few months—and I needed that. Needed the help, since Mama wasn't able to come down then. And all this time, she talked about Libby. They'd been roommates at college since the first day of their freshman year. Honey said she walked into this tiny little dorm room, saw Libby sitting there staring daggers at the third girl in the room, Trisha Misher. Or Trisher Misher, as they referred to her. I heard so many Trisher Misher jokes, you wouldn't believe. How many Trisher Mishers does it take to screw in a lightbulb?"

I shrugged. "I don't know," I said.

"None. It's better to be in the dark."

I groaned and Jewel laughed. "Anyway, I'd seen Libby on the TV news, of course. Honey wouldn't allow us to watch any other channel. Had to watch Libby. When Carl was about three months old, Honey decided Libby and I just had to meet each other." Jewel looked at me. "I'm not sure if this happens with men, but with women it certainly does. It happens all the time. There's one person with two friends and she decides those two friends are just going to love each other because she cares for them both so much. Then the two friends meet and they can't stand each other. It's happened to me a half dozen times, either as the friend in the middle or the other. I guess it has something to do with jealousy, although I doubt if anyone would ever admit that. It's like, How can she care as much about this new friend as she does about me?

"Well, I knew that was exactly what was going to happen with Libby. That's why I'd put off meeting her. And not only that—here she was this career woman, one of the first women anchors in Houston's history, and here I was married to an accountant, with three kids. We had *so* much in common!

"And then, of course, she and Honey had this *history*, and I just knew I was going to end up sitting there listening to them talk about people I'd never heard of and being left totally out of the conversation."

Jewel sighed, then laughed, curling up on the couch, her feet tucked under her. "But Honey was so excited. She wanted us to meet so badly. And Honey's enthusiasm *is* contagious, you know."

"That I know," I said.

"So we made these big plans—Brennan's downtown, Sunday brunch. God, the place was packed. Libby's already there waiting for us. I was immediately struck by how much prettier she was in person than on TV. And I don't know how to explain it, but it just worked. I liked her immediately and she seemed to like me. I never felt like she was talking down to me, even when she asked about my kids. You get that sometimes with women who work and don't have kids. They can be very patronizing. But Libby wasn't like that. And whenever they talked about someone from their past, Libby would tell me who they were talking about and why they were saying such terrible things about them. And Honey and I would do the same when we talked about particular neighbors who deserved the treatment.

"I don't know, after that we just started seeing one another a lot. All three of us. At least once a week. And when Honey and Chuck were out of town, Libby even came over to the house for dinner. She was great with the kids. Is this helping at all?"

I shrugged. I had no idea what I was looking for. I just wanted to know her. The way Jewel had. The way Honey had. "Whatever you can tell me," I finally said.

Jewel laughed. "I remember one time the three of us went to dinner at the River Oaks Country Club. Libby's father is a big cheese at a club in New Orleans that has a reciprocal agreement with the River Oaks. Neither Honey nor I had ever been there, but Libby went to the country club a lot, at least enough for the maître d' and everyone else there to know her. Of course, that could have been TV exposure. Anyway, we had this great dinner in this posh room and we all three were dressed to the nines. And we had entirely too much wine. When we left, Libby decided to show us around the grounds of the club, and somehow—don't ask me how—a lot of that night's a blur—we ended up on the twelfth green of the golf course. Well, Libby says that a golf course is the best place in the world to practice handstands and cartwheels."

Jewel laughed. "Remember, we are seriously dressed up, right? Well, we had to take our heels off because we kept getting them stuck in the turf. Anyway, it's after midnight, and we're out on the twelfth green doing cartwheels and falling on our butts, and Libby starts walking on her hands. And Honey starts hitting me, yelling, 'Watch this! Watch this now! She can do this for miles!' And, sure enough, she just keeps walking off the green and onto the next one. Honey and I jump up and follow her, but we're laughing so hard, we keep falling down. The skirt of Libby's dress is hanging in front of her face and her bikini panties are exposed to the world. And all of sudden, we hear this voice say, 'Good evening, ladies.' Well, Libby falls right on her butt, her skirt hiked up around her neck, trying desperately to get her clothes straight. It's the security guard, and when he recognizes Libby, he says, 'Miz Fortuna, this is against club rules, you know.'

"Well, Libby gets herself untangled and stands up and puts her arm around the guard's shoulder and promises to mention his name on the news if he doesn't turn us in. He let us go, and lo and behold, the next night, toward the end of the broadcast, Libby says, 'And a special good night to my dear friend Ernie Miller.'"

Jewel got a far-off look in her eye, then sighed heavily. "I hadn't realized how much I missed Honey and Libby until I knew Libby was coming to live here. It was so great having her here. So great."

I stood up and moved over to the couch, next to my sister, and put my arm around her, pulling her to me, and kissed her on the cheek. "I'm sorry, kiddo. I really am."

Jewel wiped a tear on my sleeve and pushed away from me. "You gonna find who did this to her?"

I got up and moved to the door. "Yeah. I guess I am," I said, and took my leave.

The information on Howard Cleveland, the man with the ear bob being held in Tejas County, was in when I got to the office. He wasn't what you might call a model citizen—two years in Big Mac (the McAlester Penitentiary) for passing bad checks, arrests for petty theft, fraud, and a warrant from Texas for failure to pay child support. Not a model citizen, no. But nothing on his rap sheet showed a penchant for violent crimes. I think he was probably telling the truth about the earring—that he'd found it next to the Dumpster behind the Stop N Shop, and that meant Dalton Pettigrew and Jasmine Bodine had some serious ass-chewing coming their way.

I called Bill Williams over at Tejas County and told him what was on Cleveland's rap sheet.

"Well, I finally found me the owner of the LTD," Bill said. "Real put out that we'd found the damned thing. Had it insured—can you believe it? A car that old and beat-up! And he'd already collected, so now he has to give the money back."

"So I guess I can give the earring back to Libby's husband, if we won't need it for trial."

"I dunno, Milt, might need it to prove why we were chasing the boy in the first place. You know how the courts are getting."

"That's true, that's true," I said, shaking my head at the stupidness of it all. "Well, you check with your county attorney and let me know when I can get it back to Daniel, okay?"

"Will do. How's that wife of yours doing?"

"Fat and sassy. In a wheelchair now, she's getting so big. Screws up her equilibrium."

"What'd she have, anyway? Polio?"

"Yeah, when she was five. Her mamma and daddy didn't believe in the vaccine. It had just barely come out back then. Then she come down with it and they took the other kids in and had 'em vaccinated."

"Humph. Day late and a dollar short."

"Tell me about it."

"How bad she paralyzed, anyway?"

"Hit her from about midthigh, the way I understand it. Muscles atrophied. Not really paralyzed."

"I don't know shit about polio," Bill said.

"Me, neither, till I met Jean. Still don't know all that much."

"It gonna affect her delivering the baby?"

"She and the doctor both say no. The polio didn't affect the pelvic area, so she'll just have the regular problems any mid-forties lady would have delivering."

"Well, me and Mary Sue gonna put y'all on a prayer chain at the church."

"I surely do appreciate that, Bill. You take care of ol' Howard, here?"

"Oh, that boy's taken care of, don't you worry 'bout that."

I'd barely gotten off the phone with Bill Williams when Emmett stuck his head in my door.

"Guess what?" he said, coming into my office and closing the door and making himself at home in my visitor's chair.

"What?" I said.

"That forwarding address in the Longbranch police file for Phillip Gallagher's a phony."

"You don't say," I said.

"I do say. He didn't have a residence address to give us at the time, but he gave us the name of the hospital where he was gonna be working. I called them, just to see what ol' Phil's been up to. They never heard of him. I had the operator put me through to personnel and they never heard of him, either. So I called directory assistance and got the AMA in LA. Never heard of him. Got the number from them for the state AMA. Also never heard of him. Phillip Gallagher has never applied to practice medicine in the state of California."

"Well, now this is getting interesting," I said. "Is there a national AMA registry?"

"Yeah," Emmett said. "I called them. They need the request in writing." He handed me a sheet of paper. "I took the liberty of having Gladys type this here up."

It was a letter for my signature, asking for the whereabouts of Phillip Gallagher, M.D., OB-GYN, last known board certification in the state of Oklahoma.

I signed it with a flourish. "Randolph's Office Supplies's got a fax machine. Why don't you fax it to them and add on the bottom here that this is urgent." I figured I needed to find something wrong with what he done. Couldn't let him get too up-pity. Just good management.

"Okay," Emmett said, taking his leave.

I called Gladys on the intercom and asked her to send Jasmine Bodine into my office. I noticed when she walked in how much better Jasmine'd been looking since she divorced Lester Bodine. She'd done one of those frosting things with her hair, so now it had some blond strips in the muddy brown, and she was wearing makeup that gave a little color to her face. And I thought maybe she was losing a little weight, not that she had ever been fat or anything, but her uniform was hanging a little loose on her frame.

"Jasmine, what's on your plate right now?" I asked, indicating that she shut the door and have a seat.

"Nothing much, Milt," she said in her Eeyore voice. "I served a warrant this morning on that DUI we talked about yesterday and I was fixing to go by Mr. Abernathy's and warn him again about his dog."

"That can wait," I said. I handed her the hate mail from the Cassie Gallagher file. "See what you can find out on this stuff for me. We got one signed. Madelyn R. Carey. Check her out first. Then go by the First Baptist and the Blessed Virgin and that new fundamentalist place—"

"New Faith Congregation—"

"Right. Check out what you can about this pro-life group the churches started up. See if they can shed any light on this here."

"Well, sure, Milt, but this happened quite a while back—"

"And it should have been investigated then, but it wasn't. Now we're gonna investigate it."

"But, Milt, this didn't even happen in our jurisdiction—"

I gave her a look. The look I'd picked up at the knee of Elberry Blankenship. It was a doozy.

Jasmine stood up and headed for the door. "Well, I'll try," she said.

"And before you leave, Jasmine—"

"Yes, sir?" she said, turning back to me. First time she'd called me sir. I gotta admit I liked it.

"You and Dalton did the search around the back of the Stop N Shop, where Libby Fortuna's body was found, right?"

"Yes."

So I told her about Howard Cleveland and the ear bob. Her face went pasty under the makeup and the whine went up an octave.

"Swear to God, Milt, Dalton and I went over every inch of ground!"

"Be that as it may," I said, the first time in my memory I'd ever put those words together like that, "Howard Cleveland found the ear bob and you and Dalton didn't." I sighed. "Go on and take care of those right-to-lifers."

I turned around in my swivel chair, dismissing her. After she left, I let a little smile appear on my face. This delegating stuff was fun.

Though my next thought was enough to wipe the smile off my face. I'd delegated everything I needed to do at the moment on the Libby Fortuna case. That left me with the onerous task of spending time with Larry Joe January to discuss the multiple suicides. I just love it when I smart myself into a corner like that.

9

When Emmett Hopkins was chief of police for Longbranch, Oklahoma, there were pictures on the walls of his prizewinning flowers and even a tomato he grew one time that was the biggest damn thing I ever saw. He had a sterling silver pen and pencil set in a holder on his desk that his staff had bought him when he received honorable mention as police officer of the year for the state of Oklahoma. Other than that, you never could see much 'cause of all the papers scattered about on his desk, lying in the visitors chair, and stacked on the floor. It was the office of a busy man.

When I finally got through all the rigmarole of trying to get in to see Larry Joe January, I noticed the office was now a little bit different. For one thing, it was a hell of a lot cleaner than it should have been for somebody who ran a police department. But I'd always figured Larry Joe, if given half a chance, would be a supremo delegater. The pictures on the walls were all pictures of Larry Joe with some local dignitary, from the mayor to Billy Moulini, the guy who owned most of the property on Mountain Falls Road—my absentee neighbor. And he had one of those useless executive games with the ball bearings where you hit one and then the last one moves and the ones in the middle don't. Suppose it's got a name, but I've never really had the need to find out. I always figured people bought crap like that for other people because they didn't know them well enough to get them something personal. But I had a sneaking suspicion Larry Joe probably bought that thingamabob his ownself.

When I finally got in and seated myself in Larry Joe's visitor's chair, after charitably shaking his hand, I said, "Larry Joe, I think we got some crossover stuff going on that you and I should discuss."

"Crossover stuff?" he said.

I sighed. "Stuff happening in the county and happening in the town that may be connected."

"Oh. Yeah, right. Crossover stuff. I didn't understand you at first."

"You had that suicide a little while ago where the teenaged girl got hit by the train?"

"Uh-huh. Right. Well, I wouldn't have handled that directly, see. That would have been handled by—"

"But you know about it?"

"Well, sure, probably. A teenager?"

"Lori Nabors. Fifteen years old. Stood out in front of a train on the track behind her parents' house about two o'clock in the morning. Left a note."

"Hum. Right."

"Well, maybe you should call in whoever handled it so I can discuss it with him."

Larry Joe straightened his shoulders and frowned, causing a wrinkle in his forehead, like he was thinking or something— which I doubted. "I handle any intradepartmental communication," he said. "Any liaisoning between this department and the sheriff's department will always be handled by me. I would prefer if you didn't discuss active or inactive cases with any of my officers."

I sighed. "Well, fine, Larry Joe, but it would be real nice if you were up to speed on any of the activity going on in town— like crimes and suicides and stuff like that."

Larry Joe was busily shuffling through his in-box. There were about two items in it, and I doubted one of 'em had to do with Lori Nabors.

I finally decided to take the bull by the horns, or the idiot by his nose, as the case may be. "Larry Joe, just let me fill you in, okay? I already told you there was a suicide. Young girl—teenager. She'd been seeing my wife. She was anorexic—"

"Anna what?"

"Anorexic. Like she was starving herself to death? You *ever* watch TV, Larry Joe?"

"Yeah, right, anorexic. Okay."

"Anyway, she was seeing my wife for treatment and she was getting better, then she backslided."

"Uh-huh," Larry Joe said. The frown line on his forehead was gonna become permanent, he was concentrating so hard.

"Same thing as Shirley Beth Hopkins. Emmett said she'd been doing better, been staying off the booze for a while, and then she goes back to drinking—"

Larry Joe let loose with something that sounded like a snort. "Like you can believe the husband."

I gave him a stern look. "You can believe Emmett Hopkins." I sighed again, getting seriously tired of Larry Joe January. "Well, I had me another suicide out in Bishop—lady who'd been abusing her kid. She was seeing a shrink about it, trying to stop. Then one day she didn't stop, and that evening she killed herself."

Larry Joe laughed. "You saying these is connected, Milt? How? A suicide pact, 'cept they wait months between? And anyway, they live all over the county and they ain't got nothing in common. One's an old booze hound, nother's a skinny teenaged girl, and then you got a lady hits her kid. Where's the connection?"

"I don't know, Larry Joe. But I'd like to see your files on Shirley Beth and the Nabors girl."

He was shaking his head before I'd even finished my sentence. "Ain't been no crime here, Milt. Suicide's on the book, but I don't rightly wanna dig anybody up and throw 'em in the slam, do you?"

"Something funny's going on, Larry Joe. I just wanna take a peek at those files—"

Again the head was shaking. "No way. I believe in cooperating, Milt, but, like I said, there's been no crime here. 'Sides, Emmett Hopkins got no right looking at his wife's file."

"I wouldn't show Emmett the file—"

"Well, now, how do I know that?"

"Look, you little shit—" I was standing. I was pissed. I walked out, lest I coldcock Larry Joe January. It would have been rewarding, but hardly worth the effort.

By the time I got back from the courthouse, Jasmine Bodine was sitting in the bull pen. She jumped up when she saw me. "Milt, got a minute?"

"Sure, come on in," I said, walking on to my office. Once we got there, Jasmine sat down in the visitor's chair and I sat down in my big swivel.

"Well, I went by Miz Carey's house like you said, Milt, but she wouldn't let me in."

"What do you mean she wouldn't let you in?" I demanded.

"Well, I knocked and knocked and she wouldn't open the door. I could see her peeking at me through the curtains, but she wouldn't open up," Jasmine said, her voice getting real close to a whine.

Sometimes delegating's not what it's cracked up to be. I looked at my watch and the top of my desk. I had a choice. I could stay where I was and work on about three thousand state, federal, and county forms, or I could go roust a religious nut. Didn't seem to be much on the staying side of the scale.

Madelyn R. Carey lived across the street from the Longbranch Municipal Park & Pool. It had been built back in the fifties and I'd gone there swimming a bunch when I was a teenager. The pool was huge, the way they built them back then, with tile inlays that would cost a mint nowdays to reproduce, and an island in the middle (a round concrete thing on concrete piers, with a hole in the middle) that you could swim in and out of. Used to be a big joke to yank somebody's trunks off while they were in the middle of the island and leave 'em stranded. Thought it was real funny 'til Lynn Robinson did it to me.

You got to the pool through the park, about two acres of big trees with playground equipment, swings and jungle gyms and the like. I hadn't been near the pool in a long time and I looked over at the park while me and Jasmine got out of the car, thinking in a year or two, me and Jean could be taking Junior over here to swing on the swings and maybe even get him started in one of them water-baby classes.

I didn't remember the trailer Jasmine Bodine pointed out as belonging to Madelyn R. Carey. I think if it had been there when I was hanging around the pool, I'd a noticed. It was one of them old Air Stream types—round-edged shiny aluminum—and it was covered with bumper stickers, and I mean covered. Very little of the aluminum showed through. There was a big cross, about five feet by five feet, made out of colored lightbulbs, affixed to the side. I figured the city police must get called on a regular basis when that thing blazed away at night.

As we went up the walk to the front door of the trailer, making our way through assorted lawn gewgaws—like a pair of giant plastic praying hands, a two-foot-tall statue of Jesus, a rusty metal free-form statue thing that I finally figured out was a bunch of Christian fish symbols welded together—I saw the curtains on the little window next to the door flutter.

I took one step up the aluminum stairs and rapped smartly on the door. "Miz Carey!" I called out real loud. "I'm the sheriff of Prophesy County. We need to talk to you. Let me in now or I'm going to the judge and get me a court order. Now you don't want me to do that, Miz Carey. You truly don't."

The door opened against a chain lock. "What you want?" I

116

could see a watery blue eye and a few wisps of white hair.

"Miz Carey, we need to talk to you about some letters you sent a while back."

"See my lawyer. Garson Grange, over to Bishop." She slammed the door in my face.

I rapped on the door again. "Miz Carey, you best call Mr. Grange now, 'cause I'm heading to the courthouse to get me a court order to search your premises." I had no call to do that, but I figured the old lady didn't know that. "Now, all I really wanna do is talk to you, Miz Carey, and it'd be a lot easier on both of us if you just opened up the door."

The door opened again and a portable phone was thrust into my hand. I put it to my ear. "Hello?" I said.

"This is Attorney Grange. Whom am I speaking to?"

"This is Sheriff Milt Kovak, Mr. Grange—"

"Why are you harassing my client, Sheriff?"

"I'm not harrassing your client—"

"Miz Carey says you people have been bothering her all day. Mind telling me what this is about?" He sounded on the phone like an officious little snot, but I've rarely met a lawyer who didn't sound that way—on the phone or in person.

"My deputy came by earlier today, but Miz Carey wouldn't open the door. That's why I'm here. This is only the second time—"

"What did you say this was regarding, Sheriff?"

"I didn't, Mr. Grange. But it concerns a letter Miz Carey sent a few years ago. That's all. Nobody's charging Miz Carey with anything. We just wanted to ask her about a letter she sent."

"What was this letter and when did she send it, Sheriff?"

I sighed. "Look, Grange. I haven't got the time nor the inclination to stand out here in the heat and talk to you on the phone. Now you either tell your client to let me in so we can talk or you get your butt down here pronto, before we haul her in for obstructing justice."

"Now see here, Sheriff—"

117

I hung up on him. The phone rang almost immediately. I flipped it back on and said, "Yes?"

"Let me talk to Miz Carey," Grange said.

I knocked on the door. The old lady opened it again against the chain and I handed the phone back to her. "Your lawyer wants to talk to you," I said.

She took the phone and slammed the door. I moved off the porch to stand with Jasmine under the not-too-great shade of a scrawny little mimosa tree in the yard. Sweat was already running down my armpits and back. I hoped to hell if we ever got in Miz Carey's trailer it was air-conditioned.

Five long minutes passed before the door opened again. "Come on in if you gotta," Miz Carey said, sticking part of her head out the door. She moved away, leaving the trailer door standing partially open. Jasmine and I moved inside.

I stepped over the threshhold into the trailer and realized that not only did Miz Carey not have air conditioning, she didn't know how to open a window, either. The place was an oven—literally.

Once inside, I got the full impact of Madelyn R. Carey. Without the obvious osteoporsis, she may have been about five foot one or two; with it, she was about four-and-a-half-feet tall. She had wispy white hair, with a lot more scalp than hair showing, and her face was wrinkled like a shirt that's been in the laundry basket way too long. She was wearing denim stretch pants and a T-shirt emblazoned with the legend, "Christ Forgives the Repentant."

She sat down on the couch, which pulled her too-long pants up, exposing her bare feet. I doubted if Madelyn R. Carey could fit shoes over the cracked and yellowed toenails that hung off her feet like talons.

Jasmine and I took seats, me on the couch next to Miz Carey, Jasmine in a platform rocker. The outside of the trailer and the yard looked tame compared to the interior of Miz Carey's home. The couch, the rocker, and a small built-in dinette were the only furniture in the room. But the room was wall-to-wall junk: stacks of religious tracts and pamphlets, plastic Jesuses, antiabortion signs on wooden stakes leaning against the walls, and all manner of stuff I didn't want to try to identify.

After we got settled, I cleared my throat, trying to suck in some air, although there wasn't much in the trailer, and said, "Miz Carey, we wanted to talk to you about a letter you sent a few years back to Phillip Gallagher."

"Who?" The old lady squinted at me, breathing the word in my direction. I was lucky I'm not the type to lose my lunch— the lady's breath was that bad.

"Dr. Phillip Gallagher. He was an OB-GYN who practiced here in Longbranch couple years back. His wife and unborn child were killed in an explosion—"

"Oh," she said, a smile cracking her parched-looking lips. "That Godless heathen who kilt babies. I 'member him."

"You sent him a letter—"

"Well, 'course. I send letters to anybody kills babies. I send letters all over Oklahoma; wherever they got them clinics, I send letters. I get a listing from the national and I send out letters." She sighed and looked off into the distance. "Kinda hard sometimes coming up with the stamps, but sometimes the kids, they leave bottles over to the park and I get me a nickel here and there. That's when I send me a letter."

"Miz Carey, are you a member of the right-to-life group here in the county?"

She nodded her head. "Yes, sir. Sure am. Can't contribute much 'cept I send letters. Don't get out much. Lost my Social Security while back."

"Why's that?" I asked.

Miz Carey straightened herself as much as her body was able. A glint of fire lightened her eyes. "Cause a my convictions. Gov'ment's getting scared a us and they trying to kill us. Figure cuttin' off my money, I dry up and go away. Ain't gonna happen. I'm still here."

119

"Miz Carey," I said, trying to be reasonable, "the government doesn't do that sort of thing."

She cackled a laugh that sent a shiver down my spine. "That's what they want you to believe. They tole me it's cause I didn't qualify no more 'cause I broke one of their rules or somethin', but I know the truth. Godless Communists done took over the gov'ment and they wanna kill all the babies. No more American babies ever. That's what they trying to do. Pretty soon gonna be forced abortions, you just wait and see."

"Miz Carey, about the letter to Phillip Gallagher—"

"Who?"

Jasmine and I left. I figured there was no reason to stay around. If Madelyn R. Carey'd had anything to do with the bombing that killed Cassie Gallagher, which I didn't believe, I doubt that she would remember. Besides, I couldn't take the place or the lady a minute longer.

I had Jasmine drop me back at the sheriff's office and go on out to the New Faith Congregation Church, where the Interdenominational Right-to-Life group headquarters were located. We talked a bit about the types of questions she should ask.

"Like if they were around five years ago when Cassie Gallagher got killed. If they weren't, what members had been active before the group started up. If they got any members they think might be a little hinky. If anybody there ever heard of Phillip Gallagher. That sorta stuff, Jasmine."

"Right," she said, duly noting in her little book every word I uttered.

"And anything else you might think of," I said, hoping to spark a little initiative.

I called County Social Services and talked to a social worker there, explaining the situation with Madelyn R. Carey.

"Oh, you don't have to tell me about Miz Carey," the social worker, Lucy Silver, said. "We know all about Miz Carey."

"Well, she's a crazy old bat," I said, "but seems to me there should be some way to get her Social Security in order."

"There is, Sheriff. There are some forms she needs to fill out. But Miz Carey thinks filling out the forms means she's admitting herself into the ranks of the heathens. She won't fill them out."

"Doesn't she have any next of kin?"

"Nobody who will admit it. Would you?"

"Ah, come on, Miz Silver—"

The social worker sighed. "Sheriff, we *are* concerned about her. Somebody from this office goes out there every other week or so to check on her, but she won't let anybody in. The only other thing we can do is go for an involuntary commitment, but that's hard to get, and nobody really wants to do it, you know?"

I sighed my own sigh. "Yeah. I know. I just thought I'd call."

"I appreciate your concern, although I doubt if Miz Carey would."

I hung up the phone and went back to my three thousand state, federal, and county forms. Near to quitting time, my ex-brother-in-law, Earl "Trust Me" Conners, came by with one of his underlings, bringing me my brand-new squad car. Earl owns both the Chevy and Ford dealerships in town and can get you a deal on any other make or model you might have your heart set on—from a Hyundai to a Range Rover. When I bought my Jeep, I went up the Tulsa Highway to another dealership, but the county has a contract with Earl and he was the one who ordered my new squad car. And I gotta admit, it was a beaut.

A brand-new Chevy Caprice, all decked out with everything you need in a squad car, plus a place to put a computer, if the county ever got that fancy. I thanked Earl, asked after his wife, Francine, and their four nasty brats, all now grown up and having nasty brats of their own, then asked after LaDonna, my ex-wife.

That gave Earl the opening he needed to tell me what a wonderful thing it was having a banker for a new brother-in-law. I tuned him out about four seconds into it, knowing Earl well from actually having worked for him right after me and LaDonna got married and not wanting to hear how well my ex and her new hubby were doing. I just dearly hoped Dwayne Dickey, LaDonna's husband and owner of the Longbranch First National Bank, knew the only reason Earl took a shine to him was the proximity of all that money. Earl dearly loved to borrow money.

Earl finally left, and it was about a quarter to six when Jean called me from the hospital.

"I need to take group tonight for one of my staff. Her father's in the hospital in Taylor," she said.

"How late you gonna be?" I asked.

"Nine or ten," she said, "and remember, tomorrow's our first Lamaze class."

I sighed. "Yeah, almost forgot." I'd tried. I really had. "Don't forget to eat," I added.

"As soon as I can get rid of you, I'm going down to the cafeteria."

"They got a special on pizza and ice cream?" I asked.

"I don't find you amusing," my wife said.

"But, honey, I'm known· as the Bob Hope of Prophesy County."

"I'm fat, Milt."

"You're beautiful," I said.

I heard a sob. "Honey, what's wrong?" I said, hunching over the phone. I can't stand it when a woman cries, specially when it's probably my fault.

"My belly button became an outie today."

I suppressed the laughter. "Honey—"

"My hands and feet are swelling and my face is puffy and now I've got an outie!"

"Jean, it'll go back—"

"What if it doesn't?" she wailed.

"Honey, you're a doctor. You know it's gonna go back. Think about it. You know that."

"No I don't. I don't *know* it's going to go back. There are cases—"

"Honey . . ." I started.

Jean gulped in a breath. "I've got to go now. You get something to eat, too, okay?"

"Right. Okay. Bye."

The line went dead in my hands. Oh, well, that's life with a pregnant woman.

The door opened and Jasmine Bodine came in. "Got a minute, Milt?" she asked.

"Sure, Jasmine," I said, pointing at one of my visitor's chairs. "Have a seat. Just get back from the right-to-lifers?"

She nodded her head. "Yeah. I asked all the questions you told me to, but the guy I talked to"—she flipped her book open and ran one finger down a page—"Jimmy Sedgwick—he's the minister of the New Faith Congregation—he said they've only been officially operating for about two years and he doesn't know if any of the members were active in the movement before that time. When I asked the hinky question, he got kinda offended."

I sighed. I'd used the word *hinky*. Jasmine had written down the word *hinky*. Therefore, Jasmine used the word *hinky* when talking with the good pastor. I keep forgetting how literal a lady Jasmine is. She could have substituted "overly involved," "wound a little too tight," "nutty as a june bug," but no, Jasmine said "hinky."

"What does he know about Madelyn R. Carey?"

Jasmine's eyes got big. "Oh. I didn't ask him about Miz Carey. Was I supposed to?"

Luckily, Emmett Hopkins took that moment to pop his head in. "Got a minute?" he asked me, waving slightly to Jasmine, who got up and scampered out of the room. And I hadn't even dismissed her. Milt Kovak, the Rodney Dangerfield of Prophesy County, Oklahoma.

123

Emmett meandered in and eased himself down in my visitor's chair.

"You hungry?" I asked him.

"Hungry enough to eat dirt," he said.

I stood up. "How 'bout the Longbranch Inn?"

There'd been a time after my old friend Glenda Sue Robinson'd been killed that I found it hard to eat at the Longbranch Inn, where she'd been a waitress for twenty-some years. Then when I got where I could eat there, I stayed away from her station and away from the chicken-fried steak, fries, and cream gravy, which had always been my usual when I was waiting for Glenda Sue to get off work. But grief has a way of working itself out, specially when the Longbranch Inn makes the best damned chicken-fried steak in three states.

So I ordered that with fries and an extra side of gravy for dipping the fries, and some creamed corn, a biscuit, and a quart of iced tea, which is how it comes, anyway. Emmett had the meat loaf with red gravy, succotash, mashed potatoes, corn bread, and a quart of iced tea. We split a piece of pecan pie for dessert. 'Cept Emmett did the dividing up, and I do believe he took the larger piece.

While we settled back with the pie, I asked Emmett, "You still got a key to the courthouse?"

He gave me the evil eye. "Well, I might. Why you asking?"

"That key or another one you got get you into the police department and your office?"

He set down his jar of iced tea and sat forward, looking me in the eye. "You planning something?"

"What's the usual personnel on at night? Place crowded?" I asked.

"Got one in and one on the streets when I was there."

"Who's in?"

"Used to be Gaylor Swanson."

I smiled. Gaylor Swanson was a minute and a half away from

retirement and had had a slight case of narcolepsy for years now. "You mind loaning me them keys?"

Emmett started shaking his head. "Ain't no way. But I'll be happy to let you in. What you looking for?"

"Some files Larry Joe January didn't feel like sharing."

"What files?"

"Emmett."

"What files, Milt?"

I sighed. "The file on Shirley Beth and on that Nabors girl killed herself last week."

Emmett frowned. "What's on your mind, hoss?"

I sighed. I hadn't shared my worries about the suicides with Emmett, seeing as how his wife had been one of them. But I guess I needed to do that now. So I told him.

"What are you thinking, Milt?"

"I don't know, Emmett. I just think it's mighty strange, that's all. I think it's worth checking out."

Emmett stood up and threw some money on the table. "Let's move," he said, heading for the door, the keys to the courthouse already in his hand.

10

It was after eight o'clock and Longbranch was already half shut down. The Longbranch Inn's restaurant would be open until nine, and Bernie's Chat & Chew didn't close until ten, but other than that, the sidewalks were rolled up tight. We passed the one city cruiser on our way to the courthouse, but it was going the other way and didn't pay us any mind.

The back door of the courthouse was unlocked and would be 'til ten o'clock, so getting in the building was no big shakes. The police department was behind the stairs on the right, where the sheriff's department had been housed until we moved to the new building out on the highway twelve years before. Emmett walked me to the back entrance, which was locked, and used his key to open it.

"Go in this way. You know where the files are kept, right?"

I nodded my head. "I'll keep Gaylor busy up front while you do your thing," Emmett said while I slipped in the back way.

I passed Larry Joe January's office and the empty office Larry Joe used to have before he got bumped up to Emmett's job. Beyond that was a secretary's desk and behind that the file room. I went in and shut the door behind me before I flipped the switch for the lights. The closed door muffled the sound of Emmett's and Gaylor's voices to the point where I could barely hear them at all. That was good. If I couldn't hear them, chances were they couldn't hear any little noise I mighta made.

It took about five minutes to locate the file on Shirley Beth Hopkins and the one on Lori Nabors. I went to the door, turned off the light, and slipped into the hall. So far, all clear. I retraced my steps to the back door, passing Larry Joe's office, put my hand on the knob of the door, and slowly turned it. I noticed my hand was shaking and my mouth was dry. I figured cat burglary wasn't in my makeup. I opened the door and shut it firmly behind me, testing to make sure the lock held. It did. I skedaddled out the back door of the building, around the front, and into the front seat of my car. I honked the horn twice, hoping Emmett would know what that was about, but as we hadn't seen fit to come up with a signal for when I was through, I just hoped for the best. He came out two minutes later; I started the car and drove two miles below the speed limit back to the sheriff's office, not saying a word and sweating buckets.

Once inside, I fired up the Xerox machine and made quick copies of the files. Turning to Emmett, I said, "Now you can take 'em back."

"In a minute," he said, taking the file on Shirley Beth and sitting down at Dalton's desk in the bull pen.

"Emmett, I don't think you oughta—"

"Shut up, Milt."

Well, he was off duty. I took the copies I'd just made and read the file on Shirley Beth, getting myself prepared for whatever insensitive crap Emmett might find in there. But the file was short, sweet, and professional. Somebody other than Larry Joe January had obviously written it up. Other than the statistics of the case, in the area of remarks, the officer had written, "Victim was the wife of a police officer and used his service weapon to self-inflict bodily injury. Victim was pronounced dead at the scene by county medical examiner." The autopsy report was attached to the back. I noticed Emmett put it down before he got to that. And who could blame him.

The file on Lori Nabors was bigger. It included her suicide note and statements by her parents and the engineer who had tried to stop the train before it ran the girl down.

Her suicide note read, "Dear Mama and Daddy and Trey" (identified as her younger brother), "I'm sorry it has to be this way, but I can't figure out what else to do. I can't see my life getting any better. None of this is y'all's fault. I want you to believe that. And I want you to know that I know God is going to forgive me for this and I'll be in Jesus' sweet loving arms for all eternity. I'll say hi to Gramma Nabors for you, Daddy. All my love, Lori."

The father's statement was short and uninformative. The mother's was more detailed: "Lori ate dinner with the family around 6:30. We had fried steak and new potatoes and okra and tomatoes and I fixed an apple pie for dessert. I couldn't get her to eat the pie or any of the steak, 'cause it was fried, but she did have some of the potatoes and the okra. She seemed depressed, but she always does nowadays, so I didn't realize anything unusual was up. She went up to her room. She didn't go to the bathroom—I made sure of that. I watch her now when she goes to the bathroom. I make her keep the door open so I know she's not throwing up. Dr. McDonnell says that's what she's been doing, so I make sure she doesn't. I know it's awful not giving a teenaged girl any privacy at all, but that's what you gotta do with an anorexic. She's got a phone in her room and I heard her talking to somebody, but I didn't bother with that. I thought that was a good sign. She doesn't have a lot of friends. I thought that was a good sign. I didn't hear her leave the house. I musta been really asleep. I didn't know anything had happened until Troy Miller with the police department rang the bell around three in the morning. I tried everything I knew with that girl, I really did. I really tried."

The train engineer's statement said, "This was my regular Tulsa-to-Dallas run. Nothing unusual happened till we get to Longbranch, when, in this wooded section, I see this girl standing on the tracks. Might not of seen her except the moon was full. She had long hair and wore a light-colored nightdress and she was just standing in the middle of the tracks, with her arms down at her sides. I hit the horn and the brake at the same time. Kept hitting the horn, but she didn't budge. The train didn't stop till the engine was fifty feet or more beyond where I'd seen her. Me and my brakeman jumped out and ran down the track, trying to find her, hoping she jumped outta the way without us seeing, but then we saw her arm under car number four. Found some more of her scattered under the other cars and along the track. We radioed the police real quick, then waited for them to come. We didn't touch any of it. No way in hell I woulda. I got me a girl that age. It was terrible."

I went back to the mother's statement. "She's got a phone in her room and I heard her talking to somebody . . ." Why did that set my teeth on edge? I walked to our files and pulled out the file on Linda McKenna. Sure enough, Abel McKenna said he'd heard his wife talking on the phone in her bedroom the same night she blew her brains out.

"Hey, Emmett," I called from the file room. "Gotta ask you a question."

He stuck his head in the doorway. "What?"

"Shirley Beth on the phone the night she killed herself?"

Emmett frowned, whether from the impertinence of the question or because he was trying to recollect, I couldn't tell you. Finally, he said, "Yeah. Maybe. I'm not sure if it was that night, but she'd been talking on the phone to somebody a lot right before she died—like for maybe a month. Shirley Beth didn't use the phone much—nobody to call. No family, and she hadn't kept up with her friends in town."

"You don't know then who she was talking to?"

Emmett shook his head. "Ain't got the foggiest."

I showed him the part of Abel McKenna's statement that mentioned the phone call, and the part of Mrs. Nabor's statement. "Damn," Emmett said. "What is this?"

Good question, I thought. I handed Emmett the files that belonged to the police department. "Take these back now, okay? And don't get caught."

He took the files and looked at me. "You got 'em, why don't you take 'em back?"

I smiled. "This is called delegation of authority, Emmett," I said, slapping him on the back as I headed out the door. "Have a nice evening now, ya hear?"

I was rubbing my wife's legs with lotion, a way of keeping the atrophied muscles supple. It took her a few weeks after we were married before she let me do that. She'd been on her own and taking care of herself for so long, it was hard to let anybody else help her. It wasn't exactly a nightly ritual, but since her belly'd gotten so big, I'd been doing it more and more. Unfortunately, rubbing her legs got me horny, and there wasn't a blasted thing either one of us could do about that.

So I told her about the files and the telephone connection between the three suicides. "So what does that mean?" Jean asked, which was a disappointment, since I halfway expected her to say, "Oh. Well, that means . . ."

"Hell if I know," I said, feeling the firmness of her thigh above the polio-withered area. She hit my hand, making me move it back down. "But it's gotta mean something. Shirley Beth didn't talk on the phone much. But all three of them talked on the phone, and then they killed themselves. What's the odds?"

Jean shrugged. "Maybe somebody's done a national survey on it.

"You serious?"

"Sure. You'd be surprised what kind of stupid statistics you can find. How many suicides make phone calls right before they kill themselves is not even as stupid as some of them. Like how many of the chronically depressed were breast-fed as babies. Whether schizophrenics went to public or private kinder-

130

garten. What kind of reading material is preferred by male spousal abusers. The median age of onset of menses for women who abuse their children. I could go on and on."

"I get your drift." I finished with her legs and rolled over on my back. "This thing's got me beat, babe. Just seems to me there's too damn many suicides going on around here."

"How about other areas? Like Tejas County and Jasper County?" Jean asked. See why I married her? Smart woman.

I rolled over and picked up the phone, pulling my personal telephone book out of my hip pocket and looking up Bill Williams's home number. I dialed and Bill picked up on the second ring.

"Hey, Bill, Milt Kovak."

"What's wrong?"

"Just wanted to ask you a question."

"At eleven-thirty at night?"

I looked at the clock. "Ah, I didn't realize the time."

"Call me at the office." And he hung up. Then I remembered some married men actually got to have sex with their wives. At least I hoped that's what I'd been interrupting. I'd like to think somebody was gonna have a smile on their face later that night.

07/08/83—Honey introduced me to her new next-door neighbor today. Her name's Jewel. Real sweet, though she probably needs to get out more. Home-bound type. I have a moral dilemma with Honey. Chuck came on to me at their Fourth of July party, and he wasn't even all that drunk. Even if he was my type, which he isn't, why would he think I'd be the type to betray my best friend? God, I hate men. They are such scum. Now the moral dilemma: Do I tell Honey, or keep it to myself? Maybe if Jewel and I get to see more of each other, I can talk to her about it. But the big question is: Why tell? What would it accomplish? Would she leave him on that information alone? Or

131

would she stay with him and start seeing less of me? Make sure I'm never around her husband. That's probably what would happen. But if I keep this to myself, then I'm lying to Honey, and I haven't done that since the time our freshman year when I told her Bobby Jacobson had called when he hadn't. And I did that to make her feel better. So this lie will make her feel better, too, I guess. Damn Chuck, anyway.

I wondered if Libby'd ever mentioned the incident to Jewel. Should I ask? Then Jewel'd wonder how I had the information. I was in the same kinda moral dilemma as Libby. Except mine was a little more self-protecting than hers. Then the whole thing came to me in a flash: Chuck Lancaster, worried after all these years that Libby would tell Honey about his coming on to her, snuck away from Houston, drove to Longbranch, and murdered Libby. Unfortunately, that was the best scenario I'd come up with since the beginning of the case—and it was ludicrous.

It was three o'clock in the morning and my bride was asleep. I wasn't. Lying next to her got kinda hard every night when I couldn't touch her. So I guess I was cheating. Sitting here in the living room with the essence of Libby Fortuna, cheating on my wife. I put the journal entries back in my briefcase and went to bed.

Bill Williams called me at 8:00 A.M. the next morning. "Didn't your mama teach you not to call people later than ten o'clock at night?" he said.

"Well, since we didn't have a phone until my senior year in high school, I doubt telephone etiquette ever came up in my house," I told him, which was a lie. We got our first phone when I was six, but I figured I could make him feel bad.

"Whadja want, anyway?" he said, shying away from the telephone-etiquette question, just like I intended.

"You had any suicides in your county lately?"

"Suicides? Well . . ." There was a rustle of paper and a long pause, then Bill said, "Yeah, now that you mention it. Two. Why?"

"Mind telling me about 'em?"

"You doing a state survey or what?"

"Or what. Tell me."

"Got a fifty-year-old white male shot himself in the mouth with a shotgun, and got a twenty-seven-year-old white female slit her wrists the right way—up and down instead of across. Can I go now?"

"Why?"

"Because this is a boring conversation."

"No. Why did they do it?"

"Hell—who knows why people kill themselves! Ask your wife—she's the shrink."

I took a deep breath and counted to three. "Did any of your people interview the next of kin? If so, did the next of kin say what coulda been bothering them that they might have committed suicide?"

Again there was the sound of paper rustling in the background before he said, "Okay. The guy, Houston Flowers—his wife says he was a heavy drinker with a heart condition. Been trying to stop drinking, but it didn't seem to be working for him. That's all Bobby Ray's got in the report here. The other one, Clyde took. Like I said, a twenty-seven-year-old white female—Brenda Macon—husband says he hasn't got the faintest idea why she'd do it, but I think I could answer that one for you."

"Okay, answer away."

"Ol' Tommy Macon's been using Brenda as a punching bag for ten years now. Neighbors call the law, and then Brenda says she fell down. Either Tommy was beating up on her regular or she was the clumsiest woman God ever made," Bill said.

"Your boys mention in their reports whether either of these

two were on the phone before they did it?"

"On the phone? Talking on the phone? Who to?"

"Any mention of that, Bill?"

"Well, now." I could hear the papers rustling. "Don't rightly say anything about that, Milt. What's going on?"

So I told him about the three suicides in my county and the connection that at least two of 'em and probably all three had been on the telephone shortly before they killed themselves.

Bill Williams sighed heavy on the other end of the line. "Milt, I gotta ask you," he said. "Tell me, how many guns you think was in Dealey Plaza? Jesus, man, you are stretching it here. You truly are."

"Just talk to the families again—find out if either of these two were on the phone the night they were killed. And look back in your files—see if there have been a few more suicides than usual for this time of year."

I listened to him for a few more minutes tell me how crazy I was, then got off the phone—only to have it ring one more time. Gladys was on the other end.

"Milt, you have a call."

"Really?" I said, all sarcasticlike. "That's so unusual."

"It's Madelyn R. Carey," she said, with what sounded like relish, before the line clicked over to the old lady, who was already talking.

". . . talk to him, and if you're recording this, I'm gonna call my lawyer—"

"Miz Carey?" I said.

There was a silence. "Who is this?" she finally said.

"This is Sheriff Kovak, Miz Carey. You called me, remember?"

"I'm not some daft old lady don't remember who she called, Sheriff—if that's really who you are."

"Well, that really *is* who I am, Miz Carey. What can I do for you?"

"I know who blew up that doctor's house," she said.

I sat up a little straighter, holding my breath. "Who, Miz Carey?" I finally got out.

"Hillary Clinton," she said.

I relaxed. "Miz Carey, the First Lady didn't have—"

"Don't you ever watch Rush, boy?"

"Miz Carey—"

"I'm telling you, and you'd better listen. It was Hillary Clinton sure as I've been saved by Jesus."

"Miz Carey," I said, trying to get the subject off the First Lady, "I talked to a lady at County Services and she said all you had to do to get your Social Security payments back—"

"Is truck with the devil! That's all I gotta do, Sheriff, and I'm beginning to think you already done it. I won't be speaking to you again."

She hung up the phone. I could only hope she'd keep that last promise.

That night was our first Lamaze class. I met Jean at her office in the hospital and we took the elevator down the two floors to the room where the class was being held. Jean had brought two pillows with her from home, because that's what you're supposed to do, and I wheeled her into the room, the pillows on her lap.

We got some looks when we came in, which happens to people in wheelchairs. First people look; then they look quickly away because they think they're not supposed to do it. Kids are the best about it, though. They're honest. While back when we were in the grocery store, a kid about five, holding on to his mom's hand, turned and looked at Jean. He checked her out real good and then he said, "Hey, lady, why you in that chair?"

The mom tried to hush him, but Jean smiled and said, "That's okay. It's a good question." So then she explained to the boy about the polio and about the baby in her tummy, and why she was in the chair. Then she said, "But I'm luckier than a lot of people in wheelchairs. After the baby comes, I'll be able to get out of it and back to using my crutches."

But grown-ups don't ask. They just look the other way. And, truth is, some people in wheelchairs would probably resent the hell out of people asking them all the time. What they wouldn't resent, though, is people acting like they're real-life human beings, not just staring over their heads like they're not even there.

Anyway, I wheeled Jean into the room and the only non-pregnant woman there came up to us, smiling big. "Hi, Dr. McDonnell. Please come in." To me, she said, "Why don't you set the chair up in the corner? Dr. McDonnell, we'll be doing a lot of this work on the floor. Will you—"

"No problem," Jean said, using my arm to help her maneuver out of the chair and down to an empty mat on the floor. After she settled in, Jean introduced me to the nonpregnant lady. "Lynn, this is my husband, Milt Kovak. Milt, this is our instructor, Lynn Maizey. Lynn's an R.N. And please, Lynn, here, can I just be Jean?"

"Oh, sure, Dr. Mc—I mean, Jean. That would work fine." The woman seemed a little ill-at-ease.

There were about six other couples in the room, mamas all on mats, daddies sitting next to or behind them. One couple was two women, obviously sisters, one pregnant, the other the designated coach, I guess.

Lynn seemed to be spending more time with us than the others. "Dr. Mc—I mean, Jean, ah, if you'd like to jump in at any time. I mean, if you feel I'm not covering what I should or—"

Jean smiled. "Lynn, I'm a pregnant psychiatrist. You're the specialist here. You run this show." She looked at the rest of the group, who'd been watching us intently. "But if any of you coaches feel you can't handle this, we can always spend a few minutes in my office and I'll shrink you down to size."

Everybody laughed and the ice was broken. Any wonder

why I married this woman? The rest of the evening we spent learning how to breathe. And I thought that was one of the few things I was fairly good at. You just never know.

They say time flies when you're having fun—which is probably why the next two weeks seemed like an eternity. Jean was spending most of her time within easy rolling distance of a bathroom, since Junior seemed to like it best when he was hopping up and down on top of her bladder. The Lamaze classes were going well and I was almost okay about being in the delivery room. Almost.

Early August brought a serious heat wave, and a dry spell had the farmers up in arms and demanding I do something about it. I told 'em it wasn't my jurisdiction. Emmett repeated his request on the whereabouts of Phillip Gallagher, M.D., to the national AMA three more times, and Jasmine Bodine interviewed just about everybody who had anything to do with the Interdenominational Right-to-Life group headquartered at the New Faith Congregation Church. Nobody seemed anything more than just folks—folks who didn't approve of abortion. Except for Madelyn R. Carey, most of 'em had regular lives with regular families and outside obligations to keep them from getting too hepped up over politics. But I couldn't see Miz Carey, even five years ago, being able to accomplish all it would take to blow up a house.

But Miz Carey was one to let her presence be known, and she wasn't too good on keeping her promises, like the one to me that she wouldn't be speaking to me again. Actually, Madelyn R. Carey got to speaking to me on a regular three-times-a-week basis. So far, she accused Hillary Clinton of blowing up Cassie Gallagher, Bill Clinton of personally putting fluoride in her drinking water, and, from somewhere out of left field, announced that Nelson Mandela was the Antichrist. At least she kept up with current events.

Much as I would have liked to lock up Madelyn R. Carey for

the Cassie Gallagher bombing, I couldn't. But even if we were able to find some nut willing and able to have done the bombing, what would that have to do with Libby's death? How could it possibly connect? These were some of the questions that kept me up late at night—that and hoping my central air conditioning would manage to make it through the hot spell.

Bill Williams finally got back to me the third week in August to tell me that yeah, maybe something was going on with all the suicides.

"I was talking to Gary Booker over to Jasper County last week—telling him what an idiot you are—when he up and tells me they had two suicides in the past six months—more than they had in the last six years."

"Well, now isn't this interesting," I said, not one to give out with an "I told you so" right off the bat. "Gary say anything about any of his people being on the phone?"

"Yeah, as a matter of fact. One of 'em, this teenaged boy, was locked in his room, screaming on the phone, according to his mother. By the time she called her husband and got him to come home and break down the kid's door, he was hanging from the ceiling fan, with his belt around his neck."

What was his problem, this kid? Booze? Drugs?" I asked.

"Gary said, according to the mother, the boy'd been to a rehab center to kick crack cocaine. But she thought he might be using again. Gary said it was pretty much a given, what with all them little crack vials scattered around the kid's room."

"What about yours? Any of 'em on the phone?"

"Tommy ain't talking, and Miz Flowers, the widow of the drunk, says she didn't think so," Bill said. "So, now, where does this take us?"

"Hell if I know," I said.

The heat was so bad, it sucked your breath away when you stepped outside. The streets and sidewalks shimmered from it, and it was so dry, the earth was cracked and the local radio station was talking about wells drying up and maybe a mandatory water rationing coming along.

Emmett had been living in his RV since he'd come back, parking it in various places—sometimes behind the sheriff's department if he didn't feel like driving away of an evening; sometimes on Mountain Falls Road just for the scenery. But the August heat wave set him to looking for more permanent-type living arrangements—preferably something with air conditioning. Since he sold his car and furniture when he sold his house, just putting a few things in storage, he was having a hard time finding something.

But on the Friday of the third week of August, two things happened: Emmett found him a nice, mostly furnished apartment in a fourplex on the highway halfway between Longbranch and Bishop (it had a pool and a couple of single women sharing one of the upstairs apartments) and we got a reply from the national AMA registry on the whereabouts of Phillip Gallagher, M.D. Funny how things come together like that.

11

Billings, Montana. Long way from Los Angeles, California, or Longbranch, Oklahoma, for that matter. But that was the home, according to the national AMA registry, for Phillip Gallagher, M.D., OB-GYN. It was late Friday before Emmett made the first call to the only number we had for the good doctor, the one for his office, and all Emmett got for his trouble was an answering machine telling him to call another number in case of emergency. Dialing that number got Emmett an answering service that swore it'd pass on the message to Dr. Gallagher. Four more calls over that weekend elicited as much response as the first—namely, nothing. Phillip Gallagher opted not to answer this particular emergency.

By Monday, when we finally talked to a real live person in Gallagher's office, we found out the good doctor had been called out of town on a family emergency and wouldn't be back for a couple of weeks.

I grabbed the phone away from Emmett. "Excuse me, ma'am, but when exactly did Dr. Gallagher inform you of this family emergency?"

"He called me at home on Saturday and said there was a problem with his wife's father and they had to go there."

"Where's 'there,' ma'am?" I asked, all saccharine-sweet, butter wouldn't melt in my mouth.

"Well, Debbie's from Boise. In Idaho?"

"Debbie? That's the new Mrs. Gallagher?"

There was a slight pause on the line. "Who did you say this was calling?"

"This is the Prophesy County, Oklahoma, sheriff speaking to you, darlin'," I said, by way of keeping all the stereotypes in check, "and this is serious police business. I need a number where I can reach Dr. Gallagher."

The voice of the lady on the other end of the line lowered to a whisper. "What did you mean—the *new* Mrs. Gallagher?"

"You got a number in Boise, ma'am?"

"I can't give that out. But you may have the wrong Dr. Gallagher. This is Phillip Gallagher from Los Angeles. He and Debbie have been married for three years and they've got a baby on the way, and I just know there wasn't another Mrs. Gallagher or we would have heard about that—"

"What you say your name is, darlin'?" I asked.

Again a brief pause. "Ah . . . Melinda."

"Well, Melinda, if you got that number for Dr. Gallagher in Boise, you call him for me and tell him it's an emergency and I need him to call me right away. He can make it collect," I said, wondering how the county commissioners were going to take to them apples, "and you call me back collect and let me know what happened. Okay, Melinda?"

"What did you say your name was?"

"Sheriff Milt Kovak, Prophesy County, Oklahoma," I said.

Monday afternoon late, Melinda called back. "Sheriff?"

"Yes, ma'am."

"This is Melinda in Dr. Gallagher's office in Billings?"

"You get ahold of Dr. Gallagher for me, darlin'?" I asked.

"Not exactly. I mean, I called the number for Debbie's parents and all. Debbie and I used to be roommates when we were both working here—before she and doctor got married—so I knew her parents' number. But I called and talked to her daddy, and he said he hadn't heard from either Debbie or the doctor for a week or two. He said there was nothing wrong with him—no emergency. I'm afraid I got him and Mrs. Temple, Debbie's mama, a little upset. Sheriff, you mind telling me what's going on?"

"I wish I could, Melinda, I truly do, but this is confidential police business." I sighed. "Look, you hear from Dr. Gallagher or from his wife, you tell them to call here immediately." Wishing there wasn't a reason to, I asked, "Melinda, how far along is Debbie in her pregnancy?"

"Oh, she should pop just about any day!"

I hung up the phone, sick to my stomach with worry over a lady I'd never heard of until a few days ago and a baby that hadn't even been born yet. Two pregnant women, pregnant with one or the other of the Gallagher twins' babies, were dead. Phillip Gallagher had a lot of explaining to do. And I'd like him to do it as far away as possible from his new pregnant wife.

I called Jean from the office, telling her I'd be late getting home, and headed out toward Bishop to the long, lean ranch house Libby Fortuna had called home. The gate was locked up tight, as I hadn't called before coming out, but the honk of a horn behind me turned out to be Daniel Gallagher and Mrs. G. home from work. Daniel worked the remote control on the gate from his car and I preceded them down the long driveway to the house, parking by the front door and leaving them room to pass me to get to the garage.

Both Daniel and his mama got out of the car in the driveway and met me at the front of the house. Daniel and I shook hands.

"Hey, Milt, what brings you out?" Daniel asked.

"I need to talk to you and Miz Gallagher for a minute, if I can."

Daniel got his key out and unlocked the front door, flipping a switch on the alarm system to turn it off. Mrs. G. led the procession into the family room, dropping her purse on the couch, and asked us if we wanted anything to drink.

After about five minutes of small talk with Daniel, the three of us settled down, me and Daniel with a beer apiece and Mrs. G. with a tall iced tea.

"I'm real sorry about barging in on you people unannounced like this," I said, "but I need some straight answers and I need 'em real quick."

Mrs. G.'s eyes got big as her son's got small from frowning at me. "About what, Milt?" he asked.

"When was the last time either of you talked to Phillip?"

Mrs. G. stiffened and Daniel sighed, then looked at his mother. "Ma, we gotta tell him."

Mrs. G. folded her arms in front of her, her lips turning into thin lines across her mouth. "You do whatever you have to do, Daniel." She leaned back in her seat, eyes downcast, no longer a party to the party.

Daniel looked at me and sighed again. "We haven't heard from Phil since he left town four years ago. Mom and I tried on several occasions to reach him in LA, but he never went to work for the hospital he said he was going to work for." Daniel shrugged. "Phil's dropped off the face of the earth, Milt, as far as either of us know."

"Why?" I asked.

Daniel shook his head. "I don't know, Milt, I really don't. The thing with Cassie and the baby hit him really hard." He laughed grimly. "Now I know how hard."

"Miz Gallagher?" I asked.

She finally looked up at me. "Yes, Milton?"

"He's okay."

She sat up as briskly as her pudgy little dumplin' body would let her. "You know where he is? Is he okay? Why hasn't he called? Oh God, Danny," she said, grabbing her son's hand.

"Where is he, Milt?" Daniel asked, he and his mother both standing in their excitement.

"Well, up until my first phone call on Friday night, he was in Billings, Montana. But now he's disappeared—with his much-pregnant wife."

"Wife? Pregnant? Danny!" Mrs. G.'s knees buckled and it took me and Daniel both to get her laid out on the couch.

"Mama, it's okay. Phil's okay, Mama. This is good news, right, Ma? He's okay and he's married again and has a baby on the way—"

Mrs. G. burst into tears, her arms going around Daniel's neck. Daniel buried his head on his mother's shoulder, his own shoulders quivering with emotion. I decided to take my leave. I didn't have the heart to tell 'em my next move was to notify whatever passed for a Highway Patrol in Montana to be on the lookout for Dr. Phillip Gallagher. The good doctor had taken another hike—just like the one a year after his first wife's death. Now he had a new wife, little Debbie. I saw her in my mind's eye—young, pretty, pink, flushed with joy over her pregnancy. There was a real big part of my mind that wondered if little Debbie and that baby would ever make it to a birthing room.

The sergeant I talked to from the Montana Highway Patrol was named Ed Munroe and he was a real cooperating type. He said he'd call Melinda in the doctor's office and see if he could find out about cars and tag numbers and the like and then post a lookout. There was no reason for an APB—we both agreed on that—but I wished like hell I could tell him there was. There was a little pregnant girl out there and I knew her life was in danger. I wasn't sure why, but in my heart I knew it was.

I went on home to my own pregnant lady, wishing my first official act as the real-life elected sheriff of Prophesy County had been a serious jaywalking incident instead of the murder of Libby Fortuna.

Things were getting way out of hand. How could Libby's

death be connected to the death of Cassie Gallagher five years before? But how could it not? Could it just be a real strange coincidence? Then how come Phillip Gallagher not only high-tailed it out of town but gave a phony forwarding address and had been basically hiding out in another state? And how come now, the minute we make contact with him in Billings, Montana, he's all of a sudden up and gone again? With yet another pregnant woman?

And what did this have to do, if anything, with the suicides? Seven suicides in a little more than five months—three in Prophesy County, two in Tejas County, and two in Jasper. It didn't make any sense, not a bit of it. As far as we could tell, none of these people knew one another—they lived in different parts of the counties, had different economic backgrounds, and none went to the same churches. If it was a suicide pact, it was the strangest one I'd ever heard of. What was the connection? There had to be a connection. Only one thing stood out be-sides the fact that they were all dead—some, if not all, were on the telephone shortly before committing suicide.

Jean was in bed, trying to coax Junior into being still so she could get some sleep, and I was in the living room, drinking beer and staring at my cat Evinrude's back. He'd been pissed at me for a couple of months now, ever since I kept him locked in the house while there was somebody out on the streets tortur-ing animals. That got wrapped up quick enough and he was al-lowed to go back outside, but our relationship hadn't been the same since. Every once in a while, he'd forget himself and crawl up in my lap for some good ol'-fashioned groin kneading and an ear rub, but then he'd remember I was on his shit list, hop down, and give me his back. And a broad-beamed back it is, too, I might add. But I figured putting him on a diet right now would mean he'd just find a suitably appreciative family to move in with.

So I stared at his back. And I thought about the suicides and Libby Fortuna. My big question with Libby was how in the hell

145

could Phillip have done in Libby and why? Okay, the why had to be connected to the reason Cassie and her baby had been killed. Maybe something snapped while he was doing all those abortions in Tulsa. Who knows.

But first, how could he have found out about Libby? The paper. He could be taking the *Longbranch Gazette* or he coulda read about the famous Libby Fortuna marrying his brother in just about any paper. But the baby? How would he have found out about that? Never mind. Seems he had found out.

Okay. He comes back to Prophesy County. Why? Well, it had to have something to do with the twin thing. Twins are connected in lots of different ways, I've read. Like they can read each other's minds—one cuts their finger and the other one bleeds, stuff like that. Which, of course, is how he could've found out about Daniel's wife having a baby. A psychic connection. Okay, fine. Your basic hogwash, but fine. I'd use that as what you might call a working hypothesis.

Phillip Gallagher comes to town—he could hide just by his looks. As long as nobody saw him and Daniel in too close a proximity, they'd just assume Phillip was Daniel. The two were identical twins, so close in looks, only their mama could tell them apart.

I went in the kitchen and popped a top on another cold one. This was definitely a two-beer thinking night—or maybe three. Turned out to be five, but then, who's counting?

The next morning, Bill Williams called me from Tejas County. "Mornin', Milt," he said, all pleasantlike.

"Mornin' to you, too, Bill. What's up?"

"You know a yahoo by the name of Marvin W. Bernblatt?" he asked.

Marv Bernblatt. The *Washington Post* reporter. Lots of thoughts went through my head. The main one being that maybe, just maybe, I'd never heard of the guy.

But being your basically honest, law-abiding sort, I said, "Hum, name sounds a little familiar."

"He says he's a good friend of yours. Says you can vouch for him."

I snorted. "All I can vouch for is he's a pain-in-the-ass Yankee."

"Yep," Bill said. "We are most definitely talking about the same guy."

"What's up?"

"My blood pressure and the suicide rate of my county."

"Oh hell," I said. "What's this got to do with Bernblatt?"

"We got us another one last night."

"Tell me about it," I said.

"Sandra German, thirty-five, white female. Took a truckload of pills."

"On the phone?" I asked.

"Well, she mighta been, according to her sister. The two sisters been living together since they both moved out of their parents' house—I think she said like ten years before. Sister's name is Nita. Nita says Sandra'd been hanging out at the honky-tonks lately and picking up men and bringing 'em home."

"Why do I think this is where Bernblatt comes in?"

" 'Cause you're an intelligent, insightful kinda fella, Milt. I always said that."

"Uh-huh," I said.

"Bernblatt picks the lady up at a bar last night; she takes him home to her place; he wakes up in bed beside a corpse this morning," Bill said.

"In the same house with the sister, huh?"

"Yeah. Nita says she and Sandra'd been fighting about it regular. Sandra'd been drinking heavy and popping pills. When ol' Bernblatt starts bleating up a storm, Nita runs in and finds her sister. She figured it for an overdose till she found the note. But

147

the telephone—yeah, Nita said she'd been talking to somebody late at night on the phone. Not sure if she was talking that night, but she'd been doing it a lot lately and Nita didn't think it was one of the guys she'd been picking up from the bars 'cause she said Sandra never was much into repeaters. Doubt if she'd wanna talk to the guys after, ya know?"

"Bernblatt say anything about her being on the phone after they did the deed?"

"Think the guy was too drunk to know."

"What about the note? You got it?" I asked.

"Yeah," Bill said, "it's right here in the file." He rustled some papers, then read, " 'Dear Nita—Sorry I been such a bitch. I can't get over what Daddy done and I can't live with it no more. This letter is my will and I leave everything I got to you. Including the jerk in the bed. I love you. Sandra.' "

"What's that about the daddy?" I asked.

"Well, now, Nita says Sandra was always telling her their daddy messed with her when they were little, but Nita says she never believed it 'cause the daddy never messed with her, and Sandra was always what Nita called 'dramatic.' "

"Fits the profile," I said, mostly to myself.

"What profile?" Bill demanded.

"All these people got social problems. Alcoholics, an anorexic, a child abuser, a battered woman, maybe, in your area, and now this—a victim of possible child abuse who never got over it—took to drinking and popping pills and carousing. Social problems, Bill."

"Where does this take us?"

"Hell if I know," I said. "So, what are you doing with Bernblatt?"

"I got him in the drunk tank for the hell of it. But now he's screaming about lawyers, so I guess I'm gonna have to let him go."

"Tell him Milt Kovak vouched for him. That he's wanted in this county for ten counts of being an obnoxious asshole."

148

Bernblatt showed up two hours later. "What are you still doing here?" I asked him. "I thought you took off with the rest of your ilk twenty minutes after we buried Libby."

He threw himself down in my visitor's chair, stretching his long legs out under the desk. "I decided to stick around. Jewel and Harmon put me up for a couple of weeks, then I stayed with friends in Tulsa for a while. Then I stayed with a lady I met at the Sidewinder for a week and a half. That's a real nasty bar you got there, Kovak."

"My sister and her husband put you up for two weeks!"

"Yeah," he said, grinning. "She likes me."

"I bet Harmon don't."

"You know, it's strange," Bernblatt said, frowning. "He never did act particularly friendly."

"Ha. You're lucky he didn't gut-shoot you." I leaned back in my chair, staring daggers at Bernblatt. "Any reason why you're hanging around? You'd think the *Post* would miss your ass."

Bernblatt sat up straight in his chair. He was wearing another dirty, faded T-shirt, this one with the legend, "Vote Republican—It's Easier Than Thinking." "I decided I'd stick around when I realized you weren't going to do anything about finding Libby's killer."

I stood up. "Bernblatt, you make me tired. You really do. You won't admit that the *Post* doesn't want you, that nobody much wants you—"

He stood up, too. "Listen, you two-bit piece of shit," he said, leaning on my desk and glaring at me. "Libby was my friend. Now she's dead. You're not doing anything to find her killer. So I'm going to."

I sat back down. I tried a smile, but it came out a smirk. "Your friend? Libby Fortuna wouldn't dirty her hands by shaking yours."

He grinned. "She shook more than my hand, so to speak."

I wanted to kill him. I felt a murderous rage I hadn't felt since

Tommy Kalinsky clotheslined me during the Ardmore-Longbranch game back in 1959. Then it hit me: Maybe he *wanted* to be her friend—real bad.

"Just how long you been in my area?" I asked him, looking at him anew.

"Since the murder."

"Since right after—or right before?"

Bernblatt snorted out a laugh. "Oh, I get it. Can't find the real murderer, so now you're trying to stick it on me!"

"And just how well did you know that woman last night? Huh? Who else you been sleeping with lately?"

It was all becoming clear. What woman in her right mind wouldn't commit suicide after sleeping with Marv Bernblatt? This could take care of Lori Nabors, Sandra German, Brenda Macon—and Shirley Beth? Did I want to clear the books on these suicides so bad that I was willing to believe a lady like Shirley Beth Hopkins woulda slept with the likes of Marv Bernblatt? And what about the Flowers man in Tejas County and the teenaged boy in Jasper County?

Bernblatt leaned forward in his chair. "Look. The lady last night—I just met her. Just last night. She was okay. I mean, I was a little drunk. But she seemed okay. How was I to know she'd off herself?"

"Your compassion knows no bounds, Bernblatt."

"Jesus. Listen. I didn't know her—"

"You slept with her."

"So? Haven't you ever—" He stopped himself and leaned back, grinning. "No, probably not. You probably have to have a woman's Social Security number and rap sheet before you shake hands."

"Nowdays, a health clearance would be nice, too. But I'm a married man."

"Listen, I've been nosing around on the Fortuna thing, and I'm willing to give you what I've got for an exclusive when you—if you—ever catch the guy."

I laughed. "What could you possibly have on the Fortuna case?"

He got that sly look on his face—the one I grew to hate in about two minutes the last time I'd dealt with Marv Bernblatt. "Well," he said, "did you know, for instance, that Daniel Gallagher has a twin brother? And that this twin brother's wife was killed in a house bombing?"

I got up, taking Bernblatt by the arm, and threw him out of my office, shutting the door in his face.

We didn't hear anything from the Montana Highway Patrol on the whereabouts of Phillip Gallagher on Wednesday or Thursday. On the Friday of the fourth week of August, I had Emmett call Ed Munroe back. No word. He'd found out the doctor had three cars—a '75 Porsche, an '86 Mercedes station wagon, and a '92 Toyota Land Cruiser. The Land Cruiser was missing from the garage at the doctor's house. He got the tag numbers from the computer and they were on the lookout for the car. I figured the doctor probably wasn't even in Montana anymore, but ya gotta do what ya gotta do.

Saturday, Jean and me went to Bishop to celebrate my sister's graduation from cooking school. Harmon had supposedly talked her into doing simple—we ended up with beef Wellington (the crust was burnt on the outside and runny next to the meat), Caesar salad (heavy on the anchovies and she forgot the croutons), and scalloped potatoes (raw and runny). She bought the bread at a bakery in Bishop and it was gone in about three seconds flat.

At the dinner table, I brought up my sister's houseguest. "Hear Marv Bernblatt stayed with y'all for a while after the funeral."

Harmon snorted a laugh, then, after a look from my sister, buried his face in his food. A brave man, my brother-in-law.

"Yes, Marv stayed here for a while. He was very concerned about Libby's death. He needed someone to talk to."

151

"Oh, yeah?" I said.

"Marv is a very sensitive guy—" Jewel started.

Harmon threw his fork down on the table. "If anybody ever mentions that pus breath's name in this house again, I'm gonna puke." He looked at each one of us.

Jewel changed the subject.

Jean and me made our excuses before Jewel could bring out the baked Alaska, and we headed home.

Sunday morning, around 6:00 A.M., I got a call from A. B. Tate on the switchboard.

"Milt?"

"Yeah, A.B.?"

"We got another suicide?"

"Shit. Who? Where?"

"Dawson DeLaney's son J.R.? Over by ya'll?"

"Hank on it?"

"Well, Hank just left for breakfast? I thought since Dawson lives so close to y'all—"

"I'll take it. Have Hank come on out when he shows back up, A.B."

"Okay, Milt . . . and Milt?"

"Yeah, A.B.?"

"Seems like we been getting a lot of suicides lately, huh?"

"Yeah, A.B., seems that way."

12

I hung up and pulled my pants on, grabbed a shirt out of the closet, and headed out Highway 5 to Ranch Road 420, then down two miles to Dawson DeLaney's ranch.

Me and Dawson had played together one year on the Long-branch Cougars. Dawson was a senior and I was a sophomore, my first year to play on the A string. Dawson was six foot four and over three hundred pounds his senior year in high school, and some of those pounds were belly. But he was a real good tight end, best the Cougars ever had. Dawson was also funny. Everybody loved being in a circle around Dawson DeLaney. He could take an everyday incident you witnessed and, in the retelling of it, make it the funniest thing you ever heard of.

Dawson went on to play ball for a small state school in Texas, but he hurt his knee bad his sophomore year. He came back to live on his daddy's ranch, married Martha Haspin, his high school sweetheart, and when Dawson's mama and daddy retired and moved to south Texas in a Winnebago five years ago, Dawson took over the ranch total. I knew Dawson and Martha had a whole passel of kids and I knew J. R. DeLaney by sight. He was the great white hope of the Longbranch High School football team.

I pulled my Jeep through the ranch gate and drove the quarter of a mile up to the ranch house. The house had been built by Dawson's grandpa and added to by Dawson's daddy. I hadn't seen it since an after-game party I came to out here my sophomore year in high school. Looked like Dawson himself had added on a bit. It was a white clapboard thing, two-story, with wings off wings.

It felt strange to realize that Dawson had been living less than ten miles from me since I moved into the house on Mountain Falls Road and I hadn't once been out to see him. But then, we weren't that kinda friends. We'd see each other in town, maybe share a cup of coffee at Bernie's Chat & Chew or the Longbranch Inn of a morning, stop and chew the fat on the street, say hidy over the shelf at Millers' Drugs & Sundries. But I hadn't been to his house in almost forty years.

I pulled up next to Dr. Jim's Buick, got out, and rang the bell. Dawson himself opened the door, his shoulders slumped, his usual ruddy face white.

He squinted at me, said, "Milt?" and then went into my arms. I stood there holding on to him for a moment, that great big ol' man, crying like a baby. Hate to admit it, this day and age, but I was a little embarrassed. I patted him on the back, then pulled away, my arm still around his shoulders, and led him into the living room. Two girls were in there, one about twelve and a girl about ten or so (not real good yet on kids' ages, but I guess I'm getting ready to learn). Dawson told them gently to go out to the kitchen and get them some breakfast. The girls looked kinda lost, but the older of the two took the younger one by the hand and led her out, her still looking back at her daddy, like there were a few thousand questions she had to ask.

"Where is he?" I asked Dawson.

His head motioned toward the stairs. "Upstairs. Martha found him. Dr. Jim's in with her now. She collapsed. Don't know if she'll make it through this, Milt. I just don't know. Her health ain't been all that good lately."

I patted Dawson's hand. "I'm real sorry, Dawson. Real sorry.

I'm gonna leave you here for just a minute while I go upstairs. I'll be right back and we'll talk, okay?"

He nodded his head. "Check on Martha for me, will ya? I . . . I just don't wanna go up there now. . . ."

"Sure," I said, resisting the urge to pat him again. "No problem."

Once upstairs, I saw a boy about fourteen standing in a doorway, looking out into the hall. When he saw me, he turned and shut his door. One of Dr. Jim's assistants stood in the doorway of the room where I knew J. R. DeLaney's body could be found. It was a bathroom. The boy's body lay in the tub; a .45 automatic lay within inches of his right hand, stretched out over the rim of the tub. Blood had dried in a line from the hole in his temple, down the side of his face to the tub, and eventually to the tile floor. In death, J. R. DeLaney, maybe seventeen, eighteen years old, looked a lot like his daddy had at that age— except no belly. J. R. DeLaney was tight and muscular—very, very muscular. The only real difference between J. R. and his daddy at that same age was J. R.'s serious case of acne, standing out redder and nastier, probably, due to the paleness of death. And, even at seventeen, J. R. seemed to have less hair on his head than his daddy did now. You just never know about those throwback genes, I suppose. But the one thing I could really tell was J. R. DeLaney was definitely dead.

"Where's Dr. Jim?" I asked the assistant.

He pointed to the end of the hall, and I went down there and knocked softly on the door. Dr. Jim opened it and stepped outside with me, quietly closing the door behind him.

"How's Martha? Dawson's pretty worried."

"Yeah, well, he should be worried. The woman's sick. I called her doctor and he's coming over to look at her." Dr. Jim shook his head. "What's going on, Milt? This is four suicides in the county in—I don't know—a short time."

"Less than five months. And not only that—there've been three suicides in Tejas County and two in Jasper," I told him.

Dr. Jim looked at me. "I certainly hope you don't think this is a coincidence, Sheriff," he said, making "Sheriff" sound like some people might say "dog turd."

"Hardly," I said, and turned around and headed back downstairs to talk with Dawson DeLaney.

Dawson was stretched out on the couch, one arm over his eyes. I cleared my throat and he moved the arm and looked at me, straightening up and sitting on the couch. "How's Martha?" he asked.

"Dr. Jim called your family doctor. He's on his way over here. I hope her problems aren't serious."

Dawson shrugged. "She had a hysterectomy two years back. Asshole in Oklahoma City who did it botched it pretty bad. Almost bled to death. She's been pretty weak ever since, caused bladder problems, kidney problems. Her nerves are shot." He looked at me, the old Dawson DeLaney gleam in his eye. "I'm suing the sumbitch for every cent his insurance company's worth, I can guaran-damn-tee you that, bubba." The gleam in his eyes was quickly replaced by the dull ache of remembering where he was and what was going on in his life.

"Can you tell me what happened, Dawson? With J. R.?"

Elbows on knees, he leaned his face into his hands, covering it with the huge mitts. Rubbing at his eyes, he looked at me, his tongue darting out and licking his lips, his eyes blinking. "We were in bed. I was sound asleep. Something woke me—I didn't know what at the time. Martha was already out of bed. I heard her yelling for me and I ran in there and there he was just lying there like that. Oh, sweet Jesus." He buried his face in his hands and sobbed.

"Dawson," I said, gently placing a hand on his shoulder, "I need to ask you some questions. I know this is a bad time, and I'm really sorry, but I gotta ask."

He wiped at his streaming eyes with the palms of his hands, nodding his head several times. "Yeah, sure," he said. "Whatever."

"Had J. R. been having any problems lately? Drinking too much, drugs?"

Dawson shook his head. "No. Milt, he was a good kid. I knew most of his friends drank—he'd tell me that—but he was always the designated driver. He said his body was a temple and he wasn't gonna blaspheme against it. He didn't do drugs for the same reason."

"A girl—"

Again, Dawson shook his head. "There were girls in the group he hung with, but he wasn't serious about any of them. I'm not sure he was still a virgin or anything—I mean, he was seventeen—but there wasn't anybody he was serious about."

"You have any idea why he'd do this, Dawson?"

Dawson straightened his shoulders. "No, sir, I do not. I don't believe he did it. I think somebody snuck in the house and did it and left the gun there to look like my boy blew his brains out. My boy wouldn't do that."

"You mean you never saw that gun before?" I asked.

Dawson moved his head so he wasn't looking me in the eye. "What kinda gun was it?" he asked.

"A forty-five automatic," I said.

The big man's shoulders slumped and his head trembled on his short, almost nonexistent neck. "It's probably mine," he said, his voice barely above a whisper. He pointed toward a desk against the wall of the living room. "Check in there. Top drawer, right-hand side. Should be locked. I keep the gun there, the bullets in the buffet in the dining room."

The top-right-hand drawer of the desk was unlocked and empty. Going into the dining room, I found the box of bullets opened, shells scattered in the drawer of the buffet.

"Gun's gone and some bullets missing out of the box," I told Dawson.

"I don't understand," he said, his shoulders heaving. "Everybody and their brother knew he'd be getting that scholarship for OU next year. Remember what you and me woulda given

157

for even a chance at a scholarship to OU?"

I nodded my head. I remembered. It was the football fantasy to beat all football fantasies when you're a teenager in small-town Oklahoma.

"Dawson, I got one more question: Was J. R. on the phone to anybody last night?"

He shook his head. "I dunno. The boys have a private phone line in their room. I never know."

"I saw a boy upstairs, about fourteen—"

"Robbie. Almost sixteen. Never be a ballplayer. Too small."

"Mind if I talk with him?"

Dawson nodded mutely and I left him again, going back up the stairs. I passed Dr. Jim and his assistant bringing the boy in the body bag down the stairs. I rapped on the door to the room where I had seen the younger brother.

"It's open," came the reply.

I walked in the room. Twin beds, both unmade, a telephone on a table between the beds. A desk on one side of the room with a seriously tricked-out computer. The other side of the room had football paraphernalia and a desk heaped with books, papers, and sports equipment. You could readily tell which side of the room belonged to which son.

"Hey, Robbie," I said, holding out my hand, "I'm Sheriff Kovak. Sorry about your brother."

Robbie nodded his head, his face a teenaged mask, no emotion showing. He shook my hand, then fell back on the twin bed. His father was right: He *was* small for almost sixteen. Must be tough, I thought, being the small boy in a houseful of giant men. He was maybe five foot six, slightly built. He had curly light-colored hair like his mom's, and pale blue eyes—one of which was darkened by bruising.

"Robbie," I said, sitting down on the twin bed opposite his, "I need to ask you a few questions."

He shrugged.

"Did J. R. call anybody last night or in the middle of the

night? Did he talk to anyone on the phone?"

He shrugged again. "Yeah, maybe."

"Maybe?"

"I dunno. I think he was on the phone last night. He's always on the phone. Chicks call him all the time."

"Did he have one particular girlfriend?"

Robbie shrugged again. "Naw, I don't think so. Big football hero couldn't get tied down, know what I mean?"

"Played the field, huh?" I suggested.

"Yeah, I guess."

"Had J. R. been upset about anything lately?"

The shrug.

"You were probably closer to him than anyone else in the house," I said, smiling lightly, "being as you two shared a room and all. I'd think you'd know more than anybody else if he was having some problems."

Shrug.

"The reason I'm asking, son," I said, leaning forward and allowing myself a small frown, "is that your brother's dead. He committed suicide. You are aware of that, aren't you?"

Robbie swung his feet up and around, deftly putting his back to me, just like Evinrude. "I'm tired. Didn't get a lot of sleep. Can you go away now?"

I got up and moved to the other side of the room so that Robbie was facing me again. "Robbie," I said, putting my hand on his shoulder, "I really need to know what was going on with J. R."

Robbie shrugged off my hand and stood up, moving to his desk and computer.

"I don't know jackshit," the boy said, firing up the computer. "Me and him weren't close. We shared the room because we had to. See that?" he said, pointing to the floor. "See that invisible line between the two beds? I didn't cross that line unless I needed to go out the door. And ol' Jock Breath never crossed it to my side."

159

"Then how'd he manage to give you that shiner?" I asked.

Robbie shrugged, his back to me again as he brought up a screen on the computer. "Just lucky, I guess," was all he said.

I took my leave, again wondering what in the hell was going on.

Hank Dobbins was knocking on the front door when I got downstairs. I let him in, introducing him to Dawson. After that, with Dawson still holding on to his head in the living room, I took Hank into the foyer and said, "See what you can do—see if Dawson needs the kids taken to a relative's or whatever. And keep an eye on the boy upstairs—the kid brother. He's got something to tell; I'm just not sure what yet—or when he plans on telling it. You got your swabs?"

"Yes, sir," he said, patting the pack on his hip.

"Then do nitrate tests on everybody. May not be able to get to the mother, but try, just for form's sake, okay?"

Hank nodded and I went out to the Jeep and got in and headed back to Mountain Falls Road. Hank would take care of things. Even in the short time he'd been with the department, I could tell Hank was gonna work out fine—probably too fine. He'd be the first one recruited for bigger and better things.

By the time I got home, Jean was up and fixing breakfast. I told her about J. R. DeLaney, about the woman in Tejas County, about Mary Bernblatt still hanging around, and about my theory that Marv had killed everybody, up to and including Jimmy Hoffa and President Kennedy.

"Boy, when you don't like somebody," she said, "you *really* don't like them."

"This is not personal."

Jean laughed, patting me on the head like a slow beagle. "Of course not, honey."

"No, now, Jean, look at the facts."

"What facts?"

"He used to be Libby's lover."

"He says," she said.

"Okay, he was definitely sleeping with that Sandra German woman in Tejas. He was found in bed with her dead body."

Jean shrugged. "Maybe I'm just dumb, Milt, but it seems to me that most people, even homicidal types, would leave after killing someone, not crawl into bed with them. Even necrophiliacs don't hang around and sleep with the body."

"Yeah, well, Marv Bernblatt isn't most people."

She shook her head, then leaned across the table, where we'd sat down with our breakfast, and touched my hand. "Milt, Marv is just your typical A-type obnoxious personality."

"Huh," I said. I'm known for my witty repartee.

"Okay, following through on your hypothesis," Jean said, "why and how did he do in J. R. DeLaney?"

I stuffed oatmeal in my mouth. Around it, I said, "I'm working on that. Give me time."

We spent the rest of the morning with the Oklahoma City paper, reading the funnies to each other and working the crossword puzzle together. I'd never paid much attention to the crossword before, but Jean likes 'em fine and she's got to where she pretends she needs my help. It's one of them married kinda things, I guess. Sometimes I wonder how I managed to be married to LaDonna for over twenty years without getting to know all that much about married things. If LaDonna couldn't clean it or complain about it, it didn't exist—and, except for the occasional complaining, I guess I just didn't exist.

Sunday evening, I drove back over to Dawson DeLaney's ranch to see how he was holding up. The boy, Robbie, was the only one home. Martha'd been taken to Longbranch Memorial Hospital, Dawson sitting by her side, and the girls were staying with Martha's mama and daddy out the other side of Bishop. I wondered about the wisdom of leaving the boy alone under the circumstances, but, not being a parent yet myself, I let it alone. The boy was almost sixteen, after all.

"So how's your mama?" I asked.

"I dunno," Robbie said, shrugging. His slight frame was trying mightily to block the doorway, but I managed to get around him without too much trouble, then settled myself down in a living room chair. Other than being a lot ruder than his mama's upbringing would allow, Robbie had no choice but to come in and perch on the couch to keep me company.

"I'm really sorry about what's happening with your family," I told him.

He shrugged.

"What'd the doctor say about your mama?"

"Nobody tells me squat," Robbie said, leaning back on the couch and glaring at me. "Something I can do for you, Sheriff?"

I leaned forward in my chair. "Yeah, Rob, there surely is. You can tell me what your big brother was into that woulda made him take his own life—and you can tell me how come you got that lovely shiner," I said, indicating the bruised eye.

Robbie leaned forward, too, for all the world like he was mimicking me, which he probably was. "Well, I'll tell you what my brother was into, Sheriff. He was into football. Period. Oh, and lifting weights so he could be stronger for football. And watching what he ate so he'd be stronger for football. And running so he'd be stronger for football. And occasionally doing homework so he could stay eligible for football. Anything else you wanna know about, Sheriff? Anything at all?"

"Yeah, I'd like to know why you got that great big chip on your shoulder, boy."

Robbie stood up and walked to the door, opening and holding it open—obviously for me to use. "That's not a chip, Sheriff. That's a football."

I left. It seemed the thing to do.

Monday morning, I went with Jean to her doctor's appointment. We were doing the sonogram thing again and I truly did love to see that. They hooked her up and we looked at Junior floating around inside. This time, he was sucking his thumb.

162

Well, we'd have to put a stop to that, I figured, but maybe not for a year or two.

When I got back to the office, I decided it was time to fire Gladys. Marv Bernblatt was sitting in one of my visitor's chairs.

"Get out," I greeted him.

Marv stretched his legs out farther under the desk. "Seems to me you've got some explaining to do, Sheriff. Do you realize how many suicides there have been lately in your county?"

"Get out," I said, walking around and sitting in my desk chair.

"And, here's something for you—don't say I'm not generous, Kovak. Daniel Gallagher's twin brother, whose name is Phillip, by the way—was supposed to have left Longbranch for Los Angeles. Guess what?"

"Get out," I said, picking up a form that needed filling out and finding my pen in my lap drawer.

"He's not there. I have my sources in LA and they tell me Gallagher never registered with the AMA out there. What do you think about that?"

It was nice that my visitor's chairs have rollers on them. I got up, walked around the desk, grabbed the back of Bernblatt's chair, and pushed him out into the hall, where he landed with a resounding thud against the far wall. Then I shut my door.

Emmett rolled the chair back in about fifteen minutes later. It was, thank God, unoccupied. He came in to inform me that he had already tried calling Montana Highway Patrol again but discovered they'd found out a big fat nothing about Phillip and Debbie Gallagher. I told him to call 'em back and have 'em check a three-state area for babies being born. Melinda had said Debbie was about to pop any day—maybe Phillip would take her to the hospital. Chances were real good, however, being an OB-GYN himself and all, that the baby would be delivered by Phillip wherever they happened to be. But Emmett said he'd already thought about that and so had the Montana HP—and they had the word out. But all agreed that if Phillip was really, truly in hiding, he'd deliver that baby himself—if it lived to be delivered.

That evening, Jean and me were just sitting down to one of our few evening meals together when the doorbell rang. I said a few choice words (we were having this recipe Jean got from a friend in Chicago who is originally from Nepal—of real live homemade chicken curry—and I'd been looking forward to it for a week and a half, even if I didn't know we were having it tonight, if you get my drift) and went to answer the bell. Dawson DeLaney and his son Robbie were standing on the porch. I opened the door.

"Well, hey, Dawson," I said, trying to curb my natural inclination to tell them to come back in an hour.

"Robbie's got something to tell you," Dawson said, gently encouraging his son to enter my house.

I led them into the living room and waved them to sit down. I sat down on one end of the couch, the opposite end from Robbie. "So, Robbie, you got something to tell me?"

Robbie glared at his father. Dawson just sighed and said, "Go on, son, show him."

Robbie pulled two prescription pill bottles out of his pocket and handed them to me. I read the labels: Androl AD-50, 50mg; the other was a vial of oily-looking liquid labeled Deca-Durabolin, 100mg. Okay, fine, I thought. I looked from father to son. "What's this mean?" I asked.

"Robbie . . ." Dawson said.

Robbie looked at me, his face the same teenaged mask it had been at both meetings between the two of us.

"They're steroids. J. R.'d been taking 'em for months. A couple of weeks ago, he started going wiggy." Robbie shook his head, settled back on the couch, and crossed his arms—definite signs he was through talking.

Dawson sighed. "A few weeks back, Robbie sprained his shoulder. Said he fell down. Robbie, take off your shirt."

Robbie didn't budge. Dawson stood up and went over to his

son, pulling him to a standing position by one arm. He pulled the T-shirt Robbie was wearing up to expose bruising along the rib cage, a gash in his stomach, bruising around the breastbone—it was a sorry mess.

Robbie pulled away from his dad, yanking his T-shirt back in place, and fell back on the couch. "J. R. do this to him?" I asked.

Dawson nodded and went and sat back down in the chair he'd earlier vacated. I looked at Robbie. "You shoot your brother, boy?" I asked.

He and Dawson both jumped up at that one, and we might have been getting into some fisticuffs our ownselves if the sweet voice of my wife hadn't interrupted.

"You people want some iced tea?" she said from her perch on her wheelchair in the foyer. "If not, and if you don't mind, Mr. DeLaney, Robbie, I'd like to join you and help Milt understand what might have been going on."

Jean wheeled herself down the ramp into the living room and took the pill bottles off the coffee table. "How many of these was he taking, Robbie, do you know?"

"Three or four a day of the pills. I'm not sure about the other crap. He got them from other guys on the team."

"This is heavy stuff," Jean said, studying the labels. "This dosage will produce adverse symptoms in some people in as few as ten days." She looked at Dawson with sympathy. "Some people can take this stuff for a year or more without adverse reaction. I don't think J. R. was that lucky."

Dawson covered his face with his hands. "I didn't know he was taking this stuff, Milt, I swear." He looked at me. "But I gotta tell you, if I'da known, I might not've done anything about it. I mean, steroids, that's like medicine. That's not drugs, for crying out loud!"

"Steroids have their medical uses, Mr. DeLaney. But whenever someone is taking prescription medication without being under a doctor's supervision, there is cause for alarm. But steroids are being abused now, even by some doctors. They shouldn't be given as a growth hormone, but they are all the time." She looked at me, then back at Dawson. "Milt described J. R. to me. I didn't, of course, pick up on this at the time, but he said J. R. had severe acne."

"Yeah, it had gotten real bad lately."

"And he seemed to have less hair than you?"

Dawson nodded. "He'd been losing his hair. It had been receding. But my daddy's bald as an egg, I figured I'd be, too."

Jean shook her head. "Male pattern baldness comes from the maternal grandfather. But acceleration of MPB, massive acne growth, testicular shrinkage, reduced sex drive, oily hair and skin—those are all symptoms of steroid abuse. And by the behavior Robbie's described, it appears there was obviously some steroid-induced psychosis."

"Oh, sweet Jesus," Dawson muttered, his head in his hands again. Robbie sat stoically on the couch, not looking at me or Jean, or anywhere, for that matter. He was studying his kneecaps, like they were interesting.

"It's the scourge of this generation," Jean said. "Girls get eating disorders, boys develop steroid-induced psychosis. Another little splitting of the sexes."

"Is that why he killed himself?" Dawson asked.

Ignoring Dawson, Jean asked Robbie, "What happened that night? Tell me everything."

Robbie tried to shrug, but it turned into a shudder, and he hugged himself tight, wincing at the pain. "He was going on and on about how I'd been messing with his stuff, and I said I hadn't touched his stuff, but he said I had. He said he could tell things had been touched. He said he'd laid a trap for me with string and feathers and he knew I'd been messing with his stuff. I swear I hadn't touched anything. But he came at me, started hitting me in the stomach, in the sides. Said he wouldn't touch my face—that way, Mama and Daddy wouldn't know, and he said if I told, he'd kill me. He told me exactly how he'd do it. All the time he was telling me this, he was hitting me in the stomach, in the ribs. Shit." Robbie covered his face with his hands.

"Finally, when he stopped," Robbie said, "I told him he was crazy. I told him he was gonna end up like that football player we read about in *People* magazine who died from steroids. I told him that if he didn't stop doing 'em, I was gonna tell Daddy and I was gonna tell his coach and that his coach would throw him off the team and there'd be no way he'd get the OU scholarship." Robbie sighed. "This all happened pretty late—like after midnight Saturday night. Sunday morning, I guess. He came after me again, but I got away and out the door and I went and slept in the living room. The shot woke me up."

Robbie looked at me. "I didn't kill my brother, Sheriff. But I think he would have killed me eventually."

"Did he call anybody after you left the room?" I asked.

Robbie shrugged. "I'm not sure. I could hear him talking upstairs, but he coulda been talking to himself—he'd been doing that lately. Or he could have been on the phone." Again, he shrugged. "Like I said, I'm not really sure."

The DeLaneys left soon after that and Jean and I sat back down at the table. The chicken curry didn't look that good anymore and my appetite was gone. Sometimes I think I need to look into another line of work.

13

After Robbie and Dawson left, I got on the phone and called Clay Hunicutt, head coach for the Longbranch Cougars, asking if I could have a minute of his time. We agreed to meet at the Longbranch Inn at nine for a cup of decaf.

I got there about five minutes after nine, pulling my Jeep in next to Clay Hunicutt's Chevy Blazer. He was sitting in a booth along the wall, chewing the fat with Loretta Dubcheck, one of the Longbranch Inn waitresses. When she saw me, she said, "Iced tea or a decaf, Milt?"

"Decaf, extra cream," I said, sliding into the seat across from Clay. Clay Hunicutt tried real hard to look like Jimmy Johnson, the ex-coach of the Dallas Cowboys, and he succeeded with the haircut, but Clay didn't have the spirit or the orneriness to really carry off a good Jimmy Johnson imitation.

Clay'd come to Oklahoma three years ago from a school in Kansas that had gone to State championships three times. Word was the Longbranch ISD had paid royally for the chance at him, after old Coach Warton had up and retired. But in the three years Clay'd been in Longbranch, we'd been pretty near 6–2, 6–3 the whole time.

Loretta brought my coffee. After she left, I leaned forward and said, "Got some news you probably ain't gonna like, Clay."

He frowned. "What's up?"

"Good chance J. R. DeLaney died in the middle of a steroid-induced psychosis. And there may be other boys on the team doing steroids, as well."

Clay was shaking his head sharply before I even got the words out. "No way," he said. "Absolutely no way. My boys are clean—all of them."

"J. R. wasn't," I said. "You notice the acne, the hair loss? A good sign of steroid abuse, Clay. That and the fact he had the pills on him and his brother says he'd been taking them for months. Robbie says he was getting them from other guys on the team."

"No," Clay said.

"Clay, now listen. What I'm telling you is true. The boys in training now?"

"Started the first of August. But they're clean, Milt. I swear to you, they're all clean."

"You been doing drug tests on 'em?"

Clay sighed. "No. But listen—"

"Look," I said, "I gave you the information. Now you gotta do something about it. Keep me posted. If I don't hear from you in a week, I'm going to the school board. You understand, Clay?"

He nodded his head. "This is the pits, Milt. The absolute pits."

I got up and patted his shoulder. "Yeah. But we got one boy dead, Clay. Let's not make it more than that, okay?"

Steroid abuse. Did that fit the pattern? It was a socially unacceptable problem. But the others, at least the ones I knew about, were trying to stop their socially unacceptable behavior. They were in therapy, or seeing doctors, or trying to quit drinking, or whatever. There was no sign J. R. DeLaney had been trying to stop. He may have been on the phone—or he may have been in a steroid-induced snit, just talking up a storm to himself.

When I was in high school, we had some big boys, boys like Dawson. The other teams had big boys. But nature had made those boys big. Most of 'em went to seed the minute they stopped playing football and practicing every day. Some Augusts, when we'd get back to training, the big boys would have to work their tails off to get rid of the guts they got from December through July. Now athletes worked out every day. They had to be bigger and bigger and bigger. And there was a lot more riding on their success now than there had been in my day. Multimillion-dollar pro contracts, millions off endorsements for everything from running shoes to chewing gum. Nowadays, they started 'em in kindergarten, getting 'em ready for the big time. I had to think now if I wanted Junior ever to play ball. I'd thought I wanted that—to spend my Friday nights in the old stadium, yelling for my kid. But now I wasn't so sure.

My kid. God, the thought. I had so much to learn, so much I needed to tell him. I'd be fifty-six years old when he was born—seventy-four when he graduated from high school. Lot of responsibility here. Needed to lose weight, start taking vitamins if I wanted to be around to watch him strut his stuff in the Longbranch High School Auditorium that spring. I needed to tell him about moderation. That was a good one. Moderation in all things. Needed to tell him never to trust anybody who said "trust me." That was important. I needed to tell him to be a kid while he could be, because you're an adult for a whole lot longer. And it's not near as much fun. Then there was the thing about not putting beans up his nose, being kind to animals, respecting his mother, treating girls with consideration and never, ever even think about hitting one.

Driving back to Mountain Falls Road, I tried to remember any pearls of wisdom my father had passed on to me, but I couldn't think of anything he'd actually said. It was more his actions—the things he did—and the things he didn't do. My parents didn't show a lot of affection—to each other or to me. But I knew they loved me. Knew they loved each other. Sometimes on a summer night when I was supposed to be in bed but the sun wasn't entirely down yet, I'd hear them. Mama would be out on the porch and she'd say, "John, come sit with me. Watch this sunset—God's making his colors." And I'd hear Daddy's weight making the porch swing groan as he sat next to Mama. I'd hear them talking softly, never able to make out the words, and then Mama would laugh and I'd hear Daddy's deep chuckle. That they loved each other was never in doubt to me.

How would Jean and I hold up over the years? Would we get that gentle familiarity between us that my parents had had? Our marriage may not have started out exactly the way it should have. She might not have married me at all if it wasn't for Junior being on the way and all. But I'm pretty sure I woulda kept at her. Would have pursued the lady 'til she had no choice other than shooting me or marrying me. Would Junior know his mama and daddy loved each other? I hoped so. One thing I did know, though: The kid was sure gonna know he was loved—every day of his life.

By the time I got home, Jean was already asleep. I pulled off my clothes, brushed my teeth, and crawled into bed beside her, trying not to shake the bed. At this stage of her pregnancy, actually falling asleep was a miracle. I didn't want to interfere with that.

I was at that stage where you're not quite asleep but not really awake, either—you know the one?—when the thought hit me so hard, I sat straight up in bed: If Robbie DeLaney was sleeping in the living room that fateful night, how did J. R. DeLaney get the gun that was kept in his daddy's desk drawer in the very same room?

On the way to the station the next morning, I stopped by Dr. Jim's morgue to see if he had any results on the autopsy of J. R. DeLaney. I planned on calling Dawson later in the day to find out when was the last time he actually saw that gun in his desk drawer. There was always the possibility J. R. had taken the gun out the day before, a week before, anytime.

Dr. Jim was his usual cheerful self when I walked in. "Hey, Sheriff," he said. "I'm busy. What do you want?"

"How's the autopsy going on the DeLaney kid?" I asked.

He gave me one of his looks—the kind that says just how stupid he thinks me and the rest of my ilk (being live human beings and all) are. "Have I sent you the results? Are they on your desk? If not, chances are I'm not through yet."

"Anything you can tell me now? Anything at all?"

Dr. Jim leaned forward on the examining table, where the body of an old lady lay, his hands resting on her naked thighs. "You know I don't give out results 'til I'm finished, but I will tell you one thing."

He stopped talking and just looked at me. I know a cue when it slaps me in the face. "What's that, Dr. Jim?"

"That boy didn't commit suicide."

Well, talk about slaps in the face. "What makes you say that?"

Dr. Jim was obviously getting bored with the subject. He stopped leaning on the cadaver's thighs and went back to doing disgusting things to the hole in the poor old lady's chest. "No back splash," he said, his eyes on his work.

"No what?" I asked.

He looked at me and sighed. "No back splash." He pointed his index finger like a gun and held it to his temple. "You shoot yourself here, the bullet goes in, breaking through tissue and bone, and so on, that stuff's gotta go somewhere. The blood and tissue comes back, gets all over the hand holding the gun." He went back to the lady's chest cavity. "J. R. DeLaney's shooting hand was clean as a whistle. I mighta noticed it at the scene," he muttered, half under his breath, "if his mama hadn't kept me so damn busy being sick and all."

I drove to the office and looked through the incoming mail to see if we'd gotten the reports on the nitrate tests done on the DeLaney family. I hadn't marked it an emergency, so chances were slim to none that they were in. They weren't. The nitrate test is really an atomic absorption analysis and the machine that does it is so damned expensive that there was only one for the entire state, and that was in Oklahoma City. In an emergency, they can get to it in forty-eight hours; otherwise, it takes four to six months. The analysis done on Emmett had come in only the week before. And it was, by the way, clean. I put a call through to the lab in Oklahoma City and had 'em put a rush on it. I thought it would be a real good idea to see if anything showed up on the hands of any member of the DeLaney family.

First call I got when I got back to the office was from Madelyn R. Carey. No matter what I said to Gladys, she continued to put Miz Carey's calls through to me. That Gladys has a mean streak wide as a Buick.

"Hey, Miz Carey," I said, doing a real good imitation of Jasmine Bodine's Eeyore voice.

"I've fallen and I can't get up," she said, then giggled.

"Ma'am?"

"I don't feel real good, Sheriff. I wouldn'ta called you, being in league with the devil like you are, but your number's the only one I could remember." She let out a moan.

"Miz Carey, are you hurt?"

She sighed. "Evil and stupid, too, huh? I told you I fell down and I can't get up."

"I thought you were kidding."

"What eighty-five-year-old woman would joke about a thing like that?"

I heard the phone fall to the floor. I jumped up, yelling at Gladys to send an ambulance out to Miz Carey's, then headed my brand-new squad car in that direction.

I beat the ambulance by about five minutes. The door to Miz Carey's trailer was locked. I called out to her and got a moan in response. It's hard to kick a door open when you're standing on a two-inch-by-two-inch aluminum step. I fell on my keister in

Miz Carey's yard after my first attempt. I went to the living room window, took out my nightstick, and broke the glass. Cleaning off the shards with my shirt, I booted myself up. Trailer windows are small—too small. I got my head and my shoulders in, but the rest of me wouldn't budge. Not in and not out. I could see Miz Carey where she was lying on the floor. Unfortunately, she could see me, too.

"Well, Sheriff," she said between moans, "I've done decided you ain't in league with the devil. He's too smart to truck with the likes of you."

When the ambulance got there, precious time was wasted with the EMTs laughing their butts off at my predicament. If I coulda reached my gun, I mighta shot one of 'em, and I have a feeling a jury of my peers woulda let me go free. As it was, the boys finally decided to calm down, and with some pushing and shoving, I fell on through to the couch in Miz Carey's living room. My stomach, which had been balanced on the narrow windowsill, hurt like a son of a bitch, my shoulders ached, and my legs were cramping. But other than that, I was doing fine. I got up and opened the door to let the EMTs have a look-see at Miz Carey.

They got her to the hospital, and by the time I got back to the office, word had already spread about my imitation of Winnie-the-Pooh and the honey pot. I figured that was one story Junior wouldn't get read to him by his daddy.

At noon, we got the call from Sergeant Munroe at the Montana Highway Patrol. "Sheriff, got some news for you on the Gallaghers," he said by way of greeting.

I straightened up in my chair, ready for the worse. "Whatja got?" I asked.

"Debbie Gallagher's at a hospital in Seattle. Mother and daughter doing fine."

I let out a breath I didn't realize I'd been holding. It was at that moment it dawned on me just how sure I'd been that Debbie and her baby would never live long enough for the child to be born. "Phillip Gallagher?" I asked.

"The ER people said he dropped her off at the door two days ago. She signed in under her maiden name. I got to thinking that she might, so yesterday I had the search include that name. Came up this morning that she was registered at the hospital in Seattle."

"Have you talked to her?"

"Just got off the phone with the little lady. Says she has absolutely no idea where her husband is. Has no idea why he's running. Never heard about the fact that he had a wife before her. Says he told her to register at the hospital under her maiden name, so she did."

I sighed. "You think she's telling the truth?"

"Who knows. Like I said, it was just a telephone interview. Sheriff, I don't have any reason to go to Seattle. No reason my department would buy, anyway. You understand that?"

"Yeah, Seargent, I understand. My department wouldn't buy a trip to Seattle, either, and I got more reason to go than you do."

"But I do have a brother-in-law on the Seattle PD. Got a call into him now. If it's okay with you, I'll tell him what's going on, have him go have a face-to-face with little Miss Debbie and then call you direct."

"That's great. Really. What's his name?"

"Randy Hobbs. He's a public-affairs officer, but he's got a real badge, so there's no reason Debbie has to know he's not official."

"I owe you one, Ed, I truly do."

"Don't worry. I'll collect—you can bet on that."

I hung up the phone and ruminated a while. Phillip Gallagher was loose as he'd ever been. But what did that mean? He'd taken Debbie to the hospital to have her baby—that was a good sign. Nothing, at this point, made a hell of a lot of sense. But, then, I was getting used to that.

But there was one thing I could take care of—and that was the murder of J. R. DeLaney.

14

By Thursday, the first of September, I had the results of the nitrate tests on the DeLaney family. I needn't have waited. Everybody was clean. But that didn't change my mind about what I knew had probably happened.

I drove out to the old DeLaney farmhouse. Dawson was at home, sitting in the living room, staring at the TV—I guess the modern man's way of grieving. It was time for fields to be harvested, but Dawson DeLaney was sitting in front of the TV. I knocked on the screen door and asked him if I could come in. He pulled himself up from his recliner chair like an old man, using his hands to push himself up by the armrests.

"Hey, Milt," he said, a small smile on his face. "What brings you out here?"

"How's Martha?" I asked, coming inside. Martha Haspin had been in my class in school. She'd been a pretty thing, a majorette for the band. Used to strut around in a little skirt with her baton and a great big smile. Pretty as she was, nobody ever thought about hitting on Martha—she'd been Dawson's true love since grammar school. And nobody'd been fool enough to mess with Dawson DeLaney.

Dawson shook his head to my question. "Not doing too good, Milt. Not good at all. It's her heart, and all the rest. Putting too much of a strain on it, and then this thing with J. R. ... well ..."

"Dawson, Robbie around?"

Dawson glanced at me and then away. "Yeah," he said, "he's upstairs in his room. Want me to call him?"

"If you would, please, I'd sure appreciate it. Then if I could talk to the two of you—"

"Robbie!" he called up the stairs. "Son, come on down here a minute."

Dawson and I went and sat in the living room. Dawson used the remote control to turn off the TV and we sat silently, waiting for Robbie to join us. In a minute or two, he did. When he saw me, he stopped for a second, then came on in the room and sat down.

"Dawson, I gotta ask you when was the last time you saw the gun that you kept in that desk over there," I said, pointing at said desk.

Dawson looked at his son, then down at the floor. "Don't rightly know, Milt. It's not like I took it out and played with it or anything. Coulda been weeks since I seen it."

"Well, we got a problem, Dawson. Seems J. R. didn't kill himself."

Dawson, who only days before had been opting for that very scenario, only looked at the floor, not saying a word.

"What makes you say that, Sheriff?" Robbie asked.

"Technical stuff, Robbie. From the autopsy. Stuff I'm not at liberty to go into at the moment, but your lawyer should be able to get all that information before this here goes to trial."

Robbie looked at his father, but Dawson just kept on looking at the floor. "Daddy?" he said, a scared note in his voice.

"I'll get you a lawyer, son. A good one. If I gotta hock the farm."

"Daddy—"

I knew I didn't have anything that I could arrest the boy

with—just like I knew the boy was guilty as hell. I had to hope that a good upbringing would tell. "Robbie," I said, "you wanna tell me what really happened that night?"

"Daddy," Robbie whispered.

Dawson stood up, his bulk shadowing the boy and me. "Robbie, it was self-defense. I know it and you know it, and so does Milt. So just tell him what the hell happened. And pray this don't kill your mama."

Everything the boy had told me earlier still stood: J. R. beat the crap out of him. J. R. was abusing steriods. J. R. told him in detail how he was gonna kill him.

"Then he just went limp," Robbie said, shuddering at the memory. "He did that sometimes—I guess when the stuff was wearing off. He just walked off to the bathroom and slammed the door." Robbie looked from his father to me. "I was scared. Sheriff, he was gonna kill me—if not with one great big whack, then little by little. But the end result was gonna be the same no matter what—I was gonna be dead."

I stole a furtive glance at Dawson. He was sitting on the couch, elbows on knees, his head in his hands. He was a smaller man than the one I remembered from high school. He was shrinking as Robbie spoke.

"I ran downstairs. I wasn't thinking about getting the gun, at least I don't think so. Just all of a sudden it was in my hand and I was in the dining room, where Daddy keeps the ammunition, and I was loading it." He took a large gulp of air and said, "Then I went up the stairs and to the bathroom door. I figured if it was locked, I'd just stand there and wait for him, but it wasn't. Locked, I mean. So I opened it. He was lying there in the tub, his eyes closed, mouth open. His face was all red from the hot water and his zits were standing out, all scummy-looking. And I hated him. I really hated him. I just walked up to him and stuck the muzzle on his temple and fired."

Dawson's body jerked, probably much the same way J. R.'s

had when the bullet struck him. He took a breath and raised his head from his hands, reaching out one arm to stroke Robbie's head. "It'll be okay, boy. It'll be okay."

Robbie looked at his daddy and his face began to crumble, tears welling up and spilling down it. "Daddy, it's my fault Mama's sick."

"Hush, boy," Dawson said, pulling Robbie to him.

Robbie pulled away. "No, Daddy. Listen. Mama saw."

Dawson pulled away. "What?"

Robbie sniffed, gulping in air. "I was just standing there. I heard this noise by the door to the bathroom and turned, and there was Mama. She just looked at me for a second; then she came in and got a towel and took the gun from my hand, told me to wash real good with Lava soap, wiped the gun down and pressed it in J. R.'s hand, then let it fall to the floor. Then she pushed me toward my bedroom—said to get in there and keep my mouth shut. Then she hollared for you, Daddy. It's all my fault—"

I decided Martha must have been thinking about all the other suicides lately, because that's the bandwagon she'd jumped on. She had one son left to save, and by God, she was gonna save him—even if it killed her.

I read the boy his rights and drove him to the station and booked him. I could only hope that having the secret out now would help Martha, that she'd be able to survive now that she didn't have to bear this burden.

After juvenile services came and got Robbie, I picked up my messages. One was from the social worker at County Social Services. I called back.

"Hey, Sheriff," Lucy Silver said, "thought you might want to know about Miz Carey."

"Yeah, how's she doing?"

"Well, other than still talking about you getting stuck in her window, she's doing okay," she said with a not-so-well-suppressed giggle.

"That's real funny," I said, indicating it wasn't. "She break anything?"

"Yeah. Her hip. I know this is going to sound awful, but it's probably the best thing that could have happened to her. She was suffering from malnutrition; she was dehydrated. In pretty bad shape. The county's going to take it to court, get her declared a ward of the county, and then we can place her in a nice home where she'll be cared for."

What was the alternative? I wondered. Just getting a call from a neighbor someday complaining of a bad smell. I knew Miz Carey, and she wasn't going to like this. She'd take it as "gov'ment innerfernce," but maybe she could start her own little group of loony reactionaries. Somehow, I figured, she'd survive us all.

That Saturday, me and Jean drove up to the new factory-outlet stores on the Tulsa Highway and spent entirely too much money getting ready for Junior. We had about two weeks to go before Jean's due date, and it was time to start getting things together.

We had the cradle my daddy and me had built when Jewel was on the way. That would take care of the boy when he was real little, but we needed a crib and a layette, and a good rocking chair. Not to mention receiving blankets, baby T-shirts, diapers, cloth and disposable, nursing bras, a nursing pump (that was a new one on me—can't wait to see how that works!), and then, of course, we had to hit the bookstore and pick up every book ever written on caring for babies and raising children. I mentioned to Jean that I never saw even one book on child rearing in my mama's house, but she just gave me one of those looks, so I let it go.

We went to Jean's church on Sunday for early Mass (we settled on church twice a month—once hers, once mine—things'll change, though, when it's time to decide which church Junior's going to) and I spent a lot of time on my rickety knees, praying for the DeLaney family. I figured they were gonna need it.

We spent the rest of Sunday getting the little room next to ours set up as the nursery. Jean had these feelings about raising a son without sexual bias (whatever the hell that means), so she'd declined the football wallpaper I'd originally wanted for the room. A few months back, we'd painted the walls blue and Jean had bought some old Winnie-the-Pooh prints (illustrations from the original books, not from the Disney stuff), which she'd framed. We set up the furniture and put up the hooks and hung the prints. The room looked great. All it needed was a baby.

That evening, all hell broke loose. Cases break in strange ways, as any police person is likely to tell you. But I never thought Loyle Parker killing his wife, Flo Ella, would clear the books on eight suicides. But like they say, life's a strange little puppy and sometimes it's just gotta pee on your leg.

You never heard of Loyle Parker? Well, maybe that's because he's mostly famous only in Oklahoma because of the Oklahoma Evangelical Christian Cable Network. He's on the Reverend Tatum Pickering's show—him and Flo Ella. Loyle's one of those weight lifters for Jesus, but he sings like a bird, and he and Flo Ella were the music directors and musical stars of the *Pickering Christian Hour*. Listening to them was like knowing the angels themselves had come to visit, they sang so pretty.

The two of them bought a ranch right here in Prophesy County about five years ago, and you'd have thought Jesus himself had moved in, the way the folks around here reacted. There were Loyle and Flo Ella sightings coming up in every conversation for about the first year, until people got used to seeing them around.

Loyle was thirty-five, Flo Ella thirty-two, and they had three little children, ranging in age from two to eleven. Everybody who watched the Evangelical Christian Cable Network was all atwitter two years before when Flo Ella gave birth to little Angela ("for Angel") Marie ("for Mary, the mother of our Lord

Jesus"). It was the talk of Longbranch, since everybody got to know every little detail of the pregnancy three nights a week on the *Pickering Christian Hour*. When Flo Ella almost lost the baby early on in the pregnancy due to a car wreck, the good Christians of Prophesy County held candlelight vigils.

What they didn't know, what only me and Mike Neils knew, was that Flo Ella hadn't been in a car wreck. Flo Ella had had a mud hole stomped in her middle. We knew it was Loyle, and both of them knew we knew, but Flo Ella wasn't talking and Loyle sure as hell wasn't.

When she turned up with a broken arm, broken ribs, and fractured clavical at Longbranch Memorial Hospital a week after Angela Marie was born, the doctor at the ER called me. I went down to the hospital and looked her over, knowing Loyle had done it to her. Flo Ella said she fell down the stairs to the storm cellar. Laughing, she said, "Sometimes I'm just the clumsiest thing."

Loyle had been there with her, stroking her hair and smiling. "We're thinking of having bumpers put on her," he said, and they both laughed.

I'd called the Reverend Tatum Pickering at the station in Tulsa, telling him what I knew, but couldn't prove, was going on. Brother Pickering said he appreciated my call, said he doubted seriously if there was any validity to my statement, and said he'd speak to Loyle about my concerns and that he'd talk to Flo Ella to make sure she was being a good Christian wife.

It's been hard keeping my mouth shut at my church and at the station when people go on and on about Loyle and Flo Ella Parker and the wonderful Brother Pickering. My idea of Christian and their idea of Christian seemed to be about twenty miles and a few thousand years apart.

But that Sunday night, I got a call from A. B. Tate at the station. Dalton Pettigrew had gone out on a call from one of the Parker children, saying there was trouble at their house.

I got there about a minute behind Dalton, to find Loyle

183

Parker standing over his wife's body, a shotgun in his hand. There wasn't much left of Flo Ella. A little girl about seven was holding the two-year old and the eleven-year-old boy was standing between them and his daddy and the shotgun.

I moved in front of Dalton, my hand on the weapon in the holster on my hip. I motioned Dalton toward the children, and he edged around, getting himself between the shielding boy and the gun.

"Loyle, put the gun down," I said, my voice as steady as I could get it. "We gotta see what's going on here and I need you to put the gun down."

Loyle looked at me, his eyes red-rimmed from crying. "I had to do it, Milt. It was the only way. She kept tempting me to hit her, and if I hit her, I knew I'd die, so it was her or me, don't you see? I had to do it."

I moved toward him slowly, my gun still holstered but my hand still on the butt. "Well, we need to talk about that, Loyle," I said, "so just go ahead and put the gun down now, okay?"

Slowly, he leaned over from his waist, putting the shotgun down on the blood-soaked wall-to-wall carpet.

"Dalton, get the kids out of here," I said, moving the shotgun farther away from Loyle with my foot as I grabbed him by the arm. I moved him away from Flo Ella's body and bent and picked up the shotgun he'd used, taking out my handkerchief to lift it by its still-hot barrel. Dalton came back in the room and I handed him the gun, telling him to get it out to the squad car and lock it up, then come back.

"Who can we call to come get the kids, Loyle? Your mama? Flo Ella's?"

He shook his head. "They'll both be real mad when they see what she made me do," he said. "Call Brother Tatum. He'll come with Sister Pearl and they can take the kids back to Tulsa with them for the night." He smiled. " 'Til you and I get this straightened out."

It amazes me sometimes what people think they can get

away with. Loyle Parker seemed to think this was gonna all blow over, like the beatings he'd been giving Flo Ella for God only knew how long.

I sat Loyle down on one of the white couches in the living room and sat down next to him. "Why, Loyle?" I asked. "Why'd you shoot her?"

He sighed, leaning back. "Well, Milt, you see, she was always tempting me to hit her. And I'd been trying real hard not to do that. Haven't you noticed that she hasn't been in the hospital for almost a year?" he said, his voice showing exasperation at the audacity of his victim. "It has been the hardest trial of my life—I want you to know that—but with the help of the Lord Jesus, Brother Tatum, and the hot line, well, I've been resisting her temptations—"

"Hot line?"

"Well, now, I'd just as soon you didn't tell Brother Tatum I've been calling the hot line. It's pretty much a humanist organization, and you know how he feels about that. But it seemed to help some, and Bob was like a lifeline to me, Milt. I want you to know that."

"Who's Bob?"

"My counselor at the hot line. A good Christian. Whenever Flo Ella started tempting me, I'd call Bob and he'd talk me through it. But then this last time, yesterday, when it just got too much for me to bear and I hit her, well, I called Bob right up and he said that what I was doing wasn't right and that if she kept tempting me like that, I had to take responsibility. He thought that maybe the best thing would be if I wasn't around to do that to her anymore. Well, I'll tell you, Milt, in a way he was right, you know? He talked to me for hours and I began to see it was either her or me. I couldn't let that woman destroy everything I've built. Do you understand that? And if she kept tempting me to hit her the way she did, why, I'd have no choice, Bob said, but to take myself away to my Heavenly Father. But I'm not ready for that yet, Milt, do you see? I'm not

185

ready, but I do believe Flo Ella is." He looked at his wife's body lying in a large, deep pool of her own blood. He smiled. "Doesn't she look peaceful?"

"Tell me about Bob," I said. "Tell me all about Bob."

15

All Loyle Parker could tell me was the first name Bob and two phone numbers, one of which was the number of the hot line. Both were Tejas County exchanges. I left Loyle Parker to the benevolent ministrations of Dalton Pettigrew and made a quick run to the office, where I called Bill Williams, who luckily was still at the office. One number definitely belonged to the hot line, but the other, according to the county crisscross directory, belonged to one Eugene Baker at an address in Taylor.

"Not Bob, huh?" I said.

"Not Bob. But I think maybe we can find out something from Audrey Whitehead. She's the director over at the hot line. You come on out first thing in the morning and we'll deal with it. I'll call Gary Booker over in Jasper and have him meet us here."

"Just give me the address and I'll meet you over there."

"Can't do it, hoss. The Tricounty Crisis Hot Line address is confidential. Can't just give it out over the phone."

"Hell, Bill, this is serious business."

"So's the hot line, believe it or not. See you in the morning," and with that, he hung up in my ear, the ungrateful turd.

Eight o'clock the next morning, bleary-eyed from lack of sleep, I got out of my new sheriff's car (this was, after all, official business, and I'd be damned if I was gonna put the extra mileage on my Jeep) and wandered into Bill Williams's domain. Funny how sheriffs' offices the world over look just about the same—the cheapest of everything stuck under a dull green ceiling. Bill and I chewed the fat for the ten minutes extra it took Gary Booker to get there from Jasper County, but then we piled into Bill's official car and headed for the hot line.

Don't tell anybody, but the Tricounty Crisis Hot Line is housed in the basement of the First Methodist Church. Like Loyle Parker said, obviously a humanistic organization—you know how them Methodists are. The place was furnished in garage-sale rejects—a sofa with the stuffing coming out, an armchair with the wood showing through in places and springs popping out in the seat, a coffee table that had been out of date when my mama bought one just like it in 1955.

A lady met us at the door and Bill introduced us to her, and her to us. She was the director, Audrey Whitehead: about thirty-five, a slender, pretty lady with frizzy dark hair, pale skin and freckles, wearing a faded Dead Head T-shirt and much-washed jeans. When she spoke her accent wasn't local—more like a nonaccent, California or some other place where the locals all talk like newscasters.

"Hope you don't mind me bringing Sheriff Kovak and Deputy Booker over hear, Audrey, but we got us some big problems."

"Not at all, Bill," she said, her slight smile seeming to indicate that she minded a heap. "What can I do for you gentlemen?"

"Can we talk private?" Bill asked.

Audrey Whitehead looked from one to the other of us and then nodded, indicating her office. We followed her into a glassed-in cubicle not nearly big enough for the four of us and closed the door. Audrey sat down behind the desk and Bill chose the only other chair in the room. Gary and I held up the walls.

Slowly we mapped out what had been happening in the Tricounty area. Her already-pale face went white and pasty as mashed potatoes. Finally, she shook her head.

"No way," she said, her head moving in the negative so fast, I was afraid she'd pop her neck. "Absolutely no way. For one thing, our volunteers are strictly forbidden to give out their home numbers or to contact any of our callers in any way. It just isn't done."

I showed her the phone number I'd gotten from Loyle Parker. "You got anybody here named Bob?"

Her head jerked up at the name and, if possible, her face went even whiter. She stood up and went to a two-drawer filing cabinet against the back wall of her cubicle and checked the number I'd given her against her volunteer records. When she leaned her head against the filing cabinet, I had a feeling we'd finally hit paydirt.

She came back and sat down at the desk, a file in her hand. She handed me back the slip of paper. "Bob is a volunteer name. Each volunteer is asked to pick an alias, for their own protection, and also to ensure that we don't have duplicate first names. We only use first names on the line. Callers tend to get very close to the volunteers. After all, they're telling these people things they wouldn't want their spouses or their preachers to know." She sighed and leaned back in her chair. "Anyway, that's what we do. I guess you don't really want to know that, do you?"

"Who's Bob?" Bill Williams asked.

Audrey Whitehead glanced at the file as if she had to refresh her memory. I doubted that she did. "Eugene Baker. He's an orderly at St. Luke's Christian Hospital. He's been with the hot line for two years. He's one of my most active volunteers. If there's a time slot I can't fill, say a four in the morning on a week night, I can call Eugene and he'll be here in a heartbeat." She leaned her head back against her chair. "I think I'm going to vomit," she said. She stood up. "You guys stay here. I'll go through the records and see if I get any matches." I gave her the list of names of the suicide victims and she went out to the files.

She came back with scantily filled out sheets of paper. "We don't ask our callers for last names. They wouldn't give them, anyway. This is a confidential line. *Anonymity* is the key word around here." She sighed. "I can match up a couple of the first names. But we'll never know for sure if these are the ones. A couple of these were filled out by Bob, some by others."

I looked through the sheets. There was one filled out by another volunteer for a caller named Shirley who had a drinking problem. I wanted to cry, right there, right in front of Bill Williams and Gary Booker and Ms. Whitehead. Just burst into tears. Shirley Beth had been trying, really trying. And instead of getting well, she'd blown her brains out. All because of an asshole orderly at St. Luke's Christian.

It took a day to get all our stuff together to take it to the county prosecutors of the three counties. We called a meeting at Tejas County sheriff's department, in their big room, since Tejas County was where the Tricounty Crisis Hot Line was located. We had the case files on all the suicides, plus the sworn statement of Loyle Parker. Audrey Whitehead joined us with the confidential files from the hot line. The four of us, me, Gary, Bill, and Audrey, were concise and articulate. We outlined the whole megillah: a way any four-year-old could understand. When we were through, the three attorneys looked at one another, conferring for no more than a minute.

Finally, Herb Goodrich of the Jasper County attorney's office, said, "Well, people, this is all real interesting, but you ain't got diddly toward an indictment." He waved Loyle Parker's sworn statement. "What Mr. Parker says here doesn't give us squat. Maybe Eugene Baker tried to talk him into killing himself—who knows? Any way you look at it, though, Loyle Parker didn't kill himself. He killed his wife. And there's nothing in here to indicate Eugene Baker talked him into doing that."

"Sides," Larry Polliver, the attorney for Tejas County said, "these volunteer sheets don't say anything. We don't even have any proof here that this Baker fella even talked to any of these other suicides."

Audrey Whitehead leaned forward. "Loyle Parker had Eugene's home phone number in his possession."

"So?" said Kenneth Marshallton, my own county attorney, who I like to call Kenny 'cause it pisses him off. Kenny stood and the others followed his lead. "That, Ms. Whitehead, isn't against the law."

The three suits left, leaving the four of us alone in the conference room.

"There's gotta be a way," Gary Booker said.

Bill shook his head. "Biggest serial killer in tricounty history and we can't touch the sumbitch."

I looked at Audrey Whitehead. She saw me looking and said, "I suppose you guys would arrest me if I went to his house this evening and blew his brains out."

Us three law-enforcement types looked at one another. "Well, now," Gary finally said, "if you just hadn't announced your intentions, ma'am . . ."

Audrey waved his words away. "I've never held a gun in my life. Wouldn't know what to do with one. But at this point, I think I could beat him to death with my bare hands." She sighed. "I know I shouldn't be worrying about this now, but this will probably close the hot line down. We're always on a shoestring, and once people hear about this, we won't get a penny in donations." She shook her head and laughed, or sobbed—it was hard to tell. "All those people dead and I'm worried about my frigging job."

I cleared my throat. Three pairs of eyes looked at me. "I don't know about the rest of y'all," I said, "but I sure would like to meet Mr. Eugene Baker."

Audrey said she'd set it up and call us. We left it at that.

I wasn't real happy when I got back to the station. I had a moral dilemma. Did I tell Emmett what we'd found out? I hadn't mentioned anything yet—I'd wanted to have Baker behind bars before I told Emmett. My fear was that Emmett would go after Baker—and I think that fear was justified. If Baker had done that to someone I loved, I don't know how I could let the man live. As it was, it was hard enough.

I'd been a peace officer for some twenty years before I ever took a life. It was something you thought about a lot in my line a work. Can I do it? Will I do it? How will I handle it if I do? When circumstances conspired to make it happen, I hadn't even thought about it. A man was standing in front of me with my comatose granddaughter Rebecca slung over one arm and Jean held tightly against him, while the other held a knife to her throat. I shot him in the face.

Since that time, I've replayed that scene over and over in my head. But never once do I think about having taken that man's life. My thoughts are always, "What if I'd missed?"

But that killing was to save lives, not to avenge them.

I decided not to say anything to Emmett for a while. 'Til I'd seen Baker, and 'til I knew it was coming out in the papers or whatever. Save him from having to make the decision.

Around noon, Audrey Whitehead called to say Eugene Baker would be in her office at two that afternoon.

"You didn't tell him anything, did you?" I asked.

"Are you serious? Of course not! Dear Eugene thinks this has something to do with the Volunteer of the Year awards. He's been campaigning for it. Until yesterday," she said, "he had it in the bag."

Me and Gary met Bill at his office again and all went over in Bill's car—to make it official. It was, after all, Bill's county. Not that there was anything too official in what we were doing. We still couldn't touch the guy—but at least we'd know who he was, what he looked like.

When we walked in the hot line's office, we could see Audrey Whitehead in her little cubicle, talking with a man. She had a smile plastered on her face for all she was worth. She looked up and saw us and nodded for us to join them. We walked in the room. The man sitting at the only other chair in the room stood. He was about my height, five eleven, slender, late thirties, wearing his uniform of hospital greens. He had neatly groomed light brown hair, even features, a friendly smile showing even teeth and one slight dimple in his left cheek. Real normal-looking guy 'til you got to the eyes.

I've never seen eyes like that in my life and hope never to again. They were almond-shaped, a bluish green in color, and had as much depth and humanity to 'em as my uncle Ed's glass eye he used to take out during church and drop in the collection plate to give us kids fits.

Somebody once said the eyes are the mirror to the soul, or something like that. If that's the truth, then it was pretty obvious Eugene Baker had no soul. His were the eyes of a dead man. Vacant, empty. I wondered if I was the only one that saw that. Why hadn't Audrey Whitehead noticed those eyes?

Audrey introduced us all around and Eugene Baker held out his hand. Nobody took him up on it. He stood there for a moment with his hand outstretched, then slowly lowered it to his side. The smile never left his face and his eyes never changed.

"Well, Audrey," he said, turning to her, "since you've got company, I'll check back with you later."

"Sit down, Mr. Baker," Bill said.

Baker sat. The expression on his face never changed—and his eyes never blinked.

"You ever heard of Shirley Beth Hopkins?" I asked.

Baker's smile left his face and he took on an attitude of concentration. "No, Sheriff, I'm afraid not," he said after a moment. "Should I have?"

"How about Sandra German?" Bill Williams asked.

Baker shook his head.

"And Mickey Walthram?" Gary asked.

Baker tilted his head to the side and allowed a small smile to play across his mouth. "I'm afraid I don't know any of these people, guys. What's up?"

"You'd think he'd a heard of some of these, Sheriff," Bill said to me. "Killin' 'em and all the way he did."

Although nothing in them changed, Baker's eyes got bigger and the smile was replaced by a frown. "Excuse me?" he said.

I leaned in close to him. "How about Lori Nabors?" I asked. "Ever heard of her?"

Bill swung Baker's chair around and said, "Or Brenda Macon, ever heard of her?"

I swung the chair back toward me. "But your big problem, Baker, is good ole Loyle Parker. You ain't probably gonna believe this, but ole Loyle didn't fall for your line of crap. Well, he did, but in a unique sorta way. He didn't shoot himself, Eugene. He killed his wife instead. Then he told us all about you."

Baker stood up and leaned against the wall. "Sorry, fellas, but I had nothing to do with this Loyle person killing his wife. If he misunderstood my counseling, that's his problem, not mine."

"Did Shirley Beth Hopkins misunderstand your counseling, Eugene?"

He smiled. It didn't touch his eyes. Turning his head, he looked at Audrey Whitehead. "Audrey, I'm outta here. I'll see you tonight."

Audrey was shaking her head. "No, I don't think so, Eugene. Your services are no longer required."

He laughed. "No. I don't think so. You have no grounds."

Audrey stood up and leaned across her desk, her hands resting on forms and papers and other stuff strewn across it. "Loyle Parker was found with a sheet of paper in his possession that had your hot-line name and your home phone number. Giving out your home phone number to a caller is against the hot line's rules, Eugene. Grounds for immediate dismissal."

"We'll see what the board has to say about that," he said.

Audrey moved around her desk to the door, opening it. She smiled. "Sorry you won't be able to make it to the Volunteer of the Year banquet." Her smile got bigger. "But shit happens, ya know?"

When I walked into the office, Gladys met me with my messages. One was from Randy Hobbs, Seattle PD. I called him immediately.

"Hey, Sheriff," he said, "glad you called back, although I don't really have much for you."

"I'll take whatᵥver I can get," I said.

"Well, Mrs. Gallagher says her husband got his messages on Friday night and decided to have someone else take his calls and that they were going to go on one last fishing trip before the baby came. Fishing's real good in Montana," he said.

"That's what I hear."

"They borrowed a cabin from a doctor friend and stayed there for a few days, then she said her husband decided it would be fun to go west, so they got in the car and drove. She said she thought it was strange with the baby so close and all, but she strikes me as the type who doesn't ask her man a lot of questions." He laughed. "Wish I could say that about my wife. But it's just the opposite. She says jump, I don't even ask how high."

"Sometimes it just ain't politic," I said in agreement.

"Tell me about it. Anyway, they drove through Idaho, then on here to Seattle. Stayed out on one of the islands in the Sound for a couple days 'til she went into labor, then he took her to the hospital, told her to check in under her maiden name, gave her a wad of cash, and dropped her off. Says she doesn't know anything about him having another wife. Says she knows he was originally from Oklahoma because she filled out the paperwork to transfer his board certification when she first went to work for him. Girl's pretty upset, Sheriff, I'll tell you that. Her parents are coming in from Boise to pick her and the baby up and take them back there. Talked to her father on the phone and he's pissing vinegar." Hobbs laughed. "Old man said he never did trust doctors and that this just proves it."

195

"Well, Randy, thanks a lot. Doesn't give me much, but at least we know what we don't have," I said, then rang off.

I went through my other messages: one from Jean, saying she was going into a meeting and would call me back; one from Davis Montgomery with a complaint about his neighbor rustling his cattle again that only I could handle. I called Gladys on the intercom and told her to give it to Jasmine. Davis Montgomery didn't like women or blacks. As my two day deputies were one of each, I figured Jasmine being on the force the longest got her the privilege of dealing with Davis.

The last message was from Daniel Gallagher at his office. I called that one back immediately. Mrs. G. answered the phone. When I identified myself and asked for Daniel, she said, "Any word on Phillip?"

"No, ma'am, not yet. But your new daughter-in-law just gave birth to a little girl. Mother and daughter doing fine."

"Oh my Lord! Oh, Milton, this is wonderful news. Here, let me get you Daniel."

When Daniel came on the line, he said, "So, I got me a niece, huh?"

"Looks that way."

"Mama wants to know her name, her weight, her length." He laughed, and I could hear his mother in the background demanding more news.

"Daniel, I'm real sorry. I forgot to ask all that. I'll find out for you and let you know."

"Mama wants to know her new daughter-in-law's name and how she can call her."

I gave him the name of the hospital in Seattle. "She's registered under her maiden name. Debbie Temple." I heard him give the news to his mother. Coming back on the line with me, he laughed and said, "This is the best news Mama's had in a long time, Milt. Thanks."

"No problem, Daniel. Is that what you'd called about?"

"No, hell, I almost forgot. I sold Libby's computer equipment. I have my own at home and I couldn't see any reason to keep it around. When the kid that bought it came to pick it up, he found another disc in the second drive. I figured it might be more of the book. You want it?"

It had been days since I'd looked at any of Libby's journal. I felt like I was getting over that—whatever it had been. Now here was something new, something more of Libby's.

"Yeah, sure, Daniel," I said. "Suppose I should look at it. Maybe I'll swing by your house later in the week."

"I got it here at the office. Send one of your deputies over to pick it up, save us both the hassle. That's why us big shots have underlings, right, Milt?"

We both laughed at the grandness of being big shots and all, and I sent Hank Dobbins over to pick it up. I just wasn't sure how much more of Libby Fortuna my marriage could take.

16

After Hank brought me the disc from Daniel Gallagher, I sent him out on a call that had just come in. Gladys was in the file room and I told her I'd watch the switchboard; then I used the computer in the bull pen to boot up the new disc.

It was a J disc. More of her journal. But it was new, the stuff after she'd married Daniel and moved to Longbranch. I sped through April, May, and into June, just finding more of her daily calendar—boring stuff, like "Pick up Daniel's suits"; "Get plumber for hall bath commode"; "Friday night—dinner at Jewel's" (poor baby), and so on. But in mid-June, things changed. The journal was back.

June 14, 1994
Guess who? I'm back. I wish I could talk to Daniel about this, but I can't. His mother's driving me crazy! What a stupid idea for newlyweds to move into a house with *his* mother! She has her own wing of the house, granted, but she's still in the same house! I've never been big on having sex on the kitchen table, but knowing we can't is driving me crazy. If we go into the bedroom together for any reason, I know she thinks we're having sex! Okay, most of this is *my* problem, not hers,

but that doesn't make it any easier. And I would like to cook occasionally! I'm not the world's greatest cook, but I would like to try!

June 17, 1994
I tried fixing dinner tonight. She stayed over me the entire time—*helping*. Jesus, give me strength! If she just weren't so damned *sweet*, maybe I could deal with this— if we could argue and bicker, at least I could let some of this out! But how can you resent a woman "who's only trying to help"???? I don't know how, but, by God, I do!!!!!!

June 19, 1994
We told Mrs. G. about the baby. Daniel's so happy, he could burst. Mrs. G. seemed delighted. Said she was. I don't know why I get the feeling she isn't.

The phone rang and I picked it up.
"Sheriff's department," I said.
"Milt? Honey?" It was my wife's voice.
"Hey, babe, bet you're wondering why I'm answering the phone, well—"
"Milt, I'm bleeding."
"What? How bad? Have you called the doctor?"
"Yes, I called the doctor. It's more than spotting. It's pretty heavy. I'm on my way downstairs now. Could you meet me?"
"Where are you? Are you still at the hospital?"
"Yes. Janine's going to wheel me down to Obstetrics. She's already called Bobby—"
"I'm on my way," I said, hanging up the phone and hollering for Gladys.

Bobby Cannaway, Jean's OB-GYN, who specializes in problem pregnancies, led me out of the examining room by the arm. I was sweating buckets. Jean hadn't looked good. She was pale. Her dark red hair was matted with sweat. She was hooked up to every monitor in the book and then some.

We went outside in the hall and Bobby said, "Milt, the baby's in distress. We can't wait for full term—"

"Bobby, she's not due for two weeks."

"Babies have been born healthy at a lower gestational age than that, my man," he said, smiling bravely. I would have preferred a reassuring smile, but you take what you can get. "The problem right now is Jean. She's got a placenta previa—"

"What? What's that? Is she okay? Jesus—"

"Listen," he said, taking my arm. "The placenta is growing into the lower uterine segment, acting as a barrier to the baby. We're going to have to do a C-Section. We can't wait, Milt. We're taking her to the OR now. If you want to be there like we planned, get yourself prepped."

He handed me over to a nurse, who rushed me to a scrub room where I washed and donned the green paper gown, booties, and hat they'd shown us in Lamaze class. She gave me the mask and I put it over my nose and mouth and went into the operating room.

Jean was already there. She was conscious. They'd given her an epidural, like we'd planned all along. 'Cept we planned on waiting a whole nine months instead of just eight and a half. The lower part of her body was cut off by a drape, shielding the two of us from seeing the actual incision of the C-section. I stayed up by Jean's head, talking to her, cooing to her, telling her how much I loved her. A nurse gave me a cold compress and I wiped Jean's brow with it. Jean held my hand so hard, I thought she'd break a couple of fingers, but I didn't care. I was sharing the pain—sorta.

I can't tell you how long we were in there—maybe a week, maybe a minute and a half. Time seemed to stand still. All I know is it was the first time I'd been in the presence of Bobby Cannaway and not been eaten up with the jealousy bug. First time I didn't care that he'd known Jean a hell of a lot longer than I had, that he had interned under her in Chicago on his psychiatric rotation, and that he was half in love with her himself. All I knew was that I was damned glad he was there.

I couldn't hear much of what went on at the other end of my wife's body; Bobby and the nurses talked softly to one another and there was none of the jovial side talk you hear about during operations. This one was serious. I half-wished someone would crack a joke, just to make it not so serious. But nobody did.

At 7:52 P.M., the evening of September 6, 1994, my son was born.

"Let her sleep," Bobby said, looking at Jean in the recovery room. "She's gonna need it."

"Where's the pediatrician? When's he gonna talk to me?"

Bobby rubbed my shoulders. "Just hold on, Milt. He's with the baby now. He'll come out as soon as he can."

Bobby and I left the recovery room and went into the hall. Once there, one of the nurses grabbed Bobby. "Dr. Cannaway, we got a bad monitor in birthing room two."

Bobby patted me on the arm. "Gotta go. Good luck."

He left me alone in the hall, a semiunconscious wife in the recovery room, and a son in the nursery—in what condition, I didn't know.

Finally, Dr. Greene, the pediatrician, came up to me. He smiled. He didn't grin. Grins are for dad with babies who are okay. "Congratulations on your son, Sheriff," he said, shaking my hand.

"How is he?"

"Well, he's small—five pounds, couple of ounces. But his apgars aren't all that great, Milt—"

"What? Ap—what? Is he okay?"

"Apgars. It's a scoring system. His were three at one minute and five at five minutes. Ten's a healthy baby's apgars. Basically, his heart rate is below one hundred, his respirations are slow and irregular, his muscle tone's limp, no reflex irritability, and his color's not good. I've intubated him and we've got him on the monitor, and some of the best perinatal nurses in Oklahoma work at this hospital, Milt." He patted me on the shoulder. "We're at a wait-and-see right now, but I got real high hopes. I want you to know that."

As he walked away, a nurse came flying out of the recovery room, grabbed a phone, and called for Dr. Cannaway—stat.

Jean was hemorrhaging. Bobby told me a lot of stuff that all boiled down to the fact that they needed to do a hysterectomy and they needed to do it now. Jean wasn't conscious. I had to make the decision. Jean was forty-five years old. The chances of us having another baby were real slim. I hoped she'd forgive me for making the decision I made—but Bobby said she could die if I didn't. They took her back to the OR.

Jewel showed up fifteen minutes after I called her and held my hand while I got on the phone to call Jean's parents in Chicago. I'd never met them, but we had talked on the phone before. I told them what had happened.

"You did the right thing, Milt," Mrs. McDonnell said when I told her about the hysterectomy. "It was the only thing you could do."

"Right," Mr. McDonnell said on the extension.

"How's the baby?" Mrs. McDonnell asked. So I told her.

It was a sober call, not the call I'd expected to make, planned to make, fantasized about making.

"Get off the phone, Milt," Mr. McDonnell said. "We gotta call and make reservations. We'll grab the first plane out of here."

I gave them the office number and told them to call there when they had the arrival time of their plane and one of my deputies would go to Oklahoma City and pick them up. I figured if the county commissioners had any problem with that, they could have my badge. At the moment, the damned thing just wasn't very important.

I hung up and me and Jewel went to the nursery to look at my son. He was in an incubator, monitors hooked up to his little body, a little blue cap on his head. He was pinker than he'd been when he came out, but his arms and legs still had that bluish tinge. Tubes were in his nose and mouth. Jewel took my hand and we just stood there, leaning on the glass of the nursery window, staring at my boy.

I don't know how long we'd been standing there when I got paged to the phone. It was Bill Williams.

"What's going on, Milt? Gladys said you rushed out like a crazy man—"

"Jean went into premature labor. My son's been born—but—"

I couldn't say it, couldn't put it into words. "Jean's in the operating room, now; they gotta do a hysterectomy. She was hemorrhaging real bad."

"Jesus, man, I'm sorry. The baby?"

"He's holding his own."

"Look, I know you don't wanna worry about work now, so I'll just—"

"No, it could be hours before Jean's out. Give me something to keep me busy. Long as I don't have to leave."

"No problem. We'll come to you," he said, and hung up.

I had no idea who "we" was and didn't worry about it. I had too much to worry about as it was.

Half an hour passed, and I really didn't care about this year's brides in *People* magazine. I'd just thrown the rag back on the table when the waiting room door opened and Bill Williams, Gary Booker, and Audrey Whitehead came in. Bill and Gary shook my hand and wished my family well and Audrey Whitehead hugged me, saying how she just knew everything was gonna work out fine, just fine. I introduced Gary and Audrey to Jewel, as she and Bill had already met.

I cleared my throat and said, "So what's up?"

"We got somewhere private we can talk?" Bill asked, looking around the waiting room at the other people waiting for loved ones to make it through surgery.

I stopped a nurse in the hall and she suggested we go to the chapel. I left Jewel in the waiting room with instructions on where to find me if she got any word on either Jean or the baby.

Being a city-run institution, the chapel was nothing to brag about—institutional white walls, plain wooden pews, no stained glass, no Jesus, no Torah, nothing to indicate who could, or could not, worship or rest within its confines.

The chapel was empty, so we sat in the back, taking up two pews so we could face one another as we talked.

"Milt," Bill said, "the reason we're bothering you is that Audrey came up with an idea and we knew you needed to be in on this."

"The thing is," Audrey Whitehead said, "I got to thinking. There's this phenomenon in hot-line circles called the 'repeat caller.' Now, these run the gamut, from just people calling up every once in a while to talk, to the real pros, who are addicted to calling hot lines. The pros call a line and make up things—like suicides—just to get attention. When one line gets to the point that they can identify them, they often move on to other lines. We can get calls from just about anywhere. We've had calls we found out were coming from a repeater in California.

"But what I was thinking was, what if Baker tried his game on one of these repeaters?"

"Would a repeat caller be susceptible to Baker's kinda scam? Or are we just gonna get him on a misdemeanor?" I asked.

Her face fell. "Well, I don't know." Then her face brightened. "But we get calls from more than just the tricounty area—like Texas . . . from along the border. Sometimes the small towns on the border—it's cheaper to call our line than one of the big ones in Dallas or wherever. What if he tried that with somebody who called from a border town?"

Me and Bill and Gary looked at one another. "Y'all got contacts in north Texas?" I asked.

"I know a guy in Denton," Gary said. "Works for DPS."

"My brother's a fireman in Sherman," Bill said. "He's bound to know some cops."

"I'll call my old roommate in Wichita Falls, too," Audrey said. "Maybe she knows people in the little towns on the border—"

"Worth a try," I said. I stood. "Audrey, you go back and go over all your records. Get your volunteers in to help. Go back as long as Eugene Baker's been a volunteer. Check out that repeat-caller scenario in case that's all we can get. And see if you got anything saying any callers were calling from other than the tricounty area. We just gotta do something."

They all looked at me, and I realized I was barking orders like a marine drill sergeant. I shook my head. "Sorry, I thought maybe—"

"Good ideas, Milt," Bill said, standing. The others stood with him. "We needed your input. Thanks."

He shook my hand. Then they all wished me well and left. One of these days, I thought, I just oughta buy Bill Williams a steak dinner.

I stayed in the chapel a little longer. I figured me and God had some bargaining to do.

Bobby Cannaway found me and Jewel back at the nursery an hour later. Jean had been in surgery for over two hours.

"She's okay," he said when I saw him. He came up and gave me the man hug. "She's gonna be fine, Milt."

"Can I see her?"

"She's in recovery. She's unconscious right now. Why don't you wait until we take her up to her room?"

"Bobby—"

"What did Marty Greene say?" he asked.

"Something about aptars—"

"Apgars. What are the numbers?"

I racked my brain, trying to remember. "Three at one minute and like five, I think, at five minutes?"

Bobby nodded. "Not great. But not awful, Milt. Not awful at all."

He looked at the baby he'd delivered only a few hours earlier. "He's pinking up," he said. "Good sign."

"When will we know something?" I asked, looking at that frail little body lying in the incubator.

"It may be morning before he pulls totally out of this, or earlier. You never can tell." Bobby patted my shoulder again and took off. He didn't say it, but the implication was there: The baby might not pull out of it at all.

By eleven o'clock that evening, Jean was back in her room, fuzzy but conscious.

When I walked in, the first thing she said was, "How's the baby? Where is he? I want to see him."

How much should I tell her? What could she handle? But I knew Jean, and Jean wasn't the kinda lady you shield things from. I figured fuzzy or no, she needed the truth.

I sat down on the side of the bed and took her hand in mine. "Honey, he's holding his own, they're telling me. He's having some trouble breathing, so they got him in an incubator and he's got tubes up his nose—"

"What were his birth apgars?"

I rolled my eyes. Until a few hours ago, I'd never heard the word, but everybody around here sure seemed to put stock in it. "Three at one minute, five at five."

Jean leaned her head back against the pillows. "Not great," she said.

"Yeah, but Bobby said they're not awful, either. Dr. Greene said our boy was having trouble breathing and his color wasn't good, but just about an hour ago, Bobby and I were looking at him and he seemed to be getting real pink."

"I want to see him. Can they bring him to me?"

"Honey, he's in an incubator—"

Jean tried to swing her legs off the bed. "I want to go see him," she said.

"Honey, you know where you been for the past few hours? They tell you anything?"

She just looked at me. I sighed. I had a feeling she didn't know. "Baby, they had to give you a hysterectomy. You were hemorrhaging. I gave my permission. It was the hardest thing I've ever done in my life, honey, but I had—"

Jean took my hand. "You did the right thing." She leaned her head back against the pillow. "If Bobby said it was necessary, then it was."

She turned her head away from me, staring at the wall. I leaned down and kissed the cheek closest to me. "I love you," I whispered.

I left Jean alone so she could work out her grief over her body. Jewel met me in the hall. "How is she?" Jewel asked.

"I just told her about the hysterectomy."

Jewel walked by me to the door of the room. "Let me talk to her," she said. "I've been there."

I left the two women alone.

Fifteen minutes later, a nurse went in with a wheelchair. Five minutes after that, my sister came out, followed by Jean, who was being pushed in a wheelchair by the nurse. "I want to see my son," Jean said.

We went down the hall together to the nursery. He looked so little lying there. He was naked, except for the little blue cap, not even a diaper on him, with tubes in his nose and mouth, and monitors attached to his little chest. His legs and arms were still blue, the chest a little pinker. But he hadn't changed much since Jewel and I had been there hours earlier.

Dr. Greene came by and led us into the nursery, wheeling Jean up to the incubator. There was a little porthole through which the nurses did their thing. Jean put her hand through and took hold of the baby's tiny fingers. He wrapped his little fingers around her bigger one. Jean took my hand and I just stood there next to her wheelchair, staring at my boy.

I slept in a chair next to Jean's bed. It was a fitful night, mostly for me, because I didn't have the benefit of the pain medications they were giving Jean. In the morning, Harmon showed up with Jewel's kids and I took them down to the nursery to check on the baby. Marty Greene, the pediatrician, met me in the hallway.

"He's looking good, Milt," he said, smiling. "We're going to extubate him now, see how he breathes on his own."

I nodded and took my niece and nephews to look in the nursery at their new cousin. We got only a glimpse of him as they wheeled the incubator out of the main room and behind closed doors to remove the breathing tubes.

"He's so tiny," Marlene said as she stood beside me, holding my hand. "Is he going to be okay, Uncle Milt?"

I smiled down at her, hopefully showing more assurance than I felt. "He's gonna be fine," I said. "Just fine."

We went back to Jean's room to tell her about the extubation. She sighed with relief. "Thank God," she said, smiling at me. "That's a good sign, Milt."

I kissed her lips. "I know, baby. He's gonna be fine."

Fifteen minutes later, Marty Greene was in our room and the kids were sent out in the hall to be with Jewel and Harmon.

Marty was shaking his head. "I extubated, Jean, but the poor little fella just couldn't do it on his own. I had to reintubate. But his color's getting better, his heart rate's pretty good, muscle tone's improving, and there's a little reflex irritability. So he's holding his own. We get his respirations up, we're gonna have us a new halfback for the Longbranch Cougars, huh, Milt?"

I nodded and looked at my wife. She knew what the guy was talking about. She could interpret all the medical gobbledygook, and she didn't look any happier than I felt. Marty Greene left and Jean and I sat there some more, holding hands and feeling grim.

Everything about that little boy in the nursery had been a miracle. The mere fact that his mother and I met was a miracle in itself. That he was conceived the first time his virgin mama had ever had sex was a Catholic-school horror-story miracle. That he was conceived of two aging parents such as Jean and me was a miracle. I prayed to God. Just one more miracle. Just one more. To let my son live.

Emmett came by around noon, kissed Jean, and then went with me to look at my son. He was still in the incubator, a diaper covering him now, but monitors and tubes were still hooked up to him.

Emmett looked at my boy and said, "He's gonna be okay, Milt. Somehow I just know it."

I don't know why I believed Emmett Hopkins more than the doctors, but I did.

At six o'clock that evening, twenty minutes after I met my in-laws for the first time ever, they extubated the baby again. He breathed on his own. At eight, they brought him to his mama and Jean nursed for the first time. Watching my wife hold our son to her, I wondered if life could ever get better than that.

The baby spent the night in the incubator, and I stayed the night in Jean's room again. Jasmine Bodine had come and taken Mr. and Mrs. McDonnell out to our house and given them the key to my Jeep so they could drive themselves back to the hospital in the morning.

Marty Greene came in at seven o'clock, along with Jean's breakfast, to let us know the baby had done well in the night.

209

"That's one ornery little boy you got there, Jean," he said, smiling. "For somebody's whose respirations were low only hours ago, he's screaming like he's got the lungs of a marathon runner."

Jean left her breakfast and we took the wheelchair down to see the baby. He was doing great. As I wheeled my wife back into her room, the phone was ringing.

I picked it up. "Hello?" I said.

"I hear he's okay," Emmett said.

"Yeah, he had a good night and he's off the tubes and on the nipple. Can't ask for more than that."

"Amen," Emmett said. "So, if you got a minute, you wanna come by the office?"

"Emmett, I'm kinda busy—"

"I know. But I thought you might want to say hidy to Phillip Gallagher. He just walked in here about five minutes ago."

I left Jean and my son to the loving ministrations of my in-laws and drove to the sheriff's department. I walked in my office, where Gladys said Emmett and Gallagher were, and pretty near shot one theory straight to hell. If Phillip Gallagher had been hiding in Longbranch, it wasn't because of his great resemblance to his twin brother. The man I saw was thin enough to have just survived the Holocaust, had snow white hair, a sun-dried, lined face, and looked maybe like Daniel Gallagher's dead daddy—two weeks after the burial.

"Haven't asked him a thing, Milt," Emmett said, getting out of my chair and moving to one of the two visitor's chairs, the one not occupied by Phillip Gallagher. "Thought I'd save that pleasure for you."

I moved to the good doctor and held out my hand. Phillip stood up and shook it. "Good to see you again, Milt. I understand you and I have something in common—we're both daddies."

I smiled. "Sure looks that way, Phil. Nice to see you again, too."

I moved around my desk and sat down in my big swivel chair. "So Phil, what brings you to Longbranch?"

"Heard you were looking for me."

"Woulda been easier just to pick up the phone."

"There are . . . extenuating circumstances," he said.

"Uh-huh," I said. "And what would those be?"

"I read about Libby Fortuna. But the news in Billings, and the national news, didn't mention her husband's name. It did say, however, that she died here. When you called my office looking for me, I called a nurse here who used to work for me to find out what was going on. She told me who Ms. Fortuna had married. I thought Daniel might need me."

"Right brotherly of you," I said, leaning back in my chair and propping my feet up on one of the drawer handles of my desk. "Let's see if I got this straight. I call your office and ask you to call me. Instead of doing that, you call this nurse friend, and she tells you your brother's bride was brutally murdered. So you jump in the car and go fishing. Disappear, for all intents and purposes. Then, when your wife's ready to pop, you sneak her in a hospital under her maiden name—" I straightened up and looked at Phillip Gallagher. "But I guess disappearing is something you're pretty good at, huh, Phillip? Have practice and all the way you do—"

Dr. Gallagher stood up. "If you don't mind, Sheriff, I'd like to go and see my brother, and my mother."

I stood up, too. "No problem, Dr. Gallagher. I'll be happy to drive you."

He didn't protest, just nodded and walked out of the room. I motioned for Emmett to join us, and the three of us went out and got in my shiny new sheriff's car and headed to Daniel Gallagher's office.

The front office was empty when we got there, but Daniel's

door was ajar and I could hear him on the phone. I motioned for Phillip to stay where he was and I stuck my head in Daniel's door. Seeing me, he waved, gave me the one-minute sign, and I went back to the waiting room and sat with Emmett and Phillip. In less than a minute, we heard the phone being cradled and Daniel said, "Hey, Milt, what's up?" as he came out of the door of his office.

The smile on his face faded and a look of shock took its place as Phillip stood up.

"Phil? Jesus Christ!" The brothers went into each's arms, holding on. "God, man, what happened? You look like shit!"

Phillip laughed. "Nice to see you, too, little brother."

Grinning, Daniel looked at me. "Three minutes and he thinks he's the big brother who can tell me what to do!"

"Where's Mama?" Phillip asked.

Daniel shook his head, laughing. "God, she's gonna be pissed! You just missed her. She and her friend Hattie just left for Tulsa to catch the noon flight for Boise, Idaho. She wants to see that grandbaby of hers so bad—"

Phillip Gallagher had gone white as a sheet. His knees buckled as Daniel caught his arm. Phillip turned to face me and everything clicked. I'd had the answer for days and didn't know it.

17

I turned to Emmett. "Call the Tulsa airport. Get security. Tell 'em not to let Miz Gallagher on that plane. Tell 'em to hold her. Call Eric James on the Tulsa PD. Have him meet us at the airport."

Phillip said, "Have somebody go over to Daniel's, look through Mama's stuff—"

Turning to Daniel, I said, "Daniel, do I have your permission to search your house?"

"What? What the hell's going on? Jesus, Phil—"

"Give him permission," Phil said. "Now!"

Daniel looked from his brother to me. "Yeah, okay. Sure."

"Your whole house. Your mama's apartment is a part of the main house, right? It's not a separate section?"

"No, it's part of the main house—what's going on?"

"You heard him, Emmett. Make them calls and get a car over here to take you to the house." I held my hand out to Daniel. "Keys?"

Daniel gave me his house keys and I handed them off to Emmett. "Go!" I said, shoving Emmett toward the phone.

"Hurry, Milt. For God's sake, hurry," Phil said.

I grabbed his arm and we ran out of the building, Daniel Gallagher hot on our heels.

We all three piled in my new sheriff's car and, with sirens blaring, hit the Tulsa Highway.

"I thought my life was over when I got back from that convention. I knew what I was coming home to," Phil said, "but I didn't really believe it—not until I saw the house, saw the remains of Cassie's body. Nobody wanted me to view that—not Dr. Jim or Emmett or Mama. But I'm a doctor. I thought I could handle it." He gave a bitter laugh. "Puked my guts out for days. I didn't have anywhere to go, so I moved in with Mama. Danny came home and stayed with me for a few weeks." He turned around in the front seat to take his twin's hand. "Sorry I didn't reciprocate."

I was driving ninety miles an hour down the highway, heading for the interstate, siren screaming. With the windows rolled up and the air conditioning on, I could hear Phillip fine over the wail of the siren.

"When did you find out?" I asked him.

He let go of Daniel's hand and turned back around in the seat. Daniel was leaning forward in the backseat, his breath tickling my neck.

"I stayed with Mama for about eight, nine months, trying to sort out my life. Trying to get Emmett to take me seriously about the right-to-lifers. All those threats—I'd thought they'd done it. One day when Mama was out shopping, I tore my only clean pair of pants and I went looking for a needle and thread. Couldn't find the right color in her sewing basket. Knew she kept extras in her bedroom somewhere. Started looking." He was silent for a moment as we listened to the siren scream. Finally, he said, "In one of her bureau drawers, I found a small paper sack that had the logo of her favorite cloth store. I thought I'd found her extra thread. Instead, inside it I found Cassie's wedding ring and a diamond necklace I'd given her when we found out she was pregnant. That's when I really knew my life was over."

214

"No," Daniel said from the backseat, falling back. "No way. You are out of your mind. Both of you are out of your minds! Stop the damned car! Right now!"

Phillip turned around in the seat and grabbed both of Daniel's hands. "Shut up! Listen to me! I thought at first Dr. Jim took them off the body and gave them to her and she was just waiting for the right time to give them to me. But then I noticed there was nothing wrong with the rings or the necklace. They weren't charred or bent. There was no way they came off Cassie's body *after* the explosion. No way in hell."

Daniel was trying to grab his hands back from his brother. "No!" he shouted. "How can you say that about Mama! You asshole, how can you say that—"

Phillip held on tight and his voice got low and mean. "So Mama comes home and I show them to her. She turns white. Then she gets mad. Remember, Danny? Remember her face when she was mad? That red mark that starts at her neck and works its way up and you better run for your life? Remember that? Well, Mama was mad. She grabbed the jewelry out of my hand and demanded to know why I'd been going through her stuff. I asked her where she got them. She said Cassie had given them to her the day before she died. I asked why. Mama just shrugged. I said, 'Mama, that's a crock.' She tried to walk away. I grabbed her. I said, 'Mama, where did you get the jewelry?'"

"This is crazy!" Daniel cried from the backseat, finally getting his hands away from his brother. "You're accusing our mother of—of—"

"Of killing my wife," Phillip said, his voice calm. "Yes, I accused her. You know what she said, Danny? Do you want to know what our mother said?"

"Milt, stop the car," Daniel said. "Just stop the damned car! I want out."

One good thing about a vehicle like mine, once you're in the backseat the only way out is if someone lets you out. Which was good, since I'm afraid if he coulda done it, Daniel Gallagher

215

would have been out of that car and splattered all over the interstate.

"Are you going to listen to me, Danny?"

"You're nuts," Daniel said, his voice icy. "What happened to Cassie pushed you over the edge and you are certifiable—you know that, Phil? Hell, you may have been certifiable before all that happened to Cassie. Maybe you did it yourself and now you're trying to blame Mama—"

"Listen to him, Daniel," I said. "Listen to what he has to say."

"I accused Mama of killing Cassie and my unborn child and she said, 'Well, what was I supposed to do? Just sit back and let them have it all? I knew you'd forget all about me once that blasted baby came!'"

"Why'd you run, Phillip? Why didn't you turn her in?" I asked.

He looked at me, a strange expression on his face. "She's my mother," he said, his voice quiet.

"No," Daniel said, curling up in the backseat. "No."

Phillip turned around and stared out the front window. We were heading into Tulsa.

The first leg of Mrs. G.'s flight for Boise didn't leave until noon. A quick stop at the gate told us she hadn't checked in yet. With airport security in tow, we went to the front of the terminal and waited for Eric James to arrive. He got there fifteen minutes after we did. And we walked the airport looking for her. Daniel spotted her first, sitting in the coffee shop with another old lady.

He yelled, "Mama!"

Mrs. G. looked up. Seeing all of us, including her son Phillip, she jumped up and ran out of the restaurant, her bewildered friend staring after her. Mrs. G. was old, short, had stubby legs. She didn't get far. It wasn't the greatest chase scene in the world. Fifty yards maybe before one of the security guards grabbed her. With the help of Eric James, we commandeered a security room and put Mrs. G. in it. I called the office to see what Emmett had found in his search of Mrs. G.'s apartment in Daniel's house—Libby's wedding ring, watch, and one carat diamond stud earring.

I hung up the phone and went in the security room. Mrs. G. was sitting properly, hands clasped on the table in front of her, legs crossed at the ankles. She looked at me and said, "Milton Kovak, your mother must be turning over in her grave! You treating me like a common criminal."

"We found Libby's wedding ring and the other stuff," I said.

"Where?"

"In your room."

She smiled. "You had no right to go in my room—"

"We had Daniel's permission to search his house."

"Those are my private quarters—"

"Within Daniel's house. We're legally in the right."

Mrs. G. rolled her eyes. "Well, Libby gave me that stuff."

"Just like Cassie gave you her stuff?" I said. I was being quiet. Talking softly. Out of respect for her? Or maybe for my mother. My mother, whose one real joy in her later years were the three grandchildren Jewel had given her. My mother, who'd never see my son.

"Well, for heaven's sake," she said, and sighed. "You are going to make a big thing out of this, aren't you, Milton?"

"Why, Miz Gallagher? I just don't understand—"

She laughed. "Well, of course you don't. You're a man. You've never been totally alone and abandoned. You've never worked your whole life for your children, just to discover you're going to be abandoned again."

I shook my head. "Miz Gallagher—"

"I'm not a pretty woman, Milton, never was. I spent my whole life caring for my parents. My sisters married and moved on, but not me. Then when I was in my forties, I met a man. He came to the house selling my daddy life insurance. Daddy didn't buy right away. The man kept coming back day after

217

day, night after night. And we'd talk. Finally, well"—she giggled—"I guess we did a little more than talk." She sighed. "Anyway, daddy finally bought the insurance and the man left. A
couple of months later, I find out I'm pregnant." She snorted.
"Well, you'd think I was the first one in the world to get herself
in that kind of situation, the way my daddy carried on."

"Miz Gallagher, about your daughters-in-law—"

"Milton," she said, giving me the evil eye, "I was talking. This
is the good part, anyway. Well, my parents threw me out. I
moved to Oklahoma City until it was time for my confinement.
I had to go to the charity hospital because I didn't have a lick of
money. And this was in the days before they had all these fancy
ultrasounds and all that stuff, and the doctor I'd seen never said
a thing about twins. Being small and all, they couldn't tell I was
carrying two babies. Well, when I get to the hospital, there's
this insurance man there and"—she giggled again—"you might
say I did to him what one of his ilk had done to me. Back in
those days, some insurance men would hang out in maternity
wards and try to sell twin policies to any woman who hadn't
been diagnosed with twins in her belly. So, with my last five
dollars I took out this insurance policy, and, lo and behold, I
have twins! Paid me five thousand dollars! So I went to secretar-
ial school and got me a job there in Oklahoma City and told
everyone I was a widow, and when my boss moved to Longbranch, I came with him. Worked for that dentist for twenty-
two years. Ten of 'em, he promised he'd divorce his wife and
marry me. Last ten, he just promised he'd leave something in his
will." She snorted again. "I'm not that gullible. But I did get him
to help pay for the twins' education.

"I had this plan, Milton. Those boys were going to be my
salvation. I worked my whole life supporting them, making sure
they had the best of everything. If wheat jeans were what the
'in' boys were wearing, well the Gallagher twins were wearing
them two weeks early. If the kids were going to a special summer camp, the Gallagher twins were enrolled before anybody

else. You think that kinda stuff grows on trees, Milton? It most certainly does not! I invested in those boys. I worked my whole life for those boys! I put them through undergraduate school and Phillip through medical school and Daniel through law school. Neither of those boys ever had used books! Not a one! They were both in the best fraternities. Neither one worked a lick getting through school. But I did! I worked on my feet in Dr. Warner's office and I worked on my back for Dr. Warner every Tuesday night for twenty-two years!

"And then my Phillip marries Cassie. I could just look at the girl and I knew she was trouble. She gets Phillip to buy her that fancy house, and I'm still stuck in the same little two-bedroom like your mama's. He's buying Cassie diamonds and trying to find out if I have enough retirement from Dr. Warner! Telling me I need to cut down on this and cut out that entirely!"

Her voice had gotten more and more strident, louder, angrier. The red Phillip had talked about on the ride to Tulsa was spreading up her neck.

"And then she gets pregnant! And I know what that means! I'm terrified I'll fall and break a hip! That girl would have me in a nursing home so fast, it would make your head spin!" Her hair was fast coming loose from her bun. Mrs. G. took a deep breath and poked some strands back, then placed her hands on the table, clasped together politely. "Well, Milton, it was just self-preservation. Daniel had already gone to Washington, D.C., and you'll notice he didn't invite me along! Thought he was a hot britches!" She took another deep breath. "Well, Phillip was all I had then. And I didn't want to lose him. I did what I had to do. First, I talked to her. I told her that the baby just wouldn't do. I told her she needed to get rid of the baby. She said I was crazy. Told me to get out of her house and that she was gonna tell Phillip what I'd said. Well, I didn't go over there empty-handed, Milton. I want you to know that. I wasn't born yesterday. I had this feeling she wouldn't listen to me," she said, pointing her finger at me and wiggling it. She laughed and shook her head. "Well, I showed her. We were in the kitchen. I just picked up one of her shiny copper-bottom pots—do you know how much those things cost? Why, Phillip could have bought *me* diamonds for what he paid for those stupid pots. Anyway, I just whacked her upside the head with it. Then I took the jewelry because I knew Phillip had paid a mint for that, and one thing people have always said about Lilly Gallagher is that she isn't wasteful.

"I'd read this book I got out of the back of one of those magazines for hunters? About how to make bombs. And I'd brought that bomb along and I set it and got out of there."

"What about Libby, Miz Gallagher?"

"Ha! Her! Well, when Phillip took off, I just begged Daniel to let me go visit him in Washington, and I just never left. And everything was just fine, just the two of us. I'd help him entertain and we had a lovely apartment in Georgetown. Such a lovely part of the city." The red splotches were coming back to her neck. "And then *she* shows up. So full of herself! But Danny thought he was in love," she said, the last word spoken with such derision, she almost spat it. "What can you do with a boy when he thinks he's in love? But she acted like we were just one big happy family, and acted like she was just thrilled to have me move in with them, but I knew better! Believe me, I knew better!

"We're not back in Longbranch two months before she's pregnant! Pregnant! Well, I knew I'd be out that door in a New York minute if she had her say-so. And she had Danny wrapped around her little finger." Mrs. G. smiled and shook her head. "It was so nice after she was gone. I mean, Danny was upset and all, but he calmed down. Both the boys are so much calmer when there aren't women in their lives. But they keep trying. I mean, look at right this minute. Debbie?" She rolled her eyes. "That's a situation that needs some taking care of."

"How did you take care of Libby, Miz Gallagher?"

She looked at me, cutting her eyes coquettishly in my direction. "Now, Milton Kovak, you don't think you're going to tell anybody what I been telling you, do you? Your mama was my very best friend and she would just whip your hide at the thought of you doing such a thing."

"What happened with Libby?"

She waved her hand at me. "It wasn't nearly as creative as Cassie, but I figured two bombings wouldn't be smart. With all the trouble Phillip had been having with those antiabortion people, I thought a bomb was a real good idea, don't you?"

"Well . . ."

"But then that stupid police chief, Emmett Hopkins, totally ignores those people after I set everything up to look like they did it! I even mailed letters!" She leaned toward me in a conspiratorial way. "I can't believe you hired him, Milton, I don't believe he's the smartest man in the world."

"What about Libby, Miz Gallagher?"

"Well, I just told her my car wouldn't work and asked her to drive me over to a friend's house. I bought one of those cheap, disposable plastic raincoats and, when I got her on this old country road and made her stop the car, I just put the raincoat on over my work clothes and then I just took the knife and well—" She grimaced. "If you must know, Milton, it was pretty disgusting. Then I put her in the backseat and I had to stab her a couple more times to make it look like one of those crazies you read about all the time. I buried the raincoat alongside the road and then I drove the car over to the Stop N Shop, left it behind the store, and walked to the office." She smiled. "My car was already there because I'd ridden home the night before with Daniel. And he was gone to Tulsa on a court appearance, so I went to work, and that was it." She sat back, her smile getting broader. "Fooled you, too, didn't I?"

"Yes, ma'am, you sure did."

"But, Milton, you tell anybody what I told you," she said,

smiling and wiggling a finger at me, "I'm just gonna deny it."

"Can't say as I blame you, Miz Gallagher," I said, "so would I."

I looked at the two-way mirror of the security room, wondering how Daniel was gonna take all of this.

Jean put her fork down from her tray of scrumptious lunch dishes—a gray meat patty with reddish brown gravy the hospital laughingly called Salisbury Steak, green beans that hadn't seen a vitamin since 1952, and lime Jell-O with pimentos floating around inside—and touseled what was left of my hair.

"You've really been through the wringer, haven't you, baby?" she said.

"Me?" I looked at her. "Me? How can you say that after what you've been through? I can't believe I'm burdening you with all this."

"Shut up," she said, smiling to take the sting out as she pushed her tray away from her. "I'd much rather discuss your cases than eat this garbage, and they won't bring the baby back for another forty-five minutes, so—" She pointed her long index finger at my face. "Tell all."

I told her about Eugene Baker and the fact that we probably couldn't touch him, and about Mrs. G. and her haunted sons.

Jean came back with the response I expected about Eugene Baker. She can put on her shrink hat in the strangest places.

"How does that make you feel?" she asked.

"How do you think it makes me feel?" I stood up and paced the room. "I dunno. I feel . . ."

"Impotent?"

I looked at her. "No," I said, my voice as empathetic as possible. "That's not the word I'd use."

Jean laughed. "I'm not talking about Mr. Bippy," she said. "There's more ways of being impotent than just sexually. Having your hands tied legally must make you feel incapable of action . . . unable to do your job."

I saw her point. "Yeah. Impotent," I said, clarifying, "in a nonsexual sorta way."

"After what you've told me about Eugene Baker, I'd almost like to see this guy—"

I shook my head. "No way. He's crazier than a bedbug."

"And I, of course, have no experience dealing with people who are crazier than bedbugs?"

"Not this kinda crazy," I said.

"Actually, from what you tell me, I've dealt with his type often. More in Chicago, before I came here. He sounds like classic antisocial personality disorder."

I laughed at that one. "Oh, yeah," I said. "You could say this guy is a touch antisocial."

"What we used to call a sociopath," she said, her schoolmarm hat firmly in place.

"Okay, psychopath I've heard of. What's a sociopath?"

"Basically, they are in tune only to themselves. They're wonderful mimickers, though. The outside world sees them as normal because they're able to mimic normal. They can laugh on cue, cry on cue. They marry, have children. Most lead normal lives. They might have sex outside of marriage and really be unable to understand why this upsets their spouses. They may marry and divorce several times. If they become abusers, it's usually of the emotional variety rather than the physical. They have a need to control."

She stopped and looked off into space. "Actually, not too far off from Mrs. G., if you think about it. Both of them had serious control issues. With Eugene, it was do as I say or die. With Mrs. G., it was a little more subtle." She was silent for a moment. "You spoke about her fear of abandonment," she said, her voice distant, her eyes lost in that way they get when she's wearing her shrink hat. "The twins were hers—her possessions. The wives and babies were interlopers come to steal those possessions. When it was just a wife, it was tolerable, but a baby meant total abandonment to her. Although her parents threw her out when she became pregnant with the twins, she, in essence, also abandoned them. And she would lose control over the boys. With their own families, she would be on the outside looking in." Jean shook her head. "I don't believe it's in Mrs. Gallagher's makeup to be on the outside of anything."

"What I don't understand for the life of me is why Phillip didn't turn her in in the first place! Jeez, if my mother had done that to you, God himself couldn't keep me from turning her in!"

Jean smiled and motioned me to come sit down on the chair next to the bed. She touched my cheek with her hand. "A lot of the man you are is because of your mother, and your father. The values they instilled in you would demand that you do the right thing, just as those same values in your mother would never allow her even to think about, much less commit, the crimes Mrs. G. committed.

"But think about what the twins' childhoods must have been like. Mrs. G. would have demanded total loyalty. Anyone who could eventually have done what Mrs. G. did for the reasons she did them could not have had particularly stable parenting techniques. It was probably the three of them against the world. It's hard to say how you would have reacted in Phillip's shoes—you've never been in them. You weren't raised in those shoes."

"How's Phillip going to be as a parent?" I asked. "You know, they say what goes around comes around."

"Not necessarily. I hope to have a chance to talk to Phillip before he takes off for Montana again. He needs to know this isn't his fault. He also needs to know that the old saying you just quoted is a crock. With counseling, with understanding of what he's gone through most of his life because of his mother, he can put that aside. He can be a good parent to that little girl."

"So what about Eugene Baker? What do I do with him?"

Jean shrugged. "Keep looking for a survivor, I guess. Or a repeat caller."

"That's gonna be our luck. Get that sumbitch on a misdemeanor."

Jean got that gleam in her eye. "I really want to meet this guy, Milt."

I shook my head. "Jean—"

The nurse took that minute to bring in our boy. Bobby Cannaway was hot on the nurse's heels. After the nurse handed Jean the baby, Bobby said, "You know, folks, it's about damn time you named this kid. We're tired of calling him 'Little Boy Kovak.'"

Jean and I looked at each other. Yeah, it *was* about damned time.

18

We named our son John (after my daddy) McDonnell (after Jean) Kovak. I call him Johnnie Mac, which pisses Jean off so much, I guess I'll just have to keep doing it. He's gaining weight like crazy, and talk about pinking up—when that boy cries, he's the pinkest thing you ever did see.

It's the craziest thing, but seems like when you got a kid, time moves in a different way. What used to be "last Thursday" or "back in April" now starts being "when Johnnie Mac was three weeks old" and "when Johnnie Mac was two months old." Which goes a way to explain when I say that when Johnnie Mac was three weeks old, me and Jean got Jewel to sit him and we went to a funeral—Martha DeLaney's funeral. She hadn't been able to save either of her boys, but not for want of trying. And I guess it killed her. Dawson DeLaney wouldn't speak to me at the funeral. I suppose he had to blame somebody—better me than Robbie, I guess.

The upshot of all the steroid abuse at the high school was four senior boys suspended from the team and what was shaping up to be the worst season in the Longbranch Cougars' history. As the word was spreading that it was all my fault, I was just glad I had a two-year term of office and the voting public has a real short memory.

Two months after we brought Johnnie Mac home from the hospital, Gary Booker found a lady in Sherman, Texas, who'd been telling anybody who'd listen for well over two years that some fella on a hot line had talked her into taking that dive out of the three-story window that left her a quadriplegic for life. So Jean got her wish to meet Eugene. We had a meeting back at the hot line with all the usual suspects—me, Bill Williams, Gary Booker, and Audrey Whitehead, plus Jean and a guy named Harris Quale, a homicide detective from Sherman, Texas. Old Eugene walked in like he'd been invited to a party, grinning and talking trash.

I started on him. "Wonder if your memory got any better, Eugene. Remember the name Shirley Beth Hopkins?"

He frowned in concentration. "I remember a Shirley. She was the drunk, right? Married to a cop?" He laughed. It didn't change his eyes. "God, I hope it wasn't one of you guys!" The thought seemed to crack him up, and he laughed some more.

"You killed her," I said, moving in so close, he could smell my lunch.

"Not really. She killed herself," he said, moving away from me and casually taking a chair. He sighed. "Look," he said, "I work and I work and I work with these people. I give them every opportunity to get their acts together. It's not my fault they screw up." His eyes slanted and he looked at me. "In my younger days, I got addicted to heroin. I ended up doing a two-year stint in a state rehab house. I beat the addiction. Unfortunately, one of the *unofficially* recommended ways of beating heroin was drinking to scare away the demons. So I became an alcoholic." He shrugged. "Addictive personality," he said, smiling. "Glad I never took up smoking. But I beat the booze, too. All I was asking these people to do was beat *one* little problem." He shook his head. "They didn't listen to me. They didn't do what I told them to do. It's not my fault they were all screwups."

I felt a shiver run up and down my spine. This was one seriously sick puppy. He had just explained, to his own satisfaction, the deaths of eight people.

He smiled. "You just haven't talked to my successes. I've got a lot more of those than the screwups. Why, there are people all over this county and both of your counties," he said, pointing at Gary and me, "who are clean today because of me. Now are you guys ready to give me some credit for that? Huh?" He crossed his arms over his chest and leaned back in his chair, his mouth covered in a smug smile, his eyes devoid of humanity.

Bill Williams leaned in close. "You're a killer and we've got your ass."

Baker smiled. "I'm afraid not. I haven't done anything you can prove."

Harris Quale smiled and moved into Eugene's space. "Remember a lady name of Bertha Hoffs?"

"No," said Baker, frowning.

"Oh, sure you do," Quale said, moving into Baker's face. "Real whiny lady? Addicted to Valium? You got her in to see somebody in Sherman and she kicked the Valium and took up Prozac. Remember? Coming back to you, Eugene?"

Baker tried to get out of his chair, but Quale wouldn't let him budge. "No, I don't know what—"

"She called you one night wasted on Prozac and you told her that it didn't look like she was strong enough to help herself. You told her she was a burden on her family and friends. You told her her children hated her and were ashamed of her. You told her the best thing she could do would be to leave them all, to just end it. She was drugged and vulnerable—just the way you like 'em, huh, Eugene? You told her if she just took a few more doses of Prozac, everything would be just fine. Her family would miss her and remember her kindly. But she didn't have any more Prozac. So you told her to look and see what she had in her medicine cabinet, but she told you her husband had cleared everything out. And you said there had to be a way she could help herself. You told her the best thing for her family

228

and for her was if she would just put herself out of everybody's misery. But poor old Bertha didn't even have any razor blades in the bathroom. No guns in the apartment. Stove was electric—couldn't put her head in the oven. But then she told you she was on the third floor of her apartment complex. You told her to open the window. You told her to look down. You asked her what she saw. She told you about the paved parking area right outside her window."

Quale's voice was low, but the room was hushed. The outside noises of the hot-line room were nonexistent. I could hear every word. I could see every drop of sweat on Eugene Baker's face. And for the first time, I saw an expression in his eyes: fear.

Harris Quale was so close to Eugene Baker, he could've counted his pores. Softly, he said, "Did you stay on the line and listen as she opened the window? Did you hear her as her body shuffled up on the windowsill? Did she scream, Eugene? Some witnesses said she screamed. Did you hear her scream, Eugene?"

Baker fell over backward in his chair. He scurried up and slammed himself against the glass walls of Audrey Whitehead's office. "I don't know what you're talking—"

Quale moved in again, grinning. "You should have stayed on the line longer, Eugene. Bertha lived. Bertha's alive. And, boy, is she pissed."

We turned Eugene Baker over to the Sherman authorities to do with him what they would. If we could get him on the deaths he'd caused, it would be third degree manslaughter. Since the Hoffs woman lived, and unless we could get some proof on the deaths, Texas would only be able to charge him with aiding a suicide—a couple of years if a judge didn't let him off with a slap on his wrists. But me and Bill and Gary and Audrey Whitehead were going to do what we could to keep the investigation in Oklahoma open.

That night in bed, with Jean cradling Johnnie Mac to her breast, she said, "I'm glad they're taking Baker to Texas. I hope he never gets sent back here. I think I could spend the rest of

229

my life quite peacefully never setting eyes on that man again."

I smiled smugly, but I didn't say, I told you so.

I had to tell Emmett about Eugene Baker, but luckily I was able to put it off until Harris Quale had removed Baker from the state. Emmett was gonna take off on his own and go down to Texas and have a look at Eugene, so I decided to drive him down there. No telling what Emmett was liable to do on his own.

We got down to the holding cell and Emmett just looked at Eugene Baker. Remembering what Eugene had said about Shirley Beth, I said, "Hey, Eugene, this is the cop whose wife you killed. Think it would be funny if we just opened this here cell door and let this ole boy have his way with you?"

It woulda been grand, 'cept I'm finding out sociopaths aren't a heap of fun to play around with. Old Eugene didn't move a muscle. And his eyes were just as dead as ever. No fear in 'em at all. Maybe I'd only imagined the fear before, seeing what I would have seen in a normal, walking human being. We left, and when we got back to Longbranch, Emmett asked me to take him to the Sidewinder Lounge, where he proceeded to get commode-hugging drunk. I drove him home. Three weeks later, he asked Jasmine Bodine to go to the movies over in Taylor. No accounting for taste, I suppose, but it was nice to see him taking an interest.

Mrs. G. wasn't going to be standing trial. There were the usual hearings, but even the state's shrinks said she was crazier than a bedbug, so with everybody in agreement, she was quietly put away in the state mental institution for the rest of her natural life.

And I finally found out why Marv Bernblatt had been hanging around for so long. In September, it was officially announced that he was the new owner of the *Longbranch Gazette*. His first headline was: THE SHERIFF'S DEPARTMENT—IS IT ALL IT SHOULD BE? I'm thinking of having him killed.

Around that same time, I gathered up all of Libby's book and

230

the discs of her journal entries and took them over to Daniel's. He was just back from a month in Billings with his brother, sister-in-law, and his new little niece. He answered the door when I rang the bell and I handed him the lot.

"You need to read this stuff, Daniel," I said. "Especially the journal entries. You made the lady happy."

I turned and walked to my car, heading back to Mountain Falls Road. I had a lady to make happy up there, and I surely intended to do that very thing.

This book is dedicated to George Davis and Hank Renteria—
and Sophie and Robin and Little Linda and Bernie
and Jeannette and Joan and Larry
and Mike and Big Don and Naomi
and Lou Ann and Rob
and all the other wonderful people who saved
lives and minds in those early days at
Crisis Hotline in Houston, Texas.
I will love and remember you always.

179
189
214
217
229